BRODY

R.I.S.C. DELTA TEAM
BOOK 2

ANNA BLAKELY

BRODY

R.I.S.C. Delta Team Series 2

Anna Blakely

Brody
R.I.S.C. Delta Team Series 2
First Edition
Copyright © 2023 Saje Publishing, LLC
All rights reserved.
All cover art and logo Copyright © 2023
Publisher: Saje Publishing
Cover by: Lori Jackson
Edited by: Tracy Roelle
Proofread by: Shirley Kilgore, Ann Payne, Angelia Springs, Suzie Waggoner

All rights reserved. No part of this book may be reproduced in any form or by any electronic or mechanical means, including information storage and retrieval systems—except in the case of brief quotations embodied in critical articles or reviews—without permission in writing from the author.

This book is a work of fiction. The names, characters, and places portrayed in this book are entirely products of the author's imagination or used fictitiously. Any resemblance to actual events, locales, or persons, living or dead, is entirely coincidental and not intended by the author.

The unauthorized reproduction or distribution of this copyrighted work is illegal. Criminal copyright infringement, including infringement without monetary gain, is investigated by the FBI and is punishable by up to five years in federal prison and a fine of $250,000.00.

If you find any eBooks being sold or shared illegally, please contact the author at anna@annablakelycom.

❀ Created with Vellum

ABOUT THE BOOK

Not knowing what you have until it's gone is a lesson former Navy SEAL Brody King learns the hard way in this steamy, friends-to-lovers romantic suspense by bestselling author Anna Blakely.

R.I.S.C. Delta Team operative Brody King has never seen Aurora "Ro" Weber as anything more than a friend. But when his younger sister's BFF becomes the target of an unknown assailant, he finds himself insisting on being the one to keep her safe. As the attacks on Ro escalate, everything Brody thought he knew shifts. Before long, this government-sanctioned killer begins to wonder if the one thing missing from his life was right in front of him all along.

Aurora "Ro" Weber has always spoken her mind and played it smart, refusing to acknowledge her heart's deepest desire. Not even her best friend knows about the secretly harbored feelings she's been carrying for Brody, her friend's older brother. But when the man of her dreams appoints himself her personal protector, Ro quickly discovers she's no match for the sexy former SEAL.

Unable to ignore the magnetic pull drawing them together, Brody and Ro soon find themselves caught in an unexpected storm of unbridled passion and danger. But just when they think Ro is finally safe, the unthinkable happens, and she goes missing. An ominous warning the only clue left in her place.

With Ro's life—and Brody's heart—on the line, he and the other men of Delta Team go on the hunt. Because Ro's no longer just Brody's friend. She's his *everything*.

And if he and the others can't find her before the clock runs out, he'll lose the only woman he's ever loved.

DEDICATION

To the late, great Matthew L. Perry. Your passing during the writing of this story broke my heart in ways I may never understand. There are no words to explain the blanket of sadness that fell over me when I heard the news, especially since we never met. (Seriously, could I BE any sadder?) I still can't quite comprehend the hours spent thinking about you, obsessing over what happened, and feeling how incredibly unfair it is that someone who brought so much light and laughter into our world could be filled with so many dark and torturous days.
I read your book after its release, and my heart broke over and over with each tragic story you shared. Your legacy will live on, not only through endless hours of hysterical re-runs, but also through your generous words and selfless heart.
You helped so many through humor and so much more. I know those you led to sobriety will forever be in your debt. Thanks so very much for the lifetime of smiles and laughter you've given me and so many others throughout the years.
Rest easy, my FRIEND.

AUTHOR'S NOTE

From their first shared scene in *Christian* (Delta Team Book #1), I knew Brody and Ro would end up together. The tall, dark, and sexy former SEAL falling for his younger sister's spunky best friend...I mean, come on. How could I put either of these two characters with anyone but each other?

And boy, am I glad I did.

These two gave me fits at first, but when they finally opened up, it was like a floodgate of emotions poured out of them both. The depth with which they care for one another resonated with me, and I am so excited to share their story with you.

I hope you like it as much as I do.

XO~
 Anna

PROLOGUE

HE WATCHED the group of tight-knit friends as they sat celebrating across the room from where he stood. Six men, two women. Lots of smiles, laughs, and cheers to the birthday boy.

Even from all the way over here, the men at the table looked exactly like what he knew them to be...

Former military, each with their own unique special forces background. Trained killers who went from working for Uncle Sam's nickel to joining Jake McQueen and his merry band of R.I.S.C. operatives.

From what he'd been able to find, the Chicago-based Delta Team was the fourth and most recent private security team to form under McQueen's rapidly growing empire. His operatives were supposedly the best of the best, though he'd be willing to put a wager on that bet.

No one was ever as good as they thought they were. Except for him, of course. He was better and smarter than everyone he crossed paths with. A fact that grew damn tiring if the truth were being told.

He should be used to it by now, he supposed. After all,

he'd spent his entire life being underestimated by those around him.

Family. Colleagues. People who thought they knew him. Who damn well *should* have.

Those idiots don't know me at all.

No one knew the real him. Oh, but that was about to change soon. Because he was going to show them.

The kind of man he really was. What he was truly capable of. The lengths he would go to for his voice to finally be heard. Yes, soon *everyone* would know the truth about him...

Starting with you.

His focus shifted to one of the two women sitting with the men of Delta. Hidden in the shadows of the bar's low lighting, the spot he'd chosen gave him an unobstructed view of the mouthwatering temptation while also preventing suspicion from those around him.

A rush of adrenaline brought his veins to life, his fingers twitching with the urge to act. This was it. *This* was what he'd been missing in his life.

About fucking time.

After years spent living and doing for others, he'd finally found the one thing needed to drive him forward. While his days were still filled with fake as shit smiles, condescending handshakes, and kissing the asses of the rich and famous, he also planned.

Planned. Prepared. And as soon as he got the chance, he'd move into action.

The seed for what would soon come to fruition had been planted long ago. But it wasn't until recently that he'd realized achieving his most desired goal was truly possible.

As if by divine intervention, he'd been handed the gift of opportunity right out of the blue. Just like that, he'd found his purpose once again. Something to strive for. Something to fight for. Something worth *dying* for.

And that something was currently sitting mere yards from where he stood.

So. Fucking. Close.

She *was* close. And so unsuspecting he almost felt bad about what was going to happen to her. Almost.

You don't have to wait, you know? It would be so easy to just go over there and end it all now.

The impatient voice in his head was right. Between the unsolicited distractions of the darkened ambiance and the bar's bustling crowd, it would almost be *too* easy to fast-forward to his grand finale and be done with it.

He could see it playing out so clearly, so beautifully, in his mind's eye...

Exiting his hiding spot, he would slowly begin to make his way past the bar. He might stop to order another drink. Maybe strike up a light and casual conversation with one of several obviously single women currently at the bar.

Once he felt enough time had passed, he'd then bid the woman—or women—a nice night and continue weaving through the crowd with his head down and his movements steady.

And when he was close enough to strike, he'd deliver a single, lethal stab on his way past. Then he'd walk right out the door and vanish into the night...before his victim ever hit the sticky, liquor-coated floor.

It was a solid plan, and one he was certain would work. But it wasn't time for the final kill part of the plan. Not yet. Because killing wasn't the only thing listed on his agenda...

Take.
Torture.
Kill.

Those were the steps in his plan. And step one would be put into motion before the night's end.

For now, however, he would stay in the shadows. Watching tonight's target until the time came to do more.

Aurora Danielle Tennison.

The sexy brunette had porcelain skin, striking blue eyes, and a body that would make any man in here hard as fucking steel. She also appeared to be smart, both in the ways of life and in business.

At thirty-two, the marketing and graphic design specialist was well on her way to building a very successful business. He'd seen her work first-hand and knew what a talented and savvy vixen she was.

It was a shame he was going to have to kill her.

With his eyes following her every movement, he kept his gaze locked onto his target as she turned and said something to the woman sitting to her left. Megan King, also thirty-two, was the sister to Delta's second-in-command. She was also Aurora's best friend from childhood and engaged to her live-in fiancé, Christian Hunt—the private security team's lead operator.

He blinked as Aurora pushed herself away from the table and stood. Leaning down, she said something into her friend's ear before pushing in her chair and turning away.

His feet shifted, preparing to move when the opportunity arose. A few minutes later, he saw his chance...and smiled.

1

Minutes earlier...

"Did someone say shots?" Aurora Tennison balanced the round tray full of drinks in her hands as she approached the most important people in her life.

Careful not to spill the near-overflowing shot glasses in her care, she squeezed herself between her empty seat on the right and her best friend.

"Ro! You bought an entire round?" Megan King studied the tray and its contents with a set of wide, hazel eyes and arched brows. Speaking loudly, she turned her brown brows inward with a look of disapproval. "You didn't have to do that. I told you when I invited you, tonight's on Delta."

"I know I didn't *have* to, and I know that's what you said. But Cade only turns thirty once, and his latest drink was getting close to empty." She gave her friend a casual shrug. "Figured he might be getting thirsty."

Ro glanced at the birthday boy sitting two spots down from Megan. Though it was hard to tell with the unfocused look currently spread across his attractive, drunken face, the hunky man was a top-notch sniper for R.I.S.C.'s Delta Team—one of four teams that made up the most elite private security empire in existence.

Tall. Built. Attractive. Funny. Loyal.

Deadly.

That was Cade Ellis...and every other man currently sitting at their table.

Though she had no other personal connection to the group of former military badasses, Ro and Megan were as close as if they were actually blood related. Since she spent most of her time with the other woman—and she pretty much got along with everyone as long as they didn't piss her off—it hadn't taken long for Christian and the other guys on the team to become her friends, too.

Not a massive hardship given how tall, dark, and mouth-wateringly sexy they all were. Of course, there was only one member of R.I.S.C.'s Delta Team that truly made Ro's insides quiver and her heart flip.

Unfortunately—or perhaps fortunately—the sexy, unsuspecting man she dreamed about at night saw her as nothing more than a friend.

And I get to spend the entire night tonight pretending that's all I feel for him, too.

"Hey, Cade!" Ro elevated her voice so the man they were celebrating could hear her over the music and constant buzz of conversation. "You good?"

His blank stare, heavy lids, and intoxicated sway—combined with a wide, lazy smile—said he was far better than good.

"I'm...grrreat!" The former Green Beret gave her a lazy thumbs-up.

His slow-motion movements and slurred response made Ro and the others burst into laughter.

"Dude you sound like that cartoon tiger from that one cereal commercial," Liam Cutler, the team's technical analyst, teased from his seat across from Cade's.

Everyone barked out another laugh because, yeah. The devil-may-care guy sounded almost *exactly* like that cartoon tiger.

"Okay, everybody!" Megan stood to gain everyone's attention. "Time to sing to the birthday boy!"

"But first, grab a drink!" Ro motioned to the shots.

Picking up two of the tiny glasses, she ignored the small drips of cool liquid spilling over the rounded edges as she handed them to her friend. Megan set one down in front of Cade—who was oblivious to its arrival—before stretching across to pass the second one on.

The makeshift assembly line continued until everyone around the table was ready to roll.

"Listen up!" Christian Hunt—Delta's leader and Megan's fiancé—rose to his feet. With a commanding voice, he addressed the group as a whole. "Now I know we've all enjoyed giving Ellis a hard time about being the baby of the group." His brown stare landed on Cade's. "I also know I speak for everyone here when I promise you..." A dramatic pause. "We're *still* going to give you shit for being the youngest on the team. Ain't that right, boys?"

Just as the man promised, the other Delta men joyfully hollered their own solemn vows. Christian raised his tatted arm in the air, the rest of the team followed.

Standing on Cade's other side, John Rockland—better known to the group as Rocky—cleared his throat and jutted his strong, square chin. Looking like a living, breathing

Greek statue, the blond warrior put on a serious face and then...

He began to sing.

Badly.

"Happy birthday to you..."

Thankfully the entire table, along with half the bar, quickly joined in to wish the team's gentle giant a very happy birthday. Once the singing had come to an end, Ro did her duty as Cade's friend and slammed the smooth bourbon down with a harsh tilt of her head and one big gulp.

Holy shit. That really burns!

Remembering why she stuck to the simpler things in life —like fruity drinks, wine, and the occasional beer—she did her best not to outwardly react. The last thing she needed was for present company to catch her coughing or gasping because she couldn't handle her liquor.

She'd witnessed enough razzing between the group of lethal friends over the past couple of years to know she did *not* want to make herself a target.

Taking in several slow, deep breaths to cool the liquid embers, Ro stood to the side and tried like hell not to cough. The previous conversations picked back up around her, and to her left, Megan sat back down in her seat and scooted closer to the table.

The second she did, Cade leaned toward the other woman and began slurring on and on about something Ro couldn't quite hear...which was probably for the best.

Lips twitching at the thought, she turned and glanced at the growing crowd. With everyone else in her party occupied, she decided to use the opportunity to slip back to the bar for something a little less flammable.

Resting a hand on her friend's shoulder, she leaned

down, speaking close to Megan's ear to save her already strained voice. "I'm going to grab another drink," she shared. "You want anything from the bar?"

When Megan gave a gentle shake of her head, her layered brown hair flowed back and forth in soft waves. "Thanks, but I'm good," she smiled up at Ro. "Don't worry about me, though. I'll just be sitting here, enjoying the musings of a very drunk man who will most *definitely* have one helluva hangover tomorrow."

The humored expression on the woman's slightly freckled face made Ro laugh.

"He'll probably be the first in line at Cup of Joe tomorrow," she chuckled back, referring to the quaint coffee shop Megan owned. "Lord knows he's going to need a lot of strong, black coffee when he finally decides to crawl outta bed."

"In that case, we should keep the shots coming. I mean... job security for me, right?"

"Exactly." Ro huffed out a breathy chuckle and nodded. "I'll be right back."

With careful steps, she slowly began to snake her way through the thick crowd.

This being her first time here, she absorbed her surroundings with an artist's eye as she moved. With its black walls, low lighting, and spacious seating area, the club had the perfect balance of hip, masculine lines and feminine hues and curves.

Upbeat music played from speakers scattered all throughout the Chicago bar's interior. The crowd a constant sea of movement as people walked around, danced, laughed, and drank the night away.

Black and white photos from yesteryear adorned the walls around her, some even hanging in the narrow space above the long bar's massive mirror that was now fully within her view.

It was a typical bar's bar. Several black, backless bar stools—all currently filled with people talking to those standing between said stools—lined the front of a long, shiny, wooden countertop.

Facing her from behind the bar was the gigantic mirror she'd seen earlier. Glass shelves topped with just about every liquor known to man ran filled the reflective surface.

Ro leaned her elbows on the bar's edge and released a long exhale, more than ready for another drink. She'd only had two so far...an amaretto sour when she'd first arrived, and the regrettable birthday shot.

The downtown Chicago bar scene wasn't her usual Saturday night jam. Actually the bar scene as *a whole* wasn't really her thing. Truth was, most of Ro's weekends lately had been spent at home...alone.

A fact made even sadder since she was her own boss and worked from home as well.

But between work, peeling wallpaper, and painting the walls, interior doors, and trim of the house she'd recently purchased, there just wasn't much time left for socializing. When she *did* manage a night out, it was either a girl's night with Megan or something like this.

Her, her best friend, and the men of Delta.

In the time she'd come to know them, the guys had all welcomed her into their small circle of trust. So when Megan and Christian invited her to join in tonight's festivities, Ro hadn't even considered saying no.

After all, Cade was her friend, now, too. Just like every other man on the team.

A face flashed before her eyes. Dark. Brooding. Sexy. But Ro ignored it and sidled up closer to the bar.

Her chin lifted slightly as she leaned her elbows on the smooth surface and waited. A sliver of pride sank in at how much better she'd gotten at that, lately. The ignoring, that is.

Of course, she *should* be an expert at it after all this time. It wasn't like she hadn't had time to perfect the craft.

Since she was a teenager, Ro had been ignoring her deepest, most hidden desires. She'd become a true master at schooling her expression whenever *he* was around. A savant at ignoring the way her heart stopped beating every time the intimidating man entered a room.

If there was a gold medal in the art of making oneself purposely overlook the way they ached with the need whenever a certain person was near, I'd hold the world freaking record.

Ro straightened her shoulders and lifted her spine. Yes, she *would* hold the record, if for no other reason than she'd both valiantly—and successfully—resisted the urge to throw herself into the man's arms and finally taste those bearded lips.

For. *Years.*

Which is why she considered herself quite the expert in the field of pretending not to see what was often right in front of her.

Take right now, for instance. She was standing here, actively blocking out the knowledge that the man of her dreams was back at that table with Meg, Christian, and the others right this very second.

And she couldn't care less.

Liar, liar, skirt on fire. And you do realize thinking about how good you are at not *thinking about the man means you're...well... thinking about him, right?*

Well crap. Okay, so maybe she needed a little more practice in not thinking about him...but at least she had control of her face and tongue. As long as no one could tell she wanted nothing more than to run her fingertips through that thick beard and feel it caressing her skin as he brushed his lips along her—

Damn it, Ro, this has got to stop! You need to either put up or shut up, because this whole loving-from-afar BS isn't a healthy way to live.

That pride she was feeling seconds before dissipated into an invisible vapor, vanishing into the air with the truth of her subconscious words. Because the voice in her head was right.

It was well-past time she put an end to the decades-old crush and move the hell on already. After two decades of both secretly wishing Megan's older brother would see her as more than a friend—and then being utterly terrified at the thought that he actually *would*—Ro was tired.

So, so tired.

She was also done.

"Who was next?"

Her hand shot up to signal the busy bartender she was ready to order. Yes, it was high time she quit pining away for the sexy, stoic former SEAL and moved the heck on.

Starting. Now.

This was Chicago, for crying out loud. There were hot, single men everywhere she looked, and any one of them would be lucky to have her. At least, that's what Ro told herself as the rushed redhead behind the bar appeared in front of her.

"What can I get you?" The other woman offered with a half-frenzied smile.

Shoot. Ro had been so desperate to focus on something other than her inner turmoil, she'd raised her hand without having decided on a drink.

Sounding hopeful, she asked, "Do you have something fruity you'd recommend?"

"Shot or drink?"

"Drink," Ro answered instantly.

No more shots for me, thank you, very much.

"Iced?"

She gave a quick nod. "Yes, please."

The thirty-something woman with short, spiky red hair, several earrings, and a nose ring tapped her finger on the bar as she took a few seconds to ponder. "You like coconut-flavored drinks?"

"Very much." It was one of her favorites, actually.

"I've got just the thing. Hold tight."

With a tap on the counter, the woman set about mixing a concoction that reminded her of the beach. Not the ones along the coast of Lake Michigan, but rather one along the ocean's coast.

One with soft white sand and a sea of turquoise as far as the eye could see where the bite of the sun's kisses could be felt on the skin as a warm sea breeze ruffled the large, flat leaves of nearby palm trees.

Ro could see it so clearly in her mind, she could almost smell the salty air.

"Try that."

A tall highball glass filled with a bright, iced, aquamarine concoction appeared before her. Balanced on its rim was a small orange wedge, and a bright red, stemmed cherry floating near the slim black straw.

Lifting the chilled glass from the bar's surface, she brought the straw to her lips and sucked. An explosion of tropical heaven washed over her tastebuds, the combination of coconut rum and citrus the perfect balance of sweet and tart.

"Mmm..." Ro swallowed another sip before nodding to the auburn-haired goddess. "Ohmygosh, that's delicious!" she exclaimed loudly enough for the other woman to hear. "What's it called?"

"A Blue Hawaiian," the other woman yelled back.

Taking another sip, she nodded with another show of approval. "It's perfect, thank you!"

After paying the bill with her debit card, she shoved a generous cash tip into the lidded glass jar close by before turning to make her way back to her friends. A few accidental bumps and several shoulder-brushes later, and Ro was only three tables away when she heard someone calling her name.

"Aurora!"

The imperious male voice was familiar, and one that had Ro stopping in her tracks. It was also a voice she'd been hoping to go a day without hearing.

Great. Just what I needed to deal with tonight.

Donning her perfected game face, she spun on her spiked heels and faced the man who'd flagged her down...

Clayton Yorke, sole heir to his family's billion-dollar Yorkshire Luxury Suites and Spa hotel chain. The Forbes-500 Chicago-based company was well known around the world's most rich and famous, and Clayton well...

Clayton was one of the city's most eligible bachelors and, as of a month ago, Ro's most recent client.

Tall, light brown hair and scruff that was always combed just-so and trimmed to perfection, a fit runner's build, and blue eyes that seemed to constantly be searching for their next target, the uber-rich man was even better looking in person than on any news broadcast or magazine cover.

He was also arrogant, more than a little pretentious, and

brazen as hell when it came to his unabashed flirting. Not that he would ever actually want to *date* her.

Like a man like Clayton Yorke actually dates the woman he's seen with.

Like most single women in Chicago—and probably half of the married ones—Ro had kept up on the man's bachelor status through social media and the tabloids at the news stands. But her interest was purely professional.

One of the best ways to land a client was to know as much about them as possible, using every available resource. And from everything she'd learned, there was one aspect of the billionaire heir's highly publicized life that remained consistent no matter the source...

Cayton Yorke was an F-boy of epic proportions.

The man didn't do relationships. He used beautiful, single women to suit his latest need.

According to interviews by anonymous friends and co-workers, past lovers, and even a couple unnamed relatives, Clayton would use the woman he was seen with for one of two reasons...

As eye-candy for the press or a warm and willing body in his bed.

But attempting an actual relationship with someone... one with real feelings and emotions or, God forbid, commitment...forget it.

Well hello there, Pot. Have you had the pleasure of meeting Kettle?

Okay, fine. But to be fair, Ro's harsh judgement where Clayton's love life was concerned had more to do with his revolving bedroom door and reported treatment of his former lovers than his unwillingness to settle down.

Truth be told, Ro couldn't care less about the man's sex

life. It wasn't like she was jealous or wanted him for herself. She looked at Clayton Yorke and felt...nothing.

Because you want someone very, very different. You're just too afraid to go for it.

The same image from before filtered through her thoughts. A different man.

Taller.

Darker.

Sexier.

Deadlier.

She blinked, refocusing on the man standing in front of her and doing her best to ignore his predatorial gaze. "Hey, Clayton. Sorry, I didn't see you there. How are you?"

"Much better now." A slow, cocky smile lifted the billionaire's scruff-framed lips. "And I spotted you the second I stepped through the door."

Ro let her own smile grow just a smidge, unsure of how to appropriately respond to a comment like that. Even if she was flattered by the man's blatant attraction toward her—which she was *not*—Clayton was her client.

With new advances being made in the world of graphic design and online marketing, an independent entrepreneur like herself was already about six dozen steps behind those who were part of the corporate world. She'd already worked too damn hard to destroy her small company by becoming just another notch on Yorke's high-priced bedpost.

Besides, not mixing business with pleasure was a self-imposed rule Ro refused to break. The risks simply weren't worth the cost. Not even with a handsome man as rich and powerful as Clayton Yorke.

Especially not with a man like him.

"Aurora? Are you...okay?"

"What? Oh, sorry," she apologized with an awkward chuckle.

His gaze seemed a tad glazed, his speech the slightest bit stilted, and Ro couldn't help but wonder if he'd partaken in something other than alcohol.

"I didn't realize this was a hang-out of yours."

"It's not." She shook her head, pointing a thumb behind her. "I'm just here celebrating a friend's birthday."

"Oh. Well, please be sure to pass along my wishes for a happy birthday to your friend."

"I will. Thanks."

Ro started to turn, thinking she'd gotten out of that a lot faster and easier than expected. She was wrong.

Stepping a long stride forward, Clayton shifted his stance, so he was no longer directly behind her, but rather beside her. "It's good to see you getting out and doing something other than work. I know the long hours you put in, and even someone as successful as my father would tell you taking time for yourself is important."

"He'd be right." She maintained a perfect smile. "That's why I decided to come tonight."

Her client studied her a beat, making her feel more than a little anxious. Then, totally out of left field, he popped off with an exuberant—

"I just had the most fabulous idea! Let's you and I take Monday off. We can have brunch, take a walk through the park, have dinner at the Navy Pier..."

"Oh." Ro blinked, taken off guard by the unexpected offer. "Uh..."

I believe the word you're looking for is "no".

Yes, that was exactly what she'd meant to say. What she *would* say. Just as soon as he gave her a word in edgewise.

"Or we could cruise Lake Michigan at sunset," Clayton

continued. "It just so happens I know a guy who has his own private yacht. In fact, it's docked, fueled, and ready to go." He arched a brow, flashing her a seductive smile that would probably cause most women to drop their panties and spread their thighs.

Good thing I'm not most women.

"It's a very kind offer, but we've been over this already. I don't think—"

"It's settled," he cut her off again. "I'll pick you up at ten, and you and I can head to brunch. I know this fabulous place that serves the freshest crab with its eggs and uses only the best champagne for their Mimosas. After lunch, we can spend the day on the water, and my chef can whip us up whatever you'd like for dinner."

"Clayton, that all sounds really nice, but like I was trying to say—"

"We'll eat on my private balcony." The infuriating man *still* refused to let her speak. "Just wait until you see the stars. It's incredible how differently they appear when you're away from the city lights. It's unlike anything I've ever—"

"Clayton, I said no!" Ro finally shouted.

At the exact same time, the music dropped to the soft, subtle beginning of a different song, making her booming response sound even louder than intended. Her cheeks burned from embarrassment as those in their immediate area stopped what they were doing and stared.

Everyone's looking, Ro. Including Clayton. You have to fix this. Now!

Pretending to laugh at herself, she quickly apologized with a gentle hand to the man's bicep. Not in that annoying way some women did when they were pretending to be clueless while flirting. No, hers was more of an apologetic, friends-only sort of gesture.

She hoped.

"Sorry." Ro gave another nervous chuckle. "The music was really loud, and I was trying to talk over it." Not a *complete* lie. "But I've told you before, I don't mix business with pleasure."

"The website is finished," Clayton countered. "My socials are all redesigned and ready for the public, which means our business relationship has officially come to an end."

I wish.

"There's still next week's launch party," she reminded him. "And you should probably go back over the contract you signed. I'm still on retainer for the next twelve months so I can continue to monitor and update your website as needed."

A frown created two cavernous wrinkles between his brows as he asked, "Well who's hairbrained idea was that?"

"Yours." It was the first genuine smile to grace Ro's lips since hearing him holler her name.

She turned to leave, making it three full steps before a strong hand wrapped around the wrist of her free hand.

"Aurora, wait!" The unexpected hold jerked Ro backward, spilling half her drink in the process.

She cried out, jumping out of the splash zone just in time to miss the sticky beverage from landing on her brand-new heels while doing her best not to lose her balance. "Clayton, what the—"

"Oh, my!" His eyes grew wide. "My apologies, Aurora. I didn't mean to spill your drink. Here. Let me buy you another."

When the man began trying to pull her back toward the bar, Ro locked her muscles down and resisted. "It's okay," she lied.

It wasn't. Not even a little bit. But the man could literally make or break her career with a single social media post, so she had to be very careful with how she acted and what she said.

Always putting on a show, aren't ya? If not with Clayton, then with—

"You're going to want to remove that hand before I remove it for you."

Oh, shit.

Ro's chest tightened, her stomach dropping as she turned her gaze to the man who'd just spoken the rumbled warning from behind her. Her eyes immediately lifted upward toward his, but he wasn't looking at her. No, that dark, intense glare she'd recognize anywhere had already locked with Clayton's.

And the man it belonged to looked like he was ready to kill.

2

"Brody! Hey!" Ro kept her fake as heck smile in place as she greeted the very man she'd been trying to ignore.

In her hurried attempt to keep the peace, she rushed to make introductions—and hopefully distract the man of her dreams from clocking her biggest client.

"Clayton, I don't think you've had the chance to meet my friend. This is Brody King. You met his sister, Megan. She's my friend who owns Cup of Joe."

"Ah, yes, of course." Clayton's smile looked a bit off as he very *un*hurriedly met Brody's gaze. "That adorable little coffee shop across from Millennium Park where you and I have spent many an afternoon together. How could I forget?"

Better question is how could a guy with his elevated social status be so utterly clueless when it came to reading the room?

He was clearly mistaking Brody's sudden alpha-male appearance as something more than what it actually was... an overprotective friend who'd clearly witnessed their interaction and thought she was in trouble.

And since a pissing match was the last thing *any* of them

needed—especially since neither man had a reason to be fighting over her in the first place—Ro sprang into action once more.

"That's the one!" she gave an overly enthusiastic nod in response.

Swinging her head back around to face Brody, she had to stop herself from physically recoiling. His dark, statue-like gaze was unmoving as he continued staring down a man whose family owned half of Chicago.

"You're still touching her," Brody growled.

It wasn't an exaggeration. The man had quite literally growled.

"Forgive me." Clayton finally released her wrist. "I do appreciate you looking out for the lady, but I can assure you, she's fine."

Uh...she is right here and can speak for herself.

"He's right, Brody." For once. "It's all good. Really. Clayton's a client. He recently hired me to do a whole rebranding of his personal line of spa products used and sold in his family's luxury hotel chain."

"You should give them a try," Clayton interjected. "They're cruelty-free and all-natural, which are used and sold in each of my family's forty-three luxury hotels website and social media accounts."

That's what Ro did for a living, and why Clayton had hired her in the first place. Website and social media designing and maintenance were the bread-and-butter of her business, with graphic designs adding another layer to the services she offered.

And while her client list had been slow to get started, she'd hit the jackpot when Clayton Yorke had stumbled across one of her own social media accounts showcasing some of her work.

After reaching out via her work email, they'd had an initial meeting—at Cup of Joe, of course—to discuss his plans and her ideas to bring them to fruition. The hotel heir had been impressed with her growing portfolio and had hired her on the spot.

"He was trying to get my attention, and I didn't hear him, is all," Ro further excused the inappropriate behavior to a still-stewing Brody. Facing Clayton again, she told him, "Brody's with me tonight. Well, not *me*. He's a part of the group of friends I was telling you about. His teammate's the one with the birthday."

In a move that struck her as purposely slow, Clayton held out the same hand that had grabbed her a moment earlier, his blue eyes assessing Brody's six-four frame as if he were sizing him up.

"Clayton Yorke. You're part of a team, eh? Football? I'm going to go with...quarterback. No, wait...kicker."

Though the tension between the two men was so thick she'd need a jackhammer to cut through it, Ro had to roll her lips inward to keep from smiling. "It's not exactly that kind of team."

At that, Brody turned that steely gaze of his her way. She stared back with a wide-eyed, pleading gaze, silently begging him to return Clayton's offered gesture.

One. Two. Three. Four...

Five very long, very uncomfortable seconds, Brody *finally* put her out of her misery and shook the other man's offered hand.

"Brody King." A single, tight shake. "As for me and my team, we play a very different kind of game."

Lord save me from these testosterone-driven creatures.

"Brody works for a high-end private security firm here in

town," Ro quickly shared. "R.I.S.C. Delta Team. Maybe you've heard of them?"

Clayton slid his attention to her before returning his focus to Brody. Wearing a camera-ready smile she'd seen too often, he transformed himself into his public persona.

"Of course," he nodded. "I believe the acronym stands for something like Rescue, Information, Security, and…"

"Capture." Ro couldn't help but chuckle. "And it's intel, not information. But you were close."

That's it, Ro. Correct the man who's helping pay your bills. Good choice.

"My mistake." Clayton continued to hold the weight of Brody's intense stare. "R.I.S.C.… That's the same security firm that's owned by Jake McQueen out of Dallas, right? I believe I read somewhere that every field agent within the company is former military. Is that also correct?"

Feeling as though she were watching a tennis match, Ro looked at Brody before bouncing her gaze back and forth between the two men.

"It is," Brody confirmed.

"Which branch did you serve with?"

"Navy."

The teasing tone in Clayton's voice was more than a little obvious as he jokingly quipped, "What were you, a SEAL?"

Ah, hell.

Ro cringed, not missing the way Brody's jaw muscles flexed beneath his beard.

"Yes."

Clayton started to laugh, but thankfully the idiot stopped when he realized Brody wasn't smiling. A look of surprise widened his blue gaze. "You're serious."

"Yes."

He's down to one-word answers, Ro. That's not a good sign. Not good at all.

"Oh." Clayton's brows arched in surprise. "Well...in that case, I should shake your hand again." He held his out a second time. "On behalf of myself and my family, I'd like to thank you for your service."

Ro watched breathless as Megan's brother took the other man's hand once more. The look on Brody's face said he was less than impressed by Clayton's show of appreciation.

It also says he'd rather put that fist of his through Clayton's teeth than share a handshake with the guy.

Deciding to end the bizarre interaction between the trio on a high note while she could, she inched closer and said, "Well...Clayton, it was great seeing you, but we should probably be getting back to the party."

"Of course." The wealthy man lowered his hand back to his side. "I didn't mean to keep you from your celebration."

"It's okay," she lied to him again. "Oh, Monday's meeting is still on, right? The one you told me about the other day?"

If he'd told her he'd cancelled the PR staff meeting per his request, it wouldn't be the worst thing in the world.

"The meeting is still a go, yes," he burst her hopeful bubble.

Wearing a wide, fake as heck smile, Ro was finally able to end the uncomfortable conversation. "Great. I'll see you in a couple days, then."

"Looking forward to it." Blue eyes that appeared to hold far too many secrets remained fixed on hers half a second longer before turning their attention back to the man standing beside her. "It was a pleasure to meet you, Brody. Perhaps our paths will cross again someday soon."

"Count on it." Those bearded lips curled for the first

time since he'd joined her and Clayton, his smile more sinister than polite.

"Okay, then." Ro used her free hand to pull on Brody's sinewy forearm. Ignoring the searing arc of electricity the innocent touch created, she gave him a not-so-subtle tug and a prodding, "Shall we?"

The wall of muscle could have easily stood his ground, but thank *God,* he let her guide him away. When they got back to their table, Megan spotted them almost instantly.

"There you, are!" Her friend wore a look of relief. "I was about to send the calvary after you."

"Sorry. I ran into... a client." She purposely didn't tell her it was Clayton. "We got to talking, and then Brody was there, and then the three of us talked, and now we're here."

And your hand is still curled around his arm.

As if his skin were on fire, Ro released her grip and dropped her arm back to her side. Holy hell, she needed a drink. Wait. She *had* a drink.

Don't mind if I do.

Lifting the straw to her lips, she drew in a long, refreshing pull and swallowed. Then she did it again. And then she heard Brody's deep, angry bark.

"What the hell was that?"

Ro met his steaming stare with an innocent-sounding, "What?"

Instead of referencing Clayton, as she'd expected, Megan's brother looked her square in the eyes and said, "You."

Me?

"What about me?"

"That prick put his hands on you, and instead of going all Ro on his ass, you were practically falling all over yourself to make introductions and small talk.

"Who had their hands on you?" Concern filled Meg's pretty eyes.

But Ro and Brody were too busy arguing to pay her any mind.

"One, I wasn't 'falling all over' anyone," she shot back. "Two, *you* were the one who butted into a private conversation, and three, that 'prick' is a client. And not just any client, either." Ro blew out a breath. "I know he's an arrogant ass, but the guy has the power to shoot my company to the next level."

Ten levels, really. If she was lucky.

Sure, if Brody doesn't kill him first.

A low, nerve-twisting grunt was the aggravating man's only response, destroying what was left of Ro's patience with the male species. With her back teeth grinding together, she worked to control her rising temper as she stepped closer to her most recent source of frustration.

"You got a problem with me, King, just say it."

"I don't have a problem." He shook his ruggedly sexy head with a shrug. "Just didn't figure you for a kiss ass, that's all."

Ro blinked, physically recoiling at Brody's comment. His words were like a sharp dagger slicing straight through the center of its target, and they...*hurt*.

Was that really what he thought about her? She met his cold stare again, the unapologetic look there as good an answer as any.

And Ro didn't know which angered her more, the fact that Brody had said that to her, or that he'd been right. Either way, she couldn't keep from stepping forward, placing herself smack dab in the middle of Brody's personal space.

Somewhere in the back of her slightly spinning head, Ro

knew the well-intended man didn't deserve her wrath. Deep down, she understood his aggressive behavior toward Clayton stemmed from a place of friendship and protection. And that he'd obviously seen the unsettling interaction and was just trying to help.

But the bit of alcohol she'd had was apparently starting to seep into her veins, and when it came to biting her tongue, she'd pretty much reached this evening's limit.

"I wasn't kissing his ass," she hissed the denial despite knowing the opposite was true. "I was trying to keep things civil and prevent you from jumping into the middle of it with that whole *kill first, ask questions later* attitude of yours."

Having said her piece, she turned away and put her glass on the table in front of where she'd previously been sitting. Her fingers curled around the top of the chair's wooden back, but as she began pulling it back toward her, Brody's rumbled voice reached her ears once more.

"The guy had his hands on you, Ro," he repeated as if she hadn't heard him the first time.

As if *she* hadn't been the one stopped by Clayton's near-painful grip.

She opened her mouth—to reiterate the fact that she was fine, and she could fight her own battles—but Rocky chimed in at the same time with a fierce, "Someone was messing with you? Who? Did he hurt you?"

The warrior's blue gaze locked with hers, his chiseled face twisting into a deep frown. A beat later, he looked away, scanning the crowd for the unknown offender.

"It's no one," she rushed to assure him. "And I'm perfectly fi—"

"It was Yorke, wasn't it?" Megan assumed before Ro could finish.

Hearing this, Brody's focus slid from Ro to his little

sister, and back. Serious, skilled, deadly eyes bore into hers so deeply, so *intensely*, she wanted to crawl out of her skin and hide.

"Meg!" She shot her friend a look of betrayal.

Since her meetings with Clayton had all taken place at Cup of Joe, Megan had witnessed the man's bold advances on more than one occasion. When she'd expressed her concern, Ro had insisted she could handle him and made her swear not to breathe a word of it to the guys.

"Who the fuck is Yorke?" Christian jumped in next. "And why was he touching you?"

This was followed by Jagger's nonchalantly spoken, "Don't care about the why, darlin'. Just point me in the right direction."

"Wait. We're...fightin'? Why didn't somebody tell...me?" Cade's slurring was at an all-time high as he attempted to push himself to his feet.

Attempted being the operative word.

Moving with slow, uncoordinated motions, the inebriated man knocked over an empty glass and nearly toppled his chair as he stood. Springing into action, Megan rushed to help the Delta operator back into his seat.

And still, Brody and the others were staring her down, waiting for her to answer Christian's question.

Way to go monopolize the evening, Ro. Great job. Really.

She wasn't trying to make tonight about her. Not even a little bit. But being friends with the men of Delta was like having six older, very muscular, very *overprotective* big brothers.

And right now—apart from an oblivious Cade—they all looked like they were champing at the bit to beat a certain billionaire's ass. All she'd have to do is say the word, and...

Ro raised a palm to hold off the angry mob. "Easy, fellas. It was nothing, and it's over."

Naturally, Brody disagreed.

"Clayton Yorke," he announced the name to the group. "Asshole grabbed her wrist when she tried walking away."

The rest of the group nearly exploded in a collective and pissed off, *"What?"*

Liam, who'd still been sitting, rose to his feet much faster than a man of his size should be capable.

Defuse, Ro. De-freaking-fuse!

"You came up in the middle of a conversation and then took the whole thing out of context!" she practically shouted at Brody.

The first part of what she'd said was true. The second, not so much. Not that she was about to admit it to him or the others.

"I saw and heard enough to know you turned the bastard down, and he wasn't taking 'no' for an answer," Brody seethed.

"There's a shocker."

Every man there—including Cade—spun their gazes in Megan's direction. Standing stalk still, they waited for the woman to explain while Ro closed her eyes and hung her head between her shoulders.

Damnit, Meg. You promised.

"What's that mean?" Brody demanded of his sister.

"Just that this isn't the first time the creep's made a pass at Ro."

She lifted her head and opened her eyes to find her friends looking straight at her. "Okay, fine. He's a jerk. I get that. But once his launch party has passed, my communication with Clayton will be very few and far between."

"You think that's gonna stop him?"

Meeting Brody's fuming gaze once more, Ro was serious when she vowed, "If it doesn't, I'll take the necessary steps to fire him as a client."

The tanned protector leaned in closer, his piercing eyes fixing with hers as he made his own gruff promise. "That bastard even *thinks* about touching you again, you firing him will be the least of his worries."

Ro's heart thumped hard against her ribs as she remained frozen beneath his stare. Brody had always watched out for her and Megan. But this...

His reaction to what had happened was over the top, even for him. Almost as if he'd been defending the honor of his woman, rather than a friend.

If only.

"I appreciate your concern, Brody. Really, I do." She licked her lips, her tongue feeling a bit heavier than normal. "But it's done and over with, so can we please just drop it and focus on the fact that it's Cade's birthday?"

Resorting to the basics, Ro tilted her brows up a smidge and gave the man the best pleading, puppy dog eyes she could muster. The edges of his sexy face blurred, but she blinked a few times and her vision cleared in time to see the curt dip of his chin.

"Fine."

"Great."

And for the next long stretch, that's exactly what they did. The group moved on from the tense conversation to ones filled with stories, smiles, and laughter. Soon even Ro found herself feeling relaxed and stress-free.

But when she stood to go back to the bar for a water, she realized she was a little *too* relaxed.

Whoa!

She threw a hand to the side, her fingers gripping the

table's edge to steady herself. Meg looked up at her and chuckled.

"You okay?"

"Yeah, I'm...good." She was good, right?

If good means talking with a whiskey tongue and standing with a tilt, you're right as rain.

Ro started to take a step away from the table, but stopped when the entire room began to spin.

"How much have you had to drink?" A worried Megan watched her closely.

"Just a watered down Amaretto Sour, a couple shots and that." She risked it and used the hand holding the chair to point to the glass that had once held her blue, fruity drink.

"That's it?"

"Yep." Ro nodded her heavy head.

"You don't usually get this tipsy this soon."

It was true. While she didn't do a lot of hard liquor, Ro's tolerance when it came to alcohol was typically much stronger than her present condition attested to.

"Probably just had too much on an empty stomach," she assumed. "Should've eaten more before drinking."

And you should probably head home now, before you do something stupid like drink more and pass out in the middle of the bar.

With tingling, heavy fingers, Ro reached into her skirt's pocket and retrieved her cell. She had to blink several times to get the facial recognition to accept her image and unlock the home screen.

Through heavy, fumbled movements, she managed to find and open the app to order a ride from the bar to home. Seeing an available driver only a few blocks away—one with a high customer rating, no less—Ro started to finalize the transaction.

"What are you doing?" Meg asked from the seat next to her.

Ro's finger froze over the screen as she met her friend's inquisitive stare. "Getting a ride home."

"A ride? Why?"

"The alcohol isn't settling well for some reason. I think it's best if I just go home now."

Okay, yeah. She'd *definitely* slurred those words.

"Okay, but you rode here with me and Christian," her friend pointed out. "We had full intentions of taking you home."

"But it's still early." Ro started to shake her head but realized her mistake immediately and stopped. "I don't wanna make you leave on my account. You're still having fun with everyone."

Meg waved the concern away. "Nonsense. Christian's in the bathroom, but we'll leave as soon as he gets back."

"No, really. Stay. I can find a ride home."

"I'll take you."

For the second time that night, Brody's deep, sultry voice reached her from behind. Using slow, careful movements, Ro turned her head to find him now standing by her side.

"You don't have to do that," she offered.

He really, *really* didn't.

"Not letting you take an Uber home alone when you're drunk."

"I'm not drunk." She pouted. At least, she thought she was pouting. Or was she?

Shit. Maybe I am *drunk.*

Ro felt her brows turn even further inward. That couldn't be right. Not after a measly two shots and two weak-tasting foo-foo drinks. Not to mention the glasses of water she'd purposely sipped on in-between.

She swayed again, and Brody released a rough grunt. Pulling his keys from his pocket, he turned to his sister and said, "Tell Hunt I'll see him at the range tomorrow."

"You sure?" Megan rose to her feet. "We can take her home so you can stay."

"*She's* fine and already found her own ride." Ro lifted her waggling phone in the air for emphasis.

Another double-crossing sway of her body did little to support her argument.

"I'm sure." Arching a knowing brow, Brody slid his focus back to Megan. "I was about to head out, anyway. Gonna get up and hit the gym before meeting your boy at the range."

"You still picking me up on the way?" Rocky joined the overheard conversation.

Brody gave the other man a nod. "As long as your ass is up and ready."

"I'll be ready."

"What about you?" Those dark eyes found hers once more. "You ready?"

I've been ready for you my whole life.

Ro swallowed back the words before they could leave her lips and instead gave a short and sweet, "Yep."

Because apparently she no longer had a choice in the matter of who was taking her home.

"Okay, well. Drive careful." Megan pulled her brother in for a hug.

"You, too." Brody hugged his sister back. "Love ya, Sis."

"Love you, too." After another squeeze, her friend went to her. "You sure you're okay? I worry about you being in that house by yourself if you're not feeling well."

"I ap-preciate the concern, but I'm okay. Just need food and sleep."

In that order. Or maybe she'd sleep first and then eat. Or

maybe she'd eat and then—

"Well promise you'll call if you need anything." Megan pulled her in for a hug, too.

"I will. And...sorry I'm a kiss ass."

"What?" Her friend laughed as she released her gentle hold. "You're not a kiss ass, Ro. You're driven and trying to build a business. Trust me, I understand how hard that is."

"Thank you."

"But...you do need to be careful where Clayton's concerned. The way that man blatantly flirts with you—even after you've turned him down time and again—I don't know." Megan's shoulders fell with a sigh. "It's concerning."

"I know," she admitted aloud. "And I'll keep him in line. He flirts again I'll send him on his way. Promise."

"Good." Her friend gave her another hug. "Okay, now go. Get some food and get to bed. You coming by the shop tomorrow?"

Megan's image swirled. Or maybe she was swaying on her feet again. Either way, Ro realized she needed to get home sooner, rather than later.

"You kiddin'? After tonight, I'll probably be racing Cade to the front of the line. In fact, maybe I should put my order in now instead of waiting until—"

The weight of Brody's warm, muscular arm landed on her shoulders as he gently guided her away. "Okay, Ro. Let's go."

"But..." She swung her gaze back to Megan's.

The woman was doing a poor job at hiding her amused grin as she hollered after her, "See you tomorrow!"

When Ro swung her gaze back to Brody's, she had to reach around his narrowed waist and hold on tight to keep from falling. The crowd grew thicker, making it impossible for them to continue side-by-side.

In a seamless motion, the former SEAL removed his arm from her shoulders before reaching down and taking her hand in his.

Her heart kicked, her lower belly tingling from the innocent contact, the heat radiating from his touch electric. Earlier, when she'd been holding his arm, she hadn't been able to break contact fast enough.

Now...

I wish he'd hold my hand forever.

Ro's steps faltered slightly, but she quickly recovered and blinked the crazy thought away. She didn't want forever. She just wanted...

Him.

One night. That's all she wanted. All she needed, really.

Just one night of no-strings sex to solve the mystery of what Brody King was like in bed. One night and she could finally end the decades-long obsession she'd had for this man.

A man who'd just tightened his grip as he created a pathway through the crowd.

In an effortless display of command, her friend's brother had no problem getting the sea of people around them to part ways. Soon Ro realized they'd already made it to the establishment's front door.

Using his free hand, Brody pulled on the oversized handle, propping the door open with his backside. At the same time, he slid the hand that had just held hers before placing it on the small of her back.

"Watch your step." He motioned toward the metal threshold's slight lip.

Despite the warning, Ro nearly caught the toe of her black high heel as she crossed over the strip on her way out.

She threw her hand out to the side, her fingers in a death grip on the door's thin frame.

"Okay, seriously," she slurred. "I can*not* drink on an empty stomach again."

"That won't be a problem."

The solemn vow rumbled low as Brody wrapped an arm around her waist and helped her to the sidewalk lining the building. It was a promise he never should never have made, since it wasn't like he'd be around her every time she consumed an alcoholic beverage from this point on.

Still, Ro couldn't help but find his willingness to make such a promise almost...sweet.

He's not being sweet, dummy. The man obviously doesn't see you as being capable of taking care of yourself.

She considered the point her subconscious had just made, and decided it was right. It sure didn't seem as if Brody thought she was capable, anyway.

Not when it came to getting herself home, her consumption of food or alcohol... He especially didn't think she could hold her own where Clayton was concerned.

Just didn't figure you for a kiss ass, that's all.

Ro's chest tightened, the pain from Brody's previous words returning as the two made their way to his truck. They *continued* to play inside her head on an endless, humiliating loop.

And by the time she and Brody reached his truck, she decided she wasn't going anywhere with him until she made something crystal clear.

"Wait!" she blurted as he removed his hand from her back to reach for the passenger door.

Brody halted his movements. He turned his head, concern dipping his thick, dark brows as he looked back at her from over one of his broad shoulders.

"What's the matter?"

Ignoring the void his touch had left behind and straightening her spine, she opened her lungs and pulled in the deepest breath could. When she couldn't hold another ounce of oxygen, Ro released slowly through a narrow stream between her barely parted lips.

With her shoulders back and a tone that oozed more confidence than she actually felt, she held Brody's intimidating stare and stated matter-of-factly, "I'm not a kiss ass."

"I know."

"Or maybe I am," she talked over him, having second-guessed her claim almost instantly. With a drop of her own shoulders, Ro blew out a harsh, defending breath and added, "But if I am, it's only because I'm trying to build something that will provide me with a susainab... susbainab...sutainabal..." She released a frustrated huff, going with the more easily pronounced, "A *reliable* income in the future."

Why the heck was that so hard to say?

"I kno—"

"'sides..." Ro unknowingly cut Brody off again. Continuing with the slurred, one-sided argument, she added, "S'not like you and Christian don't pucker up to some of those big-wigs Delta Team works with." She emphasized the "p" for good measure. "That's just part of running a business, you know?"

Brody's features were starting to become a bit fuzzy and unfocused. Hoping to clear her vision—because the man was far too desirable not to want to appreciate every chiseled curve—she squeezed her eyes shut and then blinked them a few times.

"I do," the man before her responded.

Ro started to keep going with, "And if you can't understand that, well then...that's your problem, not..."

Her weighted voice trailed off as everything he'd been trying to say finally began to register in her stunted brain. The man she'd spent countless nights fantasizing about wasn't only *agreeing* with her...but those bearded lips of his looked precariously close to lifting at the corners.

"Hold up." Ro frowned. "You *do?*"

"Yes." Brody turned his powerful body to face her fully. "I know you're not a kiss ass, Aurora, and I..." He ran a hand over that sexy jaw of his and sighed. "I was way out of line and never should have disrespected you the way I did. Especially in front of the others." The tip of his tongue darted out before he added and almost nervous, "I'm sorry. It won't happen again."

Holy hell in a helium balloon. Did Brody King really just apologize for being a giant ass?

Ro swallowed, her lids fluttering with several confused blinks. "Oh. Um...thanks."

Taking a step closer, his hardened expression softened, the previous anger in his eyes all but gone. "Look, Ro. I really wasn't trying to be a dick in there."

"I know." She almost shook her head again, but thought better of it at the last second. "You were just being a good friend and trying to protect me when you thought I was in trouble. I *wasn't*"—she insisted—"but you didn't know that."

Those dark chocolate eyes of his fixed with hers, the intensity of his gaze so powerful it felt as if they shared an actual physical connection.

"When I saw him grab your arm like that..." Brody's expression returned to the same hardened warrior she'd seen before. "I can't...I *won't* stand by and watch some asshat pull that shit with you. I hope you can respect that."

"I do." Ro gave the slightest of nods. "And I'm sorry, too. If I hadn't let myself get into that position in the first place, you never would've felt the need to—"

"Wrong." That deadly tone of his returned with a vengeance. "The dickhead asked you out, you said no. The rest is on him, Ro. And *only* him."

"But you said—"

"I was wrong." A stark admission. "I saw him grab you, and...I lost it." Brody shook his head as if he didn't quite understand his own reaction. "It wasn't your fault, and I never should've taken it out on you." Brody gave his jaw another rub. "I damn sure shouldn't have put the blame on you. I really am sorry, Ro."

"S'okay." She slapped a floppy hand to his chest for reassurance.

His hard, hot, sculpted chest that felt *incredible* beneath her touch.

Brody covered her hand with his. "It's not." The fabulously fit man's deep rumble vibrated against her palm. "But it won't happen again. You have my word on that. Now come on." He gave her hand a little pat. "Let's get you home so you can get some of that food and rest you promised Meg you'd get."

Right on cue, a giant yawn had Ro rushing to cover her gaping mouth. "Okay," she agreed without hesitation.

Even if she wanted to argue with his plan—which she did *not*—Ro didn't have the energy.

Taking her hand in his for the second time that night, Brody led her the few remaining feet to the truck's passenger door. With gentle, patient movements, he helped her climb inside.

Before she could do it herself, her attentive friend

reached up near her head and grabbed the seatbelt, pulling it across her lap.

"Thank you," she offered softly."

A spicy male scent filled her nostrils, and Ro drew in what she prayed was an indiscernible inhale. Clicking the buckle in place, Brody lifted his focus to hers as he whispered, "Welcome."

Their gazes lingered on one another's for several seconds. Or maybe she'd imagined it. Either way, Ro had to fight the sudden urge to reach up, grab hold of his whiskered cheeks, and pull that kissable mouth to hers.

Making the decision for her, Brody cleared his throat and muttered a low, "Better get you home," before backing away and reaching for the door.

But just as he was about to shut her in, the former SEAL paused. With his sight remaining fixed with hers, the former SEAL let their locked gazes linger a beat longer.

Ro held her breath and waited, praying to all that was holy that this would be the moment she'd been wishing for. That *this* would be the day when he finally kissed her. But with her very next breath, Brody blinked, effectively destroying the unreadable moment.

He shifted to the side and shut the door, muttering something under his breath she couldn't comprehend. From what Ro could tell through her drunken haze, the Brody that drove her mad with frustration and need was back.

Quiet, stoic, and tempting as hell.

For a minute, there, she'd been so sure he was going to kiss her. He hadn't, of course. It was silly of her to consider otherwise.

But as they drove to her house in near silence, Ro stared out the window at the passing scenery and wondered...

What would he have done if I'd kissed him, instead?

3

BRODY HELD Ro steady as he used her keys to unlock the front door to her house. Keeping an arm around her waist, he guided her into the small entryway, gently kicking the door shut behind them.

Greeted with the combining scents of fresh paint, lemon cleaning spray, and varnish, Brody reached blindly for a light switch, finding—and flipping—the nearest one with ease.

"Holy shit!" Ro used her forearm to shield her eyes from the sudden, blinding light. "Give a girl some warning, next time would ya?"

With a mumbled, "Sorry," Brody turned them both toward the opened archway on his right. Ro stumbled a bit as he led her into her living room.

Though he'd never been here, Megan had kept him abreast on all the work Ro had put into the place so far. Among the daunting tasks he recalled his sister mentioning, the woman currently struggling to walk a straight line had already removed yards of old wallpaper, had painted at least this room and the space he could see to their left, and she'd replaced some of the home's old fixtures with new.

Thanks to the light from the foyer, Brody could easily see the shadowed living room with ease. As he guided her toward the couch, he took a moment to appreciate the first house she'd ever owned.

Large bay windows faced the street out front, and Ro had utilized the curved space to create a quaint little seating area. Light gray walls, a plush, cream-colored couch, and a wooden coffee table with matching end tables gave the room what he'd seen described as a modern farmhouse sort of feel.

As for the rest of the room, that was all...

Ro.

Splashes of yellows, deep reds, and dark greens brought the otherwise ordinary space to life. Add to that the artwork Ro had chosen to adorn her walls, and Brody couldn't help but smile.

"Place looks good, Ro." He kept her steady as he helped lower her onto the couch. "Meg said you've been hard at work fixing it up."

"Thanks." She fell back against the cushion with a sigh. "It's a work in progress." Her 's' lingered much longer than necessary. "And thanks for bringing me home."

Standing over her, Brody studied Ro closely. Her movements had become sluggish, her lids were heavy, and her speech was even thicker than before.

Jesus, she's plastered.

He hadn't paid much attention to how much she'd had to drink throughout the night, but damn. It must've been one hell of a lot, because the Ro he knew could hold her own against him and most of the guys on the team.

"So good to be home."

Brody watched as the amusingly drunk woman began toeing off her high heels. First one, then the other, Ro showed no concern about where they landed as she kicked them to the side.

"There." She fell against the couch again. Resting her head on the back cushion, she closed her eyes and sighed. "That's better."

His lips twitched. "You need water and food."

"Mmm kay."

With a breathy chuckle, Brody offered a muttered, "Be right back," before leaving in search of her kitchen.

Another room that appeared to have already been redone, Ro's kitchen was white. Like *really* fucking white.

The ceiling, walls, cabinets, floors, and table were all stark white. But everything else in the room...

Candy apple red.

In a way only Aurora Tennison could imagine, the talented woman had taken what he imagined had been a very outdated space and transformed it into a work of art. From the trim to the ceiling fan, curtains, chairs, outlets, and light fixtures... Hell, even the appliances were the brightest shade of candy apple red he'd ever seen.

They make red appliances? Who knew?

Not him, but apparently they did, and damn if they weren't the coolest ones he'd ever seen.

Made to look like a vintage-style refrigerator, Ro's was the brightest shade of candy apple red he'd ever seen. Same with her stove.

Brody glanced down, nearly laughing when he read the embroidered lettering on the white and red towel hanging from the oven's handle...

IDGAF

Recognizing the acronym immediately, he snorted at the

delicate vines and flowers adorning the bottom portion of the towel.

God, I love that woman.

In his search for a glass, Brody had just started to reach for one of the cabinets near the sink when he froze. He didn't love Ro. Fuck no. He *liked* her, sure.

Of course, he did.

It was why he'd damn near gone ballistic when he'd spotted that fucknut Yorke putting his hands on her. His reaction hadn't been from jealousy. He'd never even thought about his sister's friend in that way.

But she was also his friend, and he hadn't lied when he'd told her he refused to stand by and let that shit happen. And so help him, it happens again…

Clayton Yorke will learn very quickly what a mistake it was to mess with someone I care about.

And Brody *did* care about Ro. But only as a friend, and nothing more.

That why you took so long buckling her seatbelt tonight?

He swung open the cabinet, hitting paydirt on his first try. Grabbing one of her jar-style glasses, he centered it beneath the red and silver faucet—yep, apparently that was a thing, too—and got busy filling it up.

Replaying that moment back through his head, Brody took a moment to consider the question his subconscious had posed.

After her needless but adorable rant about why she was justified in kissing Clayton Yorke's ass, he'd walked Ro over to his truck and helped her climb inside. Knowing she'd spend far longer fumbling with the buckle than if he just did it himself.

But he hadn't taken a *long* time buckling her belt. Had he?

What about those few seconds after you heard the click? You know, when you looked up and caught sight of those gorgeous eyes staring back into yours? What about then, asshole?

Shit. Maybe he had gotten caught off guard by the way she'd been staring back at him. But he'd looked up, and she was there, and for a second, Brody had been damn sure she was going to lean up and kiss him. And he...

Didn't back away.

No, he hadn't. Not at first, anyway. And that shit had been bugging him ever since. It was also one of the reasons he'd stayed quiet for most of the ride here.

One, Ro had kept her head tilted away from his the entire way. And when he did talk, he wasn't certain she'd even comprehended what he'd said.

Two, Brody had been lost in his own thoughts about what the hell that was, what it meant, what it didn't mean... and then he'd realized what an idiot he was, because it wasn't anything and meant absolutely nothing.

He'd been taken aback by a pretty set of eyes. Anyone—man or woman—would have to be blind not to see Ro's ocean blue eyes and think them anything less than gorgeous. Didn't mean those who thought that wanted to sleep with her, for fuck's sake.

Funny how you jumped straight to sex. Especially when all you were picturing in your head just now were her eyes.

Christ, maybe *he* was the one who was drunk. His thoughts were sure swirling out of control as if he was.

Brody turned off the water with a bit more force than necessary, and sat the glass down onto the—yep, you guessed it—white countertops while he went looking for a medicine cabinet.

You sure you're not drunk?

If it wasn't for the fact that he'd had the one birthday

shot with the others and nothing else besides water the entire night, he might be convinced otherwise. Because this was Ro, for crying out loud.

Ro!

She was his friend. His sister's friend, really. A good buddy who called him on his shit and made him laugh.

Oh, really? Would you have rushed to Christian's or Rocky's rescues if some pansy-ass like Yorke had been stupid enough to grab one of their wrists?

Brody ignored the unspoken question because it was like comparing apples to oranges. Of course, he wouldn't have been as concerned in that situation because those guys could handle themselves without breaking a sweat.

But Ro...

He pictured her dainty wrist in that bastard's hand. The way the muscles in her delicate forearm had become taut beneath the strain of her efforts to break free.

Even now, Brody's free hand fisted at his side while his other gripped the glass with such force, he was surprised it didn't shatter. But that was only because his protective instincts where Ro was concerned had always been on high alert.

Not because he liked her, liked her. But because she was like his family.

Like her, like her? What are you, twelve?

Ready to tell his inner voice to kick rocks, Brody was still trying not to question why the urge to pound Clayton Yorke into the ground was as strong as ever when he made it back into the living room and....

Holy. Hell.

No longer on the couch where he'd left her, Ro was standing in the middle of the room near the coffee table.

And she'd just taken off her blouse and was tossing it to the side.

Long, dark brown hair fell in a continuous wave over her shoulders, the ends of several locks brushing the tips of the dusty pink shadows he could barely make out through her bra's thick dense white lace.

Flawless porcelain skin seemed to glow beneath the room's bright light as he took in the sight of her curves. Toned yet luscious, Brody had seen them before.

At the pool. The beach.

When they were younger, he, Ro, Meg, and Christian had practically lived at the beach during the summer months. And this was no different from seeing her in a swimsuit.

A white, lacey, damn-near see through swimsuit with a skirt that hugged her hips and thighs as if it were tailored specifically for her.

Brody took in the image as a whole as he tried like hell to think of something to say.

Ro's hair was slightly disheveled, her cheeks were flushed, and she was without a shirt and barefoot. And damn if he didn't find the look sexy as hell.

Don't ever remember her looking like that at the beach.

Brody swallowed. Hard. "Uh...whatcha doin', Ro?" he choked out before finally regaining the ability to walk again.

"It's hot." Her pretty face twisted into an adorable pout. "Aren't you hot?"

Getting there.

"Nope," Brody hurried the lie. "I feel fine."

You feel something, all right.

A quick clearing of his throat kept him from verbally arguing with the voice in his head. Because that voice? It was dead fucking wrong.

He wasn't hot. He felt perfectly comfortable, in fact. Not too hot, not too cold. And his zipper sure as fuck was *not* starting to feel tighter than before.

But above all else, Brody absolutely, one hundred percent, without a fucking doubt, was not physically attracted to his little sister's best friend.

Ro was attractive, sure. But he wasn't *attracted* to her. So his dick was getting hard just thinking about how soft all that perfect, statue-like skin would feel beneath his touch. So what?

That was simply a healthy male body reacting to seeing a beautiful woman standing less than three feet away. A beautiful woman wearing nothing but a bra that cupped a set of breasts he just knew would fill his fists perfectly, a form-fitting skirt that fell mid-thigh and showcased a set of long, toned legs, and...

His gaze fell to the skirt's hem, and suddenly Brody found himself wondering what he'd find if she moved the black material up just a few more inches.

What the fuck? This isn't some random woman you picked up at the bar. She's your friend!

Blinking the inappropriate thoughts away, he realized that voice was actually right for a change. He absolutely should *not* be wondering what color Ro's panties were...or if she was even wearing any at all.

He needed to give her the water, ibuprofen, and food. That's what a good friend would do, and that's exactly what he was. A *friend*.

Nothing more, nothing less.

"You're really not hot?" Ro's dark brows turned inward. "I feel like I'm on fire. Maybe..." She fumbled around a bit, her arms moving in slow, uncoordinated motions. "Maybe if I take this off, too..."

It took Brody a second longer than it should have to realize her intent.

Ro's hands vanished behind her back, her elbows pointing out to her sides as she appeared to be struggling with...

Oh, shit!

"Ro, stop!"

In an instant, everything seemed to happen all at ounce.

Brody rushed to where she stood. In a single, fluid motion, he set the glass and pills on the coffee table behind her. At the same time, he wrapped his arms around Ro and covered her hands with his to keep her from doing something he *knew* she'd regret come morning.

"What are you—"

"Don't think you really want to do that, sweetheart."

And then he heard...

"You're so pretty."

Her voice was soft. Breathless. Her words a whisper Brody wasn't entirely certain he'd heard correctly. But when he glanced down and found those vibrant blue eyes looking up at him, he knew he wasn't mistaken.

He'd been called a lot of things in his thirty-four years, but pretty wasn't one of them.

Soft, silky hair brushed against the arm still holding her close, the ends tickling the skin on the back of his hand. A hand still holding hers—and in turn, her bra—in place.

"No, that's not right," Ro changed her mind. Tilting her head to the side, that incredible—albeit glassy—stare of hers studied him more intently. "You're not pretty. You're rough and rugged. Like a cross between a warrior and a mountain man."

"A mountain man?"

"Mmm hmm..." She nodded, her hot, sweet breath

hitting his neck as she spoke. "A dark, surly, sexy mountain man full of straight lines and angry stares."

Ro thought he was sexy? Since when?

"I'm sorry?" Brody asked, because surely he'd misunderstood.

"No, *I'm* the one who's sorry, Brody." Sliding one of her hands free from his hold, she slapped it gently over the place where his heart was wildly thumping. "I'm sorry for so...so many things."

He worked his throat and forced himself to keep his eyes on hers, rather than the luscious cleavage staring back at him from inches below. "You don't have anything to apologize for, Ro."

"But mostly..." She continued as if he hadn't spoken, her voice almost ethereal as her smoldering blue gaze dropped to his lips. "Mostly, I'm sorry I never did this."

Before he could process her intent, Ro was up on her tiptoes, and her lips—those full, perfectly bow-shaped, ruby red lips—were pressing against his.

What the...

Every muscle in Brody's body stiffened, his muscles locking down tight beneath the unexpected touch. For the next few seconds, he didn't move an inch. Didn't so much as *breathe* as he stood frozen, one arm still wrapped tightly around her while the other...

The other was clenched in a white-knuckled fist at his side.

This is nothing. Just a one-sided kiss. That's all. And any second now, Ro's going to realize what she's doing, and—

Ro slid the tip of her hot, wet tongue along the seam of his unmoving lips.

Fuuuuuck.

Brody squeezed his eyes shut, his throat suddenly desert

dry as he did everything in his power to think of *anything* other than how good her half-naked form felt against his. Desperate to ignore the scent of coconuts and vanilla coming from her silky hair, he refused to acknowledge how incredible she felt in his arms.

Or the seductive way she was teasing him with her tongue.

This is wrong. This is Ro. You can't do this with her. You can't—

"Brody," Ro whispered his name as if he were a wish she prayed would be granted. With her lips brushing against his, she added a breathy, cock-filling, "I've wanted this for so long."

After two hard swallows, Brody managed to choke out a gravelly, "This?"

You know damn well what she's talking about.

"A taste." She gave a barely-there nod. "Just one. Just one, so I can finally know."

Don't ask. Just back away, and for all that is holy... Do. Not. Ask!

"Know what?" he ignored his inner voice and asked anyway.

So maybe he was curious. So fucking what?

This was as far as he was letting things go, so why not hear what the woman wanted to know? It wasn't like he planned to do anything about it, no matter what she said.

Not like he was going to remove his hand from her back so she could finish taking off her bra. Not like Brody was standing here now, imagining the exact color of those tiny, twin shadows he'd seen earlier.

He wasn't thinking about Ro's nipples or what they'd feel like against the pads of his thumbs. He wasn't picturing himself lifting that skirt up past the curve of an ass he'd somehow missed noticing until now.

And as Brody continued to stand there, waiting for the woman's big reveal, he was *not* wondering what it would feel like to slide between those toned thighs and—

"I need to know if..." Ro's slow, husky voice trailed off, breaking through his thoughts at the exact right time.

"If what?"

Again...fucking sue him.

Eyes he felt he was seeing for the very first time stared up into his. Eyes filled with secrets Brody suddenly found himself dying to know.

The blues in those eyes darkened with so much arousal, so much *desire,* it was all he could do not to strip her down and take her right there. And then she answered his question.

"If you taste as good in real life as you do in my dreams," Ro finally revealed what she'd been trying to say.

If he tasted... In her dreams?

Ro dreams about me kissing her? Since when?

And if they kissed in her dreams, what else had they done?

With all the *what-the-fucks* rolling around in his head—and the massive hard-on filling the crotch of his jeans—Brody wasn't the least bit prepared for the next swipe of her tongue.

And when she pulled his bottom lip between her teeth in a light, teasing nibble...

He slammed his mouth to hers in a kiss so hard, so hungry, Brody felt like a starving animal in heat. He didn't think about the fact that this was Ro.

Sweet, sassy, funny as hell Ro who'd grown up with his little sister. Who'd grown up with him.

Instead Brody did something he never, ever did. He allowed himself a moment in time to simply...feel.

Not the stress that came with being a private operator for hire. He didn't feel the ghosts from his past that still haunted him most nights...and some days. He didn't even feel the guilt he knew he should possess for kissing his little sister's best friend.

In that moment, the only thing Brody felt was...

Her.

Hot. Wet. Wild.

Sweet remnants of blue raspberry, coconuts, and something uniquely Ro filled his tastebuds as her tongue swirled and danced with his. The fire from her bare skin simmered against his palms as she melted beneath his touch.

Yes, Brody felt it *all*, and for once in his life, he forgot about everything else and just...felt. But seconds later...

A tiny moan escaped the back of Ro's delicate throat. One filled with sex, passion, and promises to come.

It was a sound that *should* have spurred him on in his quest. But as it seeped into Brody's lust-filled mind, it was as if a giant wave of cold water had splashed over him, dousing the flames of a fire that never should have been ignited.

If for no other reason than the fact that Ro was clearly drunk and not acting with a clear head. And he'd just taken advantage of that. Of her.

Son of a...

"Shit." Brody pulled away, abruptly ending the kiss as he placed his hands on her bare shoulders and put several inches of distance between them.

Having only been partially unclasped before, Ro's bra remained in place. Thank fuck! But just like before, if he let himself look closely, he could still make out the circular shadows behind the—

Knock that shit off, King! The woman's your friend, and she's drunk as shit.

His subconscious was right. He was supposed to be feeding her actual food, not shoving his tongue down her damn throat or obsessing about her fucking nipples.

Nipples that were so hard right now, they were stretching the bra's white lace as if the twin nubs were trying to escape.

Stop. Looking. At. Her. Nipples. You. Asshole.

"I'm sorry," Brody blurted the lame apology. "I don't..." He blew out a breath and ran a hand over his whiskered chin before offering an equally inadequate, "Shit, Ro. I shouldn't have done that. I'm sorry."

And then...he waited.

Technically she'd been the one to kiss him, but he still deserved her angry wrath. He was the sober one, and he could've stopped it much sooner than he had. Hell he never should have let it happen to *begin* with.

There was no excuse. Except...

But she'd been standing there, in that bra and that skirt...and when she'd said that thing about tasting him and dreams, he'd lost it.

I lost control.

That had never happened to him. Not ever. And there were no excuses or fucking exceptions for what he'd just done. Not when it came to a woman too inebriated to fully consent.

Especially not when it came to Ro.

Speaking of...

Brody studied her closely, searching for the slightest sign of justified anger or remorse. The tension in his taut shoulders and neck eased slightly when he found none.

What he did find, however, concerned him even more.

Looking more confused than angry, Ro was staring up at him with a frown. The heated gaze that had been there seconds before replaced by an almost foggy look in her glassy eyes.

"Brody?" She blinked several times as if to clear her vision.

Brody felt the slight sway of her body beneath his gentle hold. "Hey." He brought his head down a bit to keep her focused on him. "You okay?"

"I..." Ro looked around them as if she were trying to figure out where she was. "I don't..."

"Ro, look at me." He lifted a hand to her chin and guided her eyes back to his. "Are. You. Okay?"

The lips he'd just tasted—could still taste—parted. The woman in his arms stared up at him blindly, and then...

Those mesmerizing eyes rolled into the back of her head, her legs gave out, and Ro passed out in his arms.

Brody Fucking King.

Fury left his back teeth grinding together as he hid in the shadows of the night and watched the nauseatingly adorable little blue house. The arrogant prick was in there right now. With her.

Talking?

Laughing?

Fucking?

No, they weren't having sex. He was surprised the woman was still conscious after downing the dose of Rohypnol he'd slipped into her drink when she wasn't looking. He'd seen the way she'd wobbled up those front steps.

And the way King had held her protectively by his side the entire time.

Fucking boy scout.

He blinked, focusing on the house once again. Though Aurora's curtains prevented a clear view inside, he could still make out the darkened silhouettes moving in the glow of the living room light.

He knew that space was the living room, of course, because he'd already been inside her house.

The work she'd put into the place so far was impressive. The freshly painted walls, shiny fixtures, red as fuck appliances, colorful paintings... Aurora's choice of décor fit the whole artist vibe perfectly, which he assumed was the unsuspecting woman's whole point.

Breaking into her place had been much easier than he'd expected. It was also a necessary step in his plan.

He'd gotten in, looked around, and got out. Didn't touch, move, or take a single item. Left no trace of himself behind. He'd simply...

Looked.

Less than an hour had been enough to time fulfill the need for his original plan. But now... Now he'd have to rework the whole goddamn thing.

All because King had to swoop in and be a fucking hero.

Anger from before returned ten-fold. Tonight had started out so perfectly, but thanks to King, it hadn't ended in the way he'd hoped.

It should be him in there with her. She should be passed out cold. Vulnerable and utterly defenseless.

Mine to do with what I want.

Oh, he'd still get what he wanted. Of that, there was no doubt. This little hiccup just made things a little trickier, that's all.

It wasn't as if he hadn't considered the possibility that King would become an issue. He absolutely had. And it wasn't like all was lost and he was throwing in the towel. Fuck no.

Who's afraid of the big, bad SEAL? Not this guy.

No, he wasn't afraid, but he *would* need to step up his game. Especially if King ended up sticking around the sexy little temptress. And as he disappeared back into the shadows and walked away, a new plan was already beginning to form.

4

The bell above Ro's pounding head announced her presence as she opened the door to Cup of Joe. The glorious scent of freshly ground coffee filled her very soul, and if there hadn't been other customers around, she was pretty sure she would've moaned.

"*Please* tell me you have a whole pot back there with my name on it," she begged Megan as she approached the shop's counter.

From the other side, her friend smiled wide and shot her a knowing grin. "Did someone drink a bit too much last night?"

"I must have." Ro leaned an elbow on the top of the small, built-in bakery display. "I woke up this morning on the couch with my shirt off, a blanket draped over me, and my small bathroom trashcan on the floor next to me. Oh..." She stood straight again. "And apparently I'd gotten myself a glass of water and some ibuprofen, but fell asleep before taking it, because it was still sitting on the coffee table when I woke up an hour ago."

And now it was after eleven, and she still hadn't had her first coffee of the day.

Laughing, Megan handed her a large cup of her favorite caffeinated beverage. "Here's your usual. And what do you mean, apparently? You don't remember getting the water and ibuprofen?"

"I don't even remember leaving the bar." A fact that had freaked her the hell out when she'd first opened her eyes and realized she was home. "And I'm really hoping I didn't throw up in your fiancé's truck."

Christian babies that thing almost as much as he does Meg.

"Kind of hard to puke in Christian's truck since Brody's the one who drove you home."

The bell above the door chimed, and on reflex, Ro turned to see who'd just walked in. As if a move designed by fate, the man himself appeared.

Dressed in jeans, a dark gray V-neck t-shirt, and a black leather jacket, he looked even more prickly than normal. Dark shadows marred the skin beneath his eyes, and the man looked exhausted.

A shot of jealously ran through her veins from the fleeting thought that another woman was likely to blame for his lack of sleep. Which was ridiculous since she held no claim on Brody.

Not like he's mine to be jealous of.

"Hey, BroBro!" Megan greeted her brother with a smile. "Me and Ro were just talking about you."

"What?" Brody blinked, his slightly widened gaze sliding to hers and then back to his sister's. "Wh-why?" Another ping-ponged gaze between the two women. "Why were you talking about me?"

If she'd thought it possible, Ro would have been convinced the man was nervous. Scared, even. But this was

Brody. Nothing made him nervous, and the only time she'd ever seen him scared was when Megan had almost been killed.

A few yards from where they stood now, as a matter of fact.

But lucky for her friend, Brody and Christian had gotten to Cup of Joe just in time to take down the man who'd been about to shoot poor Meg. And all because she'd inadvertently witnessed something she shouldn't have...and she hadn't even known it.

So yeah, Ro could appreciate the man being scared back then. But to be nervous about the mundane conversation between her and his sister...

"Relax, big guy." Ro patted his upper arm, too hungover to really appreciate how warm and incredibly tight his bicep was. "Meg was just telling me how you drove me home last night, that's all. Thanks for that, by the way." Belatedly, she added a mumbled, "Hope I didn't throw up in *your* truck."

That would be the absolute worst.

Dark eyes that were almost always unreadable stared down into hers with a look she couldn't decipher. When he didn't respond, Ro automatically assumed the worst.

Oh, no! That's why he looks so uncomfortable around me. And...ohmygod! That's why he gave me such a strange look when he first walked in.

She gasped, her hand flying up to cover her gaping mouth. "Oh, god. I did, didn't I?"

"What?" Brody frowned a millisecond before those thick brows of his shot straight up into two twin arches. "Oh...no!" He rushed to reassure her. "You didn't throw up in the truck or inside your house...or anywhere, as far as I know. At least you hadn't before I left your place this morning."

Wait a minute. Did he just say...

"This morning?" Ro's heart nearly stopped. She had to have heard that wrong. He had to have meant to say, "Last night," she corrected with a nervous chuckle. "You mean to say last night, right?"

A slight shake of his head sent her stomach to the polished concrete floor below.

"I slept on the floor after you passed out." Brody shrugged his broad shoulders. "Didn't want to leave you alone in case you got sick in the middle of the night."

Ro's throat threatened to close, but she swallowed past it and tried not to freak the heck out. Brody King had spent the night in her house...and she couldn't *remember* it?

Ohmygod. Ohmygod. Ohmygod.

Immediately she tried reaching back into her brain for something—*anything*—from the time between the bar and this morning. But she couldn't picture even the smallest of details because...they simply weren't there.

Her memory from last night was a totally blank slate, wiped clean from her ability to recall.

Ro couldn't remember a single, solitary thing from her time in Brody's truck. There were no memories of the two of them arriving at her house. Of him walking her inside.

She couldn't even remember him being inside her house...or on her living room floor. The *floor!*

Heat filled Ro's cheeks, and thanks to her pale skin, she knew she had to be blushing up a storm. But embarrassment didn't even begin to describe how she was feeling.

"Please tell me I didn't do something monumentally stupid like...dance on the coffee table or something?" She sent Brody a pleading look she prayed would yield the desired response.

Megan laughed from behind the counter, but the man's hesitation nearly gave Ro a full-blown heart attack.

"There was no table dancing," he finally confirmed.

Relief left Ro chuckling nervously. "Thank god." And then, "You really slept on my floor last night?"

Come to think of it, that *would* explain the glass of water, ibuprofen, and the trash can. All sweet, thoughtful gestures that made her fall for the man even more.

Damn you, King.

"Be right back." Megan walked away to help her manager, Kate, fill a particularly large order.

A second later, Brody tugged on the sleeve of Ro's hoodie, leading her to the end of the counter. Away from the other customers in line.

"You really don't remember?" he asked as soon as they were out of earshot from anyone else.

"I really don't." Ro glanced around and then leaned in close before asking, "And why are we whispering?"

His dark lashes lifted and fell with three long, confused blinks, his throat bobbing with a swallow that should *not* be sexy.

"What exactly *do* you remember about last night?"

Setting her lidded to-go cup onto the counter to her left, she released a breathy laugh and shoved her hands into the hoodie's large center pocket.

"Not a lot, as it turns out. I remember riding to the bar with Christian and Meg...hanging out at the bar with them, and you, and the others..." Ro frowned. "Wait. Did we sing Happy Birthday to Cade?"

"We did." A curt, too-serious nod. "What else do you remember?"

She thought back some more. Her gut clenched, her chest tightening with regret as she thought maybe, "Did you and I..." Brody's stare widened only slightly just before she finished with, "Argue?" Ro searched his guarded gaze for the answer. "For some reason, I feel like you and I got into some sort of fight. Did we?"

She couldn't imagine ever yelling at Brody like the blips and flashes her muddled mind were showing her. But—

"We butted heads over a client of yours," he offered. "You remember seeing Clayton Yorke last night?"

"Clayton?" Now Ro really *was* starting to panic. Looking away, she desperately tried to pull from her memory bank. If she'd done something to humiliate herself in front of a client as big as him... "Blue," she blurted the word as it came to her.

"I'm sorry?"

Her eyes flew back to his, her heart giving a hard kick to her ribs at his search for clarification. But she had no idea why.

Returning to her previous efforts, she concentrated on why the color blue had unexpectedly shot to the forefront of her mind. What was it about that color?

Blue. Blue. Blue...

"I-I think..." She paused. "Did I order a drink that was blue? I want to say I had something sweet, but I can't quite put my finger on the flavor."

"Blue raspberry." Brody swallowed. "And cocounts."

The man's confident answer had Ro's focus sliding back up to him. Licking her lips, it was almost as if she expected the taste to still be there.

"Blue raspberry," she mused. "It could have been that. Whatever it was, it must have packed quite a wallop. I'm just sorry you had to deal with me in that condition." Something else struck her then, another thought that left her cheeks burning with disgrace. "Did I at least wait until after you were asleep to take off my shirt?"

With his gaze still locked with hers, Brody had just

started to lean a hand onto the counter next to him when she asked the embarrassing question. Misjudging the distance between his hand and the smooth surface, he missed his intended target and instead, knocked into a plastic straw holder nearby.

The container started to tip. Almost immediately, she and Brody sprang into action, their hands shooting out lightning fast to keep the container upright.

At first, Ro thought they'd moved just in time. But when their fingers inadvertently met in the frenzied chaos, Brody yanked his hands back, sending the trove of paper covered straws flying.

"Oh, my gosh!" She bent over to start picking up the ones that had fallen to the floor.

Brody moved to do the same, and their heads hit.

"Ouch!" Ro's palm immediately went to the source of her pain.

"Shit." Brody straightened his spine and scratched a small spot on the top of his head. "Sorry."

She couldn't help but laugh. "It's okay. How about this? I'll go down. You stay up."

The man's eyes widened a hair, and though she couldn't be sure, he appeared to be struggling with his thoughts for some reason.

"I mean...if it means that much to you, *you* can get the ones from the floor, and I can handle those on the counter."

"I got 'em."

His short, barked answer was confusing to say the least, but Ro's much needed coffee was still waiting, and the straws weren't going to take care of themselves. So she squatted down and got to work.

Stacking the ones she'd collected from the floor onto the other side of the counter—because who wants straws that have been on the floor—they were putting the last of the ones from the counter back into the container when she asked him, "Are you okay? You seem a little off today."

"I'm good." A low, decidedly unconvincing rumble. "Just a long night."

Oh. That.

"I'm sorry." Guilt assaulted her, and Ro paused to offer a sincere, "It's because of me, isn't it?"

Brody's hand slipped while sliding the final straw into place, tipping the container a second time. On reflex, she grabbed hold of it...and his hands.

He froze. She froze. Their gazes became fixed, and for a split second, Ro thought she saw a flash of heat reflecting in those dark, guarded eyes. But then—

"Here ya go, BroBro!" Megan reappeared with a cheerful smile. "I've got your Americano, hot with an extra shot, Rocky's vanilla cold brew with *two* extra shots, Christian's white mocha, hot with whipped cream, Liam's regular mocha frappe, and Jagger's caramel crunch Frappuccino with extra butter toffee crunch, extra caramel drizzle, and extra whipped cream."

Brody blinked, breaking the bizarre connection they'd been sharing. "Thanks, Sis." He reached over the counter to grab the two disposable trays filled with drinks from Megan's hands. "Guess I'd better get these to the guys so we can head out."

The other woman shook her head with a grin. "I can't believe you're still going to the range after being out drinking last night."

"For the record, I only had one shot the whole night. And Cade was the only one who got trashed."

"The only one on the *team*, you mean," Megan chuckled, turning her hazel eyes in Ro's direction.

"Fine. I got wasted," Ro admitted. "I got black-out drunk and completely humiliated myself in front of your brother and...who knows who else? Now can we please be adults and just forget it ever happened? I have. Literally." A soft laugh at the not-so-funny joke.

She hated that she couldn't remember such a huge chunk of time. Hated the feeling of vulnerability she couldn't seem to shake.

"Yep," Brody agreed to her request surprisingly quickly. "I agree. Let's just forget it ever happened and move on."

"*Thank* you."

"Suit yourselves," Megan teased. "I'm totally banking this one to use the next time this one"—she pointed a thumb in Ro's direction—"gives me crap about something stupid I've done."

Ro sent her friend a deadpan expression as she pointed out, "You realize, in order for that to happen, you'll have to do something stupid in the future, right?"

"I know." Megan shrugged. "I mean, it's me. If any of us is going to do something dumb, it's gonna be me."

The three stood staring in silence for a full two seconds before both Brody and Ro nodded their heads in agreement.

"She has a point." Ro glanced up at the former SEAL.

He chuckled, but the sound was...off, somehow. Almost as if the reaction had been forced. Ro opened her mouth to make sure things really were okay between them, but he didn't give her the chance.

"I really do need to get going." Brody tipped his chin toward Megan. "Thanks for the coffee. Be sure to put it on Delta's tab."

Megan sent her brother a smile and a wave. "Already did. Have fun at the range and be careful." The adorable brunette added a belated, "And make sure my fiancé doesn't shoot himself in the foot! Or...anywhere else. He has an aisle to walk down soon, you know?"

"Oh, I know." The tall, dark, and heart-stoppingly tempting man sent his sister a wink. "Love ya, Sis."

"Love you, too, BroBro."

The close bond between the siblings both warmed and tightened Ro's chest. She loved the closeness Megan and Brody shared. After losing their parents in a freak accident—a chunk of bridge broke loose at the exact moment their car was passing underneath—the brother and sister duo were the only family the two had left.

At least they have each other.

True. Things could be worse for her friends. They could have no family left.

Like me.

"See ya, Ro."

Brody's mumbled farewell pulled her from the depressing thoughts.

"You need help with that?" She motioned toward the two trays of drinks. "I can walk with you to the office. It's the least I could do after you were kind enough to take care of me last night. Plus..." Her blue gaze slid down to the straws and back up to his. "I wouldn't want you to spill them."

That last bit had been a purposeful jab, poking fun of his sudden—and very un-Brody-like— issue with coordination.

Brody's lips didn't so much as twitch. "I'm good, but thanks."

It was all she got before he spun on his heels and walked out of the shop. Through the window, Ro followed his seemingly hastened movements until he was no longer visible from where she stood.

"Is it just me, or was your brother acting really strangely?" She turned back to her friend.

Facing away, Meg spoke while re-stocking the stack of cups near the espresso machine. "Strange how?"

"I don't know." Ro shook her head and picked up her nearly forgotten coffee. "He just seemed...distracted. Or something." Bringing it to her lips, she tested the liquid's temperature before taking a careful swig of the dark and steaming nectar of the gods. "Of course, what do I know? I don't even remember him driving me home or being in my house."

Apparently there was a lot she didn't remember. Which was so strange because that *never* happened to her. Not ever.

"If you're not feeling up to going to the movies later, we can reschedule," Meg offered. "I'm sure you're as exhausted as Brody."

Shit. She'd forgotten they'd made plans to see the newest release in their favorite scary movie franchise.

"Nope, I'm good." Or at least, she would be by the time this evening came. "What time did you say the show starts?"

"Seven."

"So...meet at the theater at, what...six forty-five?"

"I was thinking the same." Meg nodded. "Since all we'll have to do is scan the tickets on my phone and pick up the pre-ordered food and drinks. You still just want popcorn and a water?"

"Better change the water to soda. Don't want to fall asleep mid-movie."

"You'd better not! We've waited three years for this one to come out."

She released a soft chuckle. "I'm kidding. But do switch my drink, please. Theater popcorn always goes better with bubbles."

"And this is why we're best friends."

Ro's smile grew wide when she caught sight of her friend's toothy grin. "That and many, many other reasons. Ugh…I'd better go." Reaching over the counter, she gave Megan a hug before pulling back and grabbing her coffee once again. "I have to run to the post office, get groceries for the week, and I wanted to stop by that new dress shop in Block Thirty-Seven." An entire block dedicated to food, movies, and fashion in the heart of Chicago's downtown Loop.

"I wish I'd known. We could've gotten tickets for a showing at the theater there instead of the one we're going to."

"It's okay." Ro blew off the other woman's concern. "We're familiar with the other one, so it's all good."

"Next time," her friend promised.

"Next time. But for now…" A quick look at her watch. "I really do need to get scootin' if I want to have time to look for a dress."

"What's that for again?"

"Clayton Yorke's launch party."

At the mention of the other man's name, Megan's pretty face twisted into a scowl. "You're still going to that?"

Ro blinked. "Uh…yeah. Why wouldn't I?"

"After what he did to you last night?"

Confusion left her clueless, but then, "Crap. That's right. Brody said he and I butted heads over Clayton, but then we backtracked to try to figure out where my memory left off, and then he spilled the straws, and you came with the drinks, and then…"

He left.

"Well I didn't see it, but I can tell you what happened after."

"After what?"

"After that jerk, Yorke, grabbed you like some sort of possessive Neanderthal."

"He...grabbed me?"

"That's what Brody said when the two of you got back to the table. He said Clayton asked you out, you said no, and when you tried walking away, Clayton grabbed your wrist." Concern laced Megan's hazel stare. "Brody saw what happened and got in Clayton's face. But he was also mad because he said you kissed up to Clayton rather than putting him in his place."

"He...said that?"

God, I hate not remembering.

Megan nodded. "I haven't seen my brother that mad in a long time."

Great. So not only had she burdened him with her drunk ass, but she'd also prefaced that by making him mad.

"That's probably why he was acting so weird just now. He's probably still ticked off at me."

She was pretty pissed at herself now, too. For letting herself become so intoxicated, she was missing parts of the entire evening. Important parts, like her letting a client off the hook after getting physical with her, Brody King driving her home and sleeping on her floor.

Taking care of her, even though she'd apparently made him angrier than Megan had seen him in a long time.

Way to go, Ro. Way to freaking go.

"Brody?" Megan tossed a hand towel over one shoulder. "I wouldn't worry about him. You know my brother loves you."

Ro nearly choked on the sip of coffee she'd just taken. After a few coughs, she cleared her throat and composed herself. "Wow. Sorry." She patted her chest with her free hand. "Guess it went down the wrong way."

The bell on the door chimed again, and this time a large group of laughing twenty-somethings walked in. Knowing her friend was about to get very busy, Ro gave Megan another quick, final hug before leaving with a promise to see her this evening at the theater.

Four hours later, her P.O. box had been checked; she'd found a dress she was pretty sure she was going to get for Clayton's launch party. Her groceries had been bought, and she was finally back home.

Having parked next to the small, one-car attached garage that had come with the property, Ro checked her surroundings the second she got out of her car. From the time she left Cup of Joe to pulling out of the grocery store parking lot, Ro could've sworn someone had been following her.

She never actually saw anyone. Still didn't see anyone. It was just a feeling she got while walking back to her car after leaving Megan's shop. A feeling that had stayed with her throughout her time at the post office, trying on dresses, and again in the milk and bread aisles.

You're just being paranoid and feeling out of sorts because you can't remember half of last night.

Realizing the voice in her head was probably right, Ro went to work grabbing the plastic bags filled with fresh produce, meat, and a few boxed, bagged, and canned goods from her car's back seat.

With three hanging from each forearm, she fisted the milk jug's handle and righted herself before using her hip to shut the car door. Pressing the fob in her left hand, Ro locked the vehicle as she made her way through the simple wooden gate leading into her small back yard.

She let it slam shut behind her, not bothering with the latch she never used. The privacy fence was sturdy and well-built, but a metal latch wasn't going to stop someone from hopping over if they felt inclined to do so.

Her doors, on the other hand...

Ro inserted her house key into the metal lock and turned, surprised when she was met with no resistance.

What the...

She turned the knob and pushed the door open, that paranoia from before bubbling back up with the force of a tsunami. She always locked her doors. Car and house.

Always.

This was Chicago, for crying out loud. *Of course,* she kept her stuff locked up tight. It was a habit drilled into her by her parents from the time she was big enough to reach the doorknobs.

Although to be fair, she had been feeling very out of sorts this morning. Maybe...

Ro sat the milk and bags down onto the round kitchen table she'd purchased a few weeks before. Turning back, she double checked that the door was shut tight before snicking both the knob and deadbolt locks into place.

She returned to the awaiting groceries, getting halfway through putting it all away when she noticed something strange. One of her cabinets...one she hadn't opened yet... was slightly ajar.

With a frown, Ro went over to it and opened it the rest of the way. It was the cabinet where she kept her coffee mugs, only she hadn't gotten one down this morning.

It was probably Brody.

Her heart thumped at the thought, her belly swirling with regret and guilt from the previous night's events. Regret that she couldn't remember all that had happened, and guilt that she'd been so far gone Brody hadn't felt safe leaving her home alone.

Ro started to shut the cabinet when she spotted something strange. She always kept her mugs upside down on the shelf. Something her mother had always done to "keep the dust and bugs out".

Not that they had bugs. Before she got sick, her mom had been an *impeccable* housekeeper. And after...

After, Ro had taken on the role of full-time student, chef, and maid.

Her dad had done what he could. But between working overtime at the factory to help cover the bills and added medical expenses and spending nearly every minute he had at home by her mom's bedside, most of the daily chores had fallen into her young lap.

And when her mother passed away, it was as if she lost both parents that day. A few years later, her dad was gone for good.

I miss you guys so much.

Ro allowed herself a moment to picture her parents' faces, before shaking off the melancholy thoughts and returning her focus back to what had stopped her in the first place. The mug.

Her favorite mug, to be exact. And as Ro turned it upside down—the way she always kept her mugs—an uneasy feeling gnawed in her gut.

She jumped when her phone dinged with an incoming text.

"Geez, Ro," she scolded herself. "Give yourself a heart attack, why don't you?"

Reaching behind her, she pulled her cell from the back pocket of her jeans. Ro checked the screen, smiling when she saw the message had come from Megan.

Megan: *How'd dress shopping go? Find anything?*
Ro: *One. Maybe. I'll show you pics when I see you.*
Megan: *Can't wait! See you soon!*
Ro: *See you soon!*

Ending her last text with a heart emoji, she slid her phone into her hoodie's front pocket and finished putting the groceries away. With a loud exhale, her headache was finally subsiding, but the remnants were still there.

Hoping a long, hot soak in the tub before her movie night with Meg would do the trick, she went into her bedroom. Pulling her hoodie up over her head, she tossed it onto her bed.

Ro removed her jeans, laying them on the mattress next to the hoodie, before going over to her dresser and pulling open the top drawer. She started to reach for her favorite pair of panties, stopping mid-grab when she realized they weren't there.

Her brows scrunched together with confusion because she knew they'd been in there earlier that morning. She'd seen them. Had almost put them on after her shower. But at the last minute, Ro had chosen a different pair, wanting to keep the others for when she went out tonight.

Reaching inside the drawer, she began rummaging through the collection of silk, cotton, and lace. And after picking through every single pair, the result was the same.

Where the heck did they go?

One more quick search later, she finally blamed it on her still-muddled memory and picked out a different pair. Ro started for her closet, wanting to go ahead and lay out the leggings and sweater she'd picked out for later, when she noticed her closet door was cracked open.

Her steps faltered half-a-second before coming to a complete stop. Like with the locks, her habit of keeping closet doors shut was one that stemmed from childhood. One of those monsters-in-the-closet things she never quite got over.

With that gnawing feeling growing heavier in the pit of her stomach, Ro cautiously made her way across her room to the door in question. Putting her palm against the door's smooth surface, she put just enough pressure on the painted wood to slowly swing the door all the way open.

The light in the walk-in closet was off, making it impossible to see anything more than shadows. Heart racing wildly inside her chest, she used her free hand to reach for the light switch on her left. Ro held her breath and sent up a quick prayer before flipping it on.

And then...

She released the air she'd been holding in one quick, powerful exhale. "Way to freak yourself out, Ro."

Moving with rough, frustrated steps, she spent the next few minutes mentally berating herself while also changing her mind about what she wanted to wear. Going with jeans, a *different* sweater, and a pair of brown ankle boots with a slight heel, Ro laid the items neatly on her bed before heading to her jewelry chest to pick out a necklace and some earrings.

She reached for a simple gold chain, deciding it would accent her cream colored cable knit sweater well. And since the pair of diamond earrings that had once belonged to her mother had gold backs and posts, Ro thought they'd be the perfect addition to finish off the understated look.

Pulling out the first of four tiny drawers, she picked up the small white box with "Mom's" written on top. Ro lifted the lid, expecting to find the heirlooms nestled snuggly on a bed of soft cotton. Instead, she found the box empty.

Oh, the cotton was there, but her earrings? Correction, her *mother's* earrings? Gone.

What the...

A very real, very strong feeling of unease began settling in. First her door was left unlocked, then the coffee mug was right side up...her panties were missing, and now the one real piece of her mother she'd had left was gone?

Ro spun on around, doing a complete three-sixty turn, her mind whirling and swirling twice as fast as her body. One or two of those things could be explained away by coincidental happenstance. But when she put them all together...

Someone's been here.

No. No one had been here. She'd simply misplaced a couple things, that's all.

To prove her point, Ro pulled the drawer completely free of the jewelry chest and carried it to her bed. Dumping everything out onto her white down-alternative comforter, it took little effort to see the earrings she was searching for weren't with the others.

She went back to the chest and pulled out the next drawer. Giving it the same treatment as the first, Ro went through its contents as well. Her heart sank into her feet when she yielded the same results.

Her mother's earrings weren't in the second drawer, either. Or the third. Or the fourth. They'd simply vanished.

Just like my underwear.

Jumping up from the mattress, Ro marched shirtless into her bathroom. Going straight for the hamper, she picked up the small wicker-like basket and dumped its contents onto the floor. She then dropped to her hands and knees and began sorting through the few pieces of dirty clothing now splayed on the cool ceramic tile.

Her gut tightened when she realized the missing underwear wasn't there, either.

What the hell is going on?

Knowing there was still one other place to look, she pushed herself up off the floor and went in search of the laundry room. Quite generous for the home's smaller size, the eight-by-eight-foot room sat just off the kitchen toward the back of the house.

She went straight for the washing machine, which was empty. Next Ro opened the dryer. It wasn't empty, but when she pulled everything out that was in there, the only items she found were a few towels, washcloths, and her extra set of sheets.

Fear and uncertainty had her putting her back to the nearest wall and sliding down until her rear hit the floor. With trembling hands, Ro reached into her pocket in search of her phone.

Pulling it free, she entered her password and dialed the number one contact on her list. She put the device to her ear and waited, praying the person she'd called would answer.

Two rings later, they did.

"Did you change your mind about tonight?" Megan traded a more traditional salutation for a question.

"H-hey, Meg. Do you, uh…." She cleared her throat. "Do you think maybe you could come here before the movies instead of meeting there?"

A slight pause filled the phone's speakers before her friend responded with a hesitant, "Sure. Is everything okay?"

"I-I don't know. I mean, yeah. Yes. I'm sure everything's fine, I just…"

"Ro." Megan used the same kind of tone a mother would to a fibbing child.

"Okay, look. I really, really need you not to make a big deal out of this, okay?"

"I can't make that promise without knowing what's going on."

"I can't tell you what's going on without you making that promise."

Another pause. "Okay, fine. I promise I won't make whatever you're about to tell me into a big deal."

Ro felt mildly better, but there was still one other promise she needed her friend to make. "There's one more thing."

"What's that?"

"You can't tell Brody."

She could practically hear the other woman's frown when Megan said—

"Brody? Okay, now you really are starting to scare me."

Yeah, well, I'm starting to scare myself.

"Promise you won't say anything to your brother. Or Christian." How could she forget about Christian?

"I won't turn this into a big deal, and I won't tell my brother or fiancé. Now will you *please* just spill it already?"

Ro looked at the pile of clean laundry now strewn about her floor. She thought about the panties and the coffee mug. The back door and her mom's missing jewelry. That gut feeling of being followed she hadn't been able to shake most of the day.

And with a deep inhale, followed by a long, controlled exhale, she finally said aloud what she'd been afraid to admit she was thinking...

"I think someone's been in my house."

5

A FEW MINUTES EARLIER...

BRODY TIGHTENED HIS GRIP ON THE MK12 SPR, OR SPECIAL Purpose Rifle. The lightweight sniper rifle felt like home in his hands, its threaded-muzzle free floating stainless steel barrel holding steady as he brought his newest target in the center of his sights.

Knowing it was his last shot of the day, he wanted to make it count. With his belly on the ground and his trigger finger lowering, he curled it around the cool, curved metal.

Waiting for the passing breeze to calm, he took a deep breath and held it. And then he began the countdown...

Three.

Two.

One.

Brody exhaled slowly, squeezing the trigger as he emptied his lungs. Through his 1,000-yard scope, he saw the head of the targeted plywood cutout explode as his bullet struck its center with unforgiving force.

"Damn, brother." Rocky lowered his tactical binoculars and shook his head. "You got a beef with someone or something?"

Flipping up the weapon's metal stand, Brody pushed himself back up to his feet. "What makes you say that?" he asked, dusting himself off with his free hand as he started for the covered pistol range to start packing up his other weapons and ammo.

The blond explosives expert stood as well, easily catching up and walking beside him. Christian and the others had all called it a day about forty-five minutes earlier, but he'd needed a few more kills to ease the tension still rolling through him.

When Rocky volunteered to stay with him, he didn't want to be an ass and say no. Not like he owned the place.

"Just seems like most of your shots today have been a little...I don't know. Overkill."

Brody raised his scope and studied the demolished target through its lens. He'd pretty much annihilated the innocent piece of plywood.

That one. The one before that. The one before that...

"You'd rather I slap the enemy's hand and make them pinky promise to be good?" Brody snapped back. Almost immediately, he muttered a curse and offered his teammate and friend an apology. "Sorry. Didn't sleep well."

Seems like that's your excuse for everything today, isn't it?

He'd used that same line earlier in Megan's shop. With Ro.

Aurora.

Christ, he'd been such a stuttering, stumbling fool around her today. Hesitant in his answers, knocking the damn straws every which way. But fuck. He hadn't expected to walk into Cup of Joe and see her there. Not that late in the morning.

Ro's habitual morning coffee was a routine you could damn near set your watch to. It's why he'd purposely waited until the last possible minute to put in the team's order, knowing Ro typically hit the shop by nine most mornings.

Brody had been *sure* he was in the clear. He, as it turns out, was not.

Not only did he see the very woman whose face—and lace-clad breasts, and lips, and talented tongue—had been running through his mind since that mind blowing kiss... She apparently had zero recollection of the entire, intimate interaction.

Which was great news. At least, it *should* have been.

Learning Ro's memory of the kiss was non-existent should have been a massive relief. The perfect excuse to forget it ever happened. Only...

The harder I try to forget, the more I want to taste her again.

But goddamn it, he couldn't be thinking that shit. He just couldn't. Not about Ro. Any other woman in the entire fucking world, fine. But not her.

Small clouds of dust kicked up beneath his pounding boots as he reached the pistol lane he'd been shooting from earlier. Stepping beneath the metal roof onto the concrete slab, Brody moved with rough, almost angry movements as he began refilling the mags he'd brought with him.

Always keep 'em loaded and ready.

The voice from his past took him a bit off guard. It had been ages since he'd thought about his former SEAL team leader. Fleetingly Brody's mind wondered what the man was up to and mentally wished him well.

But just like every other time he tried thinking of something other than Ro, memories of her sweet taste—and the way those soft, plump lips felt against his—stormed in, threatening to take out every last one of his good intentions with the same speed and accuracy as his MK12.

And the kickass Special Purpose Rifle shot its MK262 MOD 1-C 5.56mm rounds at two-thousand, seven hundred-fifty feet per second.

"Sorry you didn't get much sleep." Rocky's deep voice broke through as the other man went to his own lane. "Not surprised, though. Heard Ro kept you up all night."

The 9mm hollow point pinched between Brody's thumb and index finger shot out, flying across the three-foot table and falling onto the ground on the other side. With a sigh, he left the sheltered area, walking around to retrieve the bullet.

Bending down, he picked it up, blew it off, and returned to his previous task.

"Ro didn't keep me up all night," he growled, shoving that same round into the mag. "Her hard ass floor did."

It was more or less the truth. Ro's floor *was* hard. And technically, since she'd been passed out on the couch the entire night, she hadn't kept him up, either.

Pretty sure your dick would disagree with that last point.

Brody's jaw grew tight as he grabbed the next box of ammo and another empty weapon. He'd promised himself he wasn't going there, and damn it, he *wasn't*.

Even as he thought it, the image of Ro sleeping peacefully on her couch that same morning filled his mind's eye. It was how she'd looked as he'd slipped away at the ass crack of dawn.

He'd returned the throw pillow and blanket he'd used to their rightful places, refilled her glass with fresh water, and moved them further down the coffee table so they were within her reach. And then he'd left.

But before he'd shut the locked door behind him, Brody had allowed himself a brief moment—no more than a handful of seconds—to look back. To take in the sleeping beauty curled beneath the soft blanket he'd found and committed the stolen image to memory.

Only in that moment, when Brody had studied all that long, dark hair, soft pale skin and lips he knew tasted like blue raspberries, coconut, and sex, he'd thought...

Ro's no Sleeping Beauty. She's my very own Snow White.

And he'd spent most of the day doing everything in his power not to think about that or the dreams that had kept him in a fitful state of unrest the night before.

Dreams where Ro's naked body had been lying on top of his. That incredible mouth of hers kissing him in places other than his hips. His hands touching, squeezing, and teasing her feather-soft skin while he drove himself deeper and deeper inside her—

"Yo, King! Have you even listened to a single word I've said?"

Shit. "Sorry, what?"

"Damn, man." Rocky's blue eyes found his as the man finished prepping his own weapons for next time. "You don't usually space out like that. Guess you really *do* need some sleep, huh?"

That and sex. Don't forget the sex.

His greedy cock twitched at the thought. It had been what...eight, nine months since he'd been with a woman? And Brody couldn't even remember how long he'd gone without before that.

Problem was casual, no-commitment sex no longer held the same appeal as it had in his twenties. Hell as recent as a couple of years ago, he'd had no problem going out and hooking up with a nice, single woman looking for nothing more than a night of consensual sex.

Those one-offs hadn't just been about scratching an itch, though. They'd gotten him through those nights when the ghosts of what he'd seen, heard, and done became too powerful to quiet all on his own.

Luckily, over time, those haunting memories had finally begun to fade. Not disappear. More like they'd go dormant for a stretch. But Brody knew they'd never, ever fully leave.

The nightmares...the *memories*... They were a part of him now. Always would be. But he was damn tired of letting the past dictate his future.

He may not know what the years ahead held for him, but one thing Brody didn't want—what he was through wasting his time with—were emotionless, meaningless hook-ups.

He wanted something real. Something lasting. A relationship that was passionate, loyal, and lasting. A life like the one his mom and dad had shared.

A love like the one Christian found with Meg.

A woman who loved and accepted every single part of him. His present. His job. His past.

Someone to wake up to. Someone to be there when he got home from work—whether that be at their office downtown or some desert in the middle of Bumfuckistan. A woman to curl up with at night, to help replace the bad memories with a lifetime of happy ones.

Christian found that with Meg. And while it was admittedly weird at first for Brody to see his friend and his little sister playing kissy face, he couldn't be happier for the two.

Jealous but happy.

If they can make it work, maybe I can have forever, too.

The thought no more struck when Ro's gorgeous face flashed through Brody's mind. Taken aback by the unexpected leap his sleep-deprived brain had decided to travel on, he lost his grip on the plastic tray filled with 9mm rounds, dumping out half-a-dozen bullets before regaining his hold.

The unspent rounds rolled every which way on the flat, wooden surface in front of him.

"Fuck!" Brody slammed the tray down so he could pick up his mess.

Mentally berating himself for not being more in control of his thoughts—and his hands—he caught one before it fell over the edge.

Jesus, what the hell was wrong with him today? Control was his thing. Always had been. Yet he'd been walking around knocking shit over and dumping stuff everywhere he went.

You know what the problem is. You just don't want to admit it.

Rocky shot him a look of concern. "You sure you're good?"

"Yeah," Brody lied. "Like you said, I just need to catch up on some sleep."

And sex. Sex would definitely help.

When Ro's princess face threatened to consume his thoughts again, he somehow found the strength to block it out. Drawing in a deep, cleansing breath to keep from letting loose the string of other curse words filling his head, Brody slowly and patiently set about picking up the spilled ammo and returned the tray to its cardboard box.

Okay, scratch that. Maybe he didn't need forever. Maybe his problem was as simple as the actions of a drunken friend clashing with his underserved hormones.

Maybe all he needed was a night of hot, wild, passionate sex.

And just like that, the memory of Ro's tongue dancing with his fell over him. A moment so deeply engrained he could almost still taste her. Even now, hours later.

Knock it the hell off, King. You're not sleeping with Aurora, and that's final!

No shit, he wasn't having sex with his sister's best friend. Because that would be...

Hot.

Wet.

Wild.

Wrong. It would be very, very wrong.

Oh yeah? Well if the idea of sleeping with Ro is so wrong, why is your dick trying to fight its way out of your zipper from just the thought?

He looked down and inwardly cursed. Christ, it was like he was a fifteen-year-old virgin again. He'd been half-hard all damn day, thanks to that one, stupid, meaningless kiss.

The kiss, her skin, those plump, lace covered breasts...

"You got any other plans for today, or can you go home and crash for a couple hours?" Rocky bent down to put several boxes of bullets into a gray backpack he'd brought with him.

"Nope. No plans."

Using the opportunity to adjust himself without being noticed, Brody reached down and fisted himself, shifting his aching erection up and over to the side. He was still uncomfortable as hell, but at least now, he might avoid having a permanent zipper impression on his dick.

"That's good." His teammate rose back to his feet. "Maybe you can call it an early night, then."

"Maybe."

Unless he got a wild hair and decided to hit the bars instead.

You really think you're gonna meet your soulmate by trolling random bars?

It happened; he assumed. Probably every damn day. But no. Loud music, sticky ass floors, and the smell of stale beer wasn't exactly the way he'd imagined meeting the love of his life.

He would have to do *something* to change up his game, however. If he didn't want casual, that meant he'd have to find the time and energy to put himself out there. Which meant he had to find the time to actually *go* out on nights other than just when it's someone's birthday or engagement party.

And some place other than his back yard or here, at Meg and Hunt's new place.

But when? Between meetings with Homeland, the day-to-day of helping Hunt run the office, and Delta taking on jobs that sometimes required them to be gone from home for days—or even weeks—at a time, his free-time was limited.

And when he did have time off, all Brody wanted to do was sit at home and relax.

God, I'm getting old.

When he was younger, there wasn't a weekend that went by without him having a date. Sometimes two.

Sometimes more.

But after high school came boot camp, and not long after that came BUD/S. Once he made it through twenty-four grueling weeks of the hardest, most intense mental and physical training he'd ever experienced, Brody's focus became centered on being the best SEAL he could be.

He'd kept in touch with his sister, of course. Going home

every chance he got. But those visits had been few and far between during his service with SEAL Team 1.

The rest of his time—his *life*—had been reserved solely for the Navy and doing all he could to protect the world from the worst it had to offer. And that's exactly what he and his former team had done.

Under the leadership of Master Chief Michael Ainsworth, Brody and the rest of SEAL Team 1 became the most coveted team on the West Coast. Especially since their assignments weren't limited to a specific country or region like other Teams.

On paper, they were responsible for the Western Pacific geographical area. But when the shit hit the fan...

We took on the whole fucking world.

And for a while, that was more than enough. Those first years as a frogman were some of the best, scariest, craziest years of his life. He'd lived on adrenaline, whiskey, and women.

But as with so many things in life, the fly-by-night lifestyle lost its boot-kicking appeal. By the time Brody left the Navy, too much had changed for him to stay.

The politics.

His team.

Me.

And after about a hundred close calls too many, he decided the risks he'd been taking...risks driven by a lethal combination of political BS, greed, and the need to be on top...simply weren't worth it.

So he'd walked away.

Did he still take chances working for R.I.S.C.? Sure. But the dangers he and the rest of Delta faced were of their choosing and—most of the time—on their terms. Even the occasional work they did for Homeland was different than when he'd been active duty.

Less red tape, more freedom, and more money. And all while doing the types of jobs that drew him to become a SEAL in the first place.

"So back to what I was saying earlier..." Rocky placed one of his long rifles into its padded case. "I really hope the situation in Libya resolves itself soon. I feel like we've been on a months-long cycle of hurry up and wait, and I wish Hunt would tell Ryker to either shit or get off the pot."

The other man pulled the zipper closed and slung the sheathed weapon over one of his broad shoulders.

"I hear ya, brother." Brody realized what Rocky had been trying to discuss earlier. "Trust me, Hunt's just as frustrated. So is Ryker."

"You guys hear from him recently?"

"Christian talked to him a couple days ago. Apparently Homeland's most current chatter makes him think we're getting close."

Jason Ryker was a Senior Special Investigator with Homeland Security. The powerful man ran a specialized task force with the agency only a few top officials knew about.

Including the President.

Going way back with Jake McQueen—the brainchild behind R.I.S.C.—Ryker had been the company's official Homeland handler since Jake McQueen first started Alpha Team.

Add in Bravo, Charlie, and now Delta Teams, and the recently promoted Ryker—along with the man's powerful contacts—had helped catapult the R.I.S.C. empire into the world-renowned security company it was today.

A few months ago, however, their handler had

announced to the team that he was stepping down as the security company's first point of contact. He'd still be there, helping from the background, but they had a new primary handler now.

A woman the team still had yet to meet.

"We've been 'getting close' since summer," Rocky grumbled. "I mean, it's almost Halloween for crying out loud."

Brody shared his teammate's frustration, but reminded the other man, "That's the downside of still working with the government. You know as well as I do the BS that comes with that."

"I know. Just sucks because we've been holding off on taking certain jobs because we keep getting told we're going to be heading to Africa, and then...nothing."

It was true, they'd first been made aware of a situation near Libya that, supposedly, was going to require their assistance four months earlier. Back when Brody was out of the country on a solo bodyguard assignment.

Back when that asshole lawyer tried to have Megan killed because he was afraid she'd be able to connect him to a murder-for-hire scheme.

He shook the unsettling memory away, refusing to think about how terrified he'd been the day he'd gotten home earlier than expected.

Meg had been working at her shop, and Christian had headed there after a meeting at the office. When Brody had shown up days earlier than planned, they'd decided he'd go with Christian to Cup of Joe to surprise Meg.

But when they'd walked in, they'd been greeted by the sound of a gunshot. Thanks to his sister's quick thinking—and Brody's and Christian's infallible aims—the prick who'd been terrorizing her while he was away had been the one to wind up dead.

"Don't worry." Brody finished bagging his pistols. "From what Christian said, Ryker's confident we'll be on the move before Thanksgiving." Sliding two rifles and a backpack over one shoulder, he bent and picked up the black duffle near his feet with his other hand.

"Sure hope so. It's been a hot minute since we've seen some real action."

Having collected their things, Brody and Rocky headed up the gravel pathway toward the small parking area Christian had put in just for the team.

He still couldn't believe his best friend and his little sister owned this place. Used as a massive—and brilliant—business expense, the ninety acres of secured, fenced land held a gorgeous, modern-farmhouse-style home with a four-car garage, separate workshop, and three stocked ponds he and the guys had been given fishing access to anytime they wanted.

But the best part, in Brody's opinion, was the spot he was standing in now.

Delta Team's very own private outdoor shooting range included the nine-hundred-yard sniper range he'd just used, as well as two rifle ranges—one that was a hundred yards, the other fifty—a fifty-yard rifle shotgun and rifle range, and a twenty-five-foot pistol range.

Hunt had even put in earthen backstops, side berms, and overhead baffles in shooting sheds for safety.

And if that wasn't enough, the brilliant team leader had also built an indoor training facility located on the back end of the property that rivaled any Brody and his former SEAL brothers had used for practice back in the day.

But today hadn't just been about practice. Not for him. No, today had been all about venting by way of spent casings and an impatient trigger finger.

"Gotta admit," Rocky spoke up beside him as the two men made their way to their vehicles. "The way you were taking out your targets today, I thought maybe you were still pissed at that Yorke guy."

Brody's fist tightened around his rifle case's thick nylon strap as he kept it steady on his shoulder. He'd been so busy fighting his own demons where Ro was concerned he hadn't given Yorke much thought aside from his and Ro's brief mention of the cocky SOB this morning.

"Dickhead probably thinks he can do whatever he wants just because he's got a billion-dollar trust fund."

"A billion?" Rocky's narrow blue eyes grew wide. "No shit?"

Brody shot his friend a look, then shook his head with a grunt. "I sometimes forget Hunt and I are the only ones on the team who are from here."

"So this Yorke guy's local?"

"Oh, yeah. His parents own the Yorkshire Luxury Suites and Spa high-end hotel chain. And he's an only child."

"Damn. So the dude's like…loaded."

"A few billion times over, yeah." Brody nodded. "And entitled assholes like that…young, good-looking, grew up with more money than God… They don't always handle rejection well."

Rocky's typically relaxed and easy-going expression hardened. That blue, knowing stare of his locked with Brody's as he gave a curt shake of his head. "No." The other man swallowed hard. "They don't."

He sensed a story there, but before he could ask his friend about it, his phone began to ring from his pocket. Recognizing the tone as Megan's, he picked up the pace to close the final distance between himself and his truck.

"Well if I don't talk to you before then, I'll see you in the office on Monday," Rocky offered as he lowered the tailgate to his metallic black Ford F150 Raptor.

Closer to the cab of his pickup than the bed, Brody opened the back driver's side door. Sliding the rifles and backpack from his shoulder, he set those in the seat and his duffle bag on the floorboard.

He shut the door and pulled his phone from his pocket just as the ringing stopped. "See you then. And hey!"

"Yeah?" Rocky, who'd just started to climb into his truck, popped his head back up.

"Nice shooting today!"

"Thanks." The other man shot him a genuine smile. "You, too."

With a parting nod, Brody opened his door and slid behind the wheel. Setting his phone on the center console, he closed himself inside and secured his seat belt. After firing up the engine, he slowly backed up the truck and waited as Rocky took the lead.

He honked as he passed by the house on his way out, knowing Christian was somewhere inside. Up ahead, Rocky sent him a wave as he turned right onto the two-lane highway that would take the other man home.

Brody lowered his window and stuck out his hand, returning the gesture as he turned his truck in the opposite direction. He tapped the large screen on his dashboard, using his truck's hands-free system to return Megan's call.

She answered on the first ring.

"Where are you right now?"

Her lack of greeting left him blinking with a smirk. "Well *hello* to you, too, Sis."

"I'm serious, Brody." She dropped to a harsh whisper. "Look, I don't have a lot of time. Where are you right this second?"

His spine stiffened, the grip on the steering wheel tightening with worry. "I just left your place. Why? What's the—"

"I need you to come to Ro's."

Ro's?

Brody's heart gave a hard thump, that grip of his growing to a near-crushing strength. "Megan, what's wrong?"

"We're fine, but—" There was a long pause and then, "Crap. I have to go. Just...get here as soon as you can."

His sister ended the bizarre call before he could utter another sound.

"Call Megan," Brody commanded his truck's system, but it went straight to voice mail. "Damn it, Meg!"

He filled his lungs and tried to remain calm. His sister had told him she and Ro were okay, and after what Megan went through over the summer, he'd like to think she would've given him more details if she or Ro were in immediate danger.

So no, he didn't think there was cause for concern as far as their physical well-being. But something wasn't right. He knew his sister better than anyone and could tell when something was wrong.

Brody pushed the accelerator to the floor. Megan may have claimed she and Ro were okay, but she'd definitely sounded off. No, that wasn't right.

She'd sounded...

Scared.

6

"So are you going to tell him, or am I?"

Ro felt her eyes double in size as she shot Megan a wide, *are you kidding me* look.

She'd asked the other woman to come over in hopes her friend would help her find her mother's earrings, and the paranoia still coursing through her would vanish. Instead her traitorous friend had apparently gone back on her word and called the very *last* person Ro wanted to see.

"Tell me what?" Brody demanded. Sliding that dark stare of his in Megan's direction, his imposing form seemed to fill her home's modest entryway. "What's the big emergency? And why the hell did you turn off your phone after you called me?"

I knew it!

Narrowing her widened eyes into an aggravated glare, Ro looked at the source of her betrayal and said, "You swore you wouldn't call him."

Megan shrugged, not looking the least bit sorry as she reached out and shut the door behind her brother. She'd come over as soon as Ro had called, and the two women had been conducting a more thorough search for the missing items ever since.

Doing her best to remember murder was illegal, Ro forced her lips to curve into a smile she didn't feel as she reached out and filled her fist with part of Megan's sleeve.

"Can I talk to you for a second?" A quick glance to Brody and back. "*Alone?*"

"I mean, you can, but it's not going to change anyth—"

"Excuse us a moment." She didn't wait for an answer before pulling her traitorous friend away from the man standing in her entryway. Yanking the other woman through the archway leading to her living room, Ro led them both around the corner so Brody couldn't see them.

"Seriously?" Her brows turned inward with a deep scowl.

"What?"

"Don't you *what* me!" She worked to keep her voice hushed. "I told you not to call him!"

Her friend's hazel eyes held swirls of greens and specs of gold, but not even a trace of remorse. "Guess it's a good thing you're not the boss of me, then, isn't it?" Megan crossed her arms at her chest. "Besides, this is what he does."

What he does...

"Meg, Delta Team takes down terrorists, not—"

"They do a lot more than that, and you know it."

"Okay, fine." Ro threw her hands out to her sides. Not stopping their fall, her palms slapped loudly against her thighs half-a-second before she thought better of it. "They do other badass protection stuff, too. But you know what I mean. Nothing of major value was stolen. *If* any of it was actually stolen in the first place."

In her gut, she knew that's exactly what had happened.

Someone had come into her house, taken a few incredibly random things, and left. But fear had her trying really, really hard to convince Megan—and herself—otherwise.

"Just because something isn't worth a lot of money doesn't mean it can't be priceless." Her friend's expression softened, Meg's knowing stare like a giant fist trying to squeeze the life from Ro's heart. "Those earrings meant the world to you. And that picture of you and your dad..." Her voice trailed off with an empathetic shake of her head.

Tears welled in Ro's eyes, but she blinked them away before any could dare to fall. As usual, the sweet, supportive woman was right.

The picture she was referring to was one she kept by her bed. Ro hadn't even realized it was also missing until after Megan got to her place, and the two had gone looking for the rest.

It was a cheap frame that had cost her maybe ten bucks, but it held one of the most precious photos she'd ever possessed. A moment captured in time Ro could remember as clearly as if it were yesterday.

Warm. Sunny. The whitest, fluffiest, most perfect clouds she'd ever seen floating high against a crystal blue sky.

She remembered thinking they'd looked absolutely perfect. So perfect, in fact, she'd pretended God had put them there. Just for them.

Ro. Her mom. And her dad...

He was so happy that day.

She could still hear the man's contagious laugh echoing through her mind. They'd been at the cancer center, her mom tearfully saying her goodbyes to other patients and staff when her dad had suggested the two of them wait for her outside.

It was the first time Ro could recall the man smiling

while on that property. And it had been a real smile, too. Not the small, forced ones he'd typically worn during their previous visits there.

But that day had been different than all the others before it. That was the day her mom's oncologist had just given them the incredible news.

Cancer-free.

That's what the doctor had called it. He'd announced it with such confidence, such pride, Ro hadn't considered the intelligent man could be wrong.

None of them had questioned the incredible diagnosis. They'd been too busy celebrating.

Her mom had cried tears of soul-lifting relief. Ro had cried, too, so very thankful to hear she wasn't going to lose her mom as she'd feared. But her dad...

She could still see him standing there, without a word, pulling her mom from her chair, and kissing her senseless. And he'd *kept* kissing her until her mom's tears—and his—were no longer falling.

Then she'd asked them to wait while she spread the wonderful news to those she'd gotten to know well during her two-year fight with ovarian cancer.

Feeling as if they had all the time in the world, Ro's dad had turned to her with that incredible smile and suggested they go walk around the center's pond. They'd made it halfway around the encircling paved walkway when her dad had stopped to take out his phone.

Ro could still hear her own laughter, thinking he was joking when he'd suggested they take a selfie with the pond in the background. Her dad had never been the selfie-taking kinda guy.

But then he'd gotten serious, saying he wanted them to remember that day—that exact moment—forever. Because, in his words, that was the first day of a future he'd thought they'd lost.

Three months later, her mother was dead. Ro lost her dad two long, soul-crushing years after that. And that picture...

That afternoon had been the last time she could ever remember hearing her father laugh.

"Besides," Megan's lowered voice ripped Ro back to the present. "I seem to recall *you* giving me all kinds of crap when I stopped to help a stranger who'd wrecked."

"Are you kidding me? That's totally different!" Ro's voice lifted an octave, but she immediately dropped it back down to a whisper. "And the guy you stopped to help turned out to be a freaking *murderer* who damn near killed you. So this is *nothing* like that."

"So far. And I pray that you're right, but—"

"But what?"

"What if you're wrong?" Megan challenged sharply. A beat later, she released a shoulder-dropping sigh, her tone returning to the soft, sweet voice Ro knew and loved. "Do you remember how upset you were when you got back from that marketing conference in Des Moines and learned about what had happened to me? Remember how pissed you got because I hadn't called to tell you about it as soon as it happened?"

The myriad of colors in her friend's pretty eyes became glassy, and Ro knew she was fighting off tattered remnants of her own demons.

"I *did* call you as soon as it happened," she pointed out. "The second I realized there were multiple things I couldn't find, and that maybe I hadn't gone batshit crazy, I called you."

"Because you thought I was going to get here, calm you

down, tell you your stuff would eventually turn up, and then we'd go to the movies as planned."

Sometimes she really hated how well Megan knew her.

"Still, that doesn't change the fact that—"

"Would you stop?" Megan cut her off, continuing before Ro could make another attempt to defend herself. "Look, I get that you didn't want me to call my brother, and I'm pretty sure I know why. But you need someone to look into this, Ro. Preferably someone who knows what the hell they're doing, which isn't me."

She also hated when the woman was right.

Relenting only slightly, she blew out a breath and crossed her arms at her chest. "Okay, fine. But *Brody?*" He was the very last person she wanted to be around, at the moment. Plus, "This is barely a case for the cops. I mean, look at the place, Meg. You can't even tell anyone was here." Ro glanced around at her tidy living room and what she could see of her spotless kitchen. "I'm sure your brother has a lot better things to do with his time than investigate some piddly little burglary."

Only it didn't feel piddly or little to her. It felt...

Personal.

"What the fuck?" The deep, booming voice reverberated from someplace close. *Too* close.

Ro squeezed her eyes shut and cringed. Lingering scents of gunpowder and the outdoors mixed with spicy male, and she knew before ever lifting her lids that Brody was standing right beside her.

She forced herself to open her eyes and meet his gaze. Angry slashes cut through the skin of his brow as he locked his dark, glowering stare with hers.

"Someone broke into your house?" His lips rolled inward with a deep inhale, his mouth nearly vanishing inside the frame of his dark whiskers. "Why the hell am I just now hearing about this?"

Great. First, I humiliate myself in front of him last night, and now he's pissed as hell. Awesome.

"Because I'm not even sure there *was* a break-in. Which is why I made your sister promise not to bother you or Christian. Not that she listened."

As she shot her friend a look, Brody widened his stance and planted his legs. Strong, capable hands came to a rest on his narrow hips as he demanded she explain.

"Start from the beginning."

Knowing he wouldn't leave until she did, Ro obeyed the order and told him everything. From the unlocked back door to the opened cabinet and right-side-up mug, her mother's missing earrings, and the picture...

She purposely omitted the MIA panties, and luckily Megan didn't bring them up, either.

Thank God for small miracles.

"You have any problems with anyone lately?"

"No." Ro shook her head with confidence. "But seriously, Brody. You don't need to—"

"Uh...that's not entirely true."

Both she and Brody turned to look at Megan.

"What's not true?" Ro frowned.

"That you haven't had a problem with anyone lately." Her friend slid her focus to Brody. "What about Clayton Yorke?"

Unable to keep from it, Ro rolled her eyes and groaned. "Clayton's not a problem."

"He was last night," Brody argued. "A big one."

That jerk, Yorke, grabbed you like some sort of possessive Neanderthal.

She'd been stewing about that all day. The entire time

she'd been dress shopping for the entitled ass's big rebranding party, she'd mentally chewed his butt a dozen different ways for thinking he could treat her—or any woman—that way.

Ro had also silently rehearsed what she would say if she ever got up the nerve to fire his entitled ass as a client. Something she was pretty sure she was going to do...after the party.

It was shallow and selfish, and yes...it probably made her a sell-out. But damn it, she'd worked her ass off to make his relaunching campaign a success, and Ro felt she deserved the public recognition his invite brought with it.

So yeah. She'd buy a pretty dress and put on a smile, but after that...

After that, her professional relationship with Clayton Yorke was done.

"Megan told me what happened." Ro maintained eye contact. "I appreciate you stepping in to help. But..." When Brody arched a dark brow, she made sure he knew, "Clayton would never hurt me."

"Asshole sure had a tight grip on you last night."

"Which is something I intend to address when I see him at our meeting first thing tomorrow morning."

"Cancel it."

"Excuse me?"

"You need to cancel your meeting with Yorke."

The man said this as if his word was law.

"He didn't do this."

"You don't know that."

"Yes, I do." She felt it to her bones.

"How?"

"I don't know, I just..." Ro growled in frustration as she broke away from the crowded triangle of friends to pace across her living room floor. "Okay, look. I'm the first to admit Clayton's a narcissistic, arrogant ass. But you seem to forget he's also a very, *very* recognizable heir to a billion-dollar hotel empire and the city's most eligible bachelor."

"And?" That damn brow of Brody's arched high once more.

"*And* guys like that don't risk embarrassing themselves or their families by getting arrested for breaking into some random woman's place and stealing her hot pink panties!"

The room grew so silent she could've heard a feather drop. Ro's pulse spiked, and she wanted to shove the words back inside her big, fat mouth. But it was too late.

Brody had already heard them, and from the way he was looking at her now, he was even more pissed off than before.

Becoming impossibly taller, the man's entire body stiffened. A handful of seconds passed before he spoke again, but when he did, his voice wasn't raised as Ro had expected. Instead Brody's words came out slow and steady.

"You want to run that by me again?"

Not really, no. "Which part?" She played dumb.

But Brody wasn't dumb. He was one of the sharpest men she knew. A trait she typically found sexy as hell.

Today was anything but typical.

"You didn't tell me he took your panties."

"I was just using it as an example."

He began walking toward her. No, not walking. *Stalking.* And with several slow, booted steps, Brody closed the distance between them.

"Hot pink." He stopped directly in front of her. "That was oddly specific."

"I'm an artist." Ro schooled her expression. "I put color in everything."

She thought maybe her acting job had been convincing,

but then Megan cleared her throat much louder than necessary, tipping Brody off to the lie.

His broad chest rose and fell with several long, deep breaths. Eyes tight with simmering rage, his tone was an eerie calm that sent shivers racing down her spine.

"Are you also missing a pair of panties?"

"Okay, seriously." Meg begged her brother from over to the side. "Can you please stop saying the word *panties*? It just sounds...weird coming from you."

One corner of Ro's lips started to twitch but fell flat again when she realized there wasn't a trace of humor to be found in Brody's stony expression. And he was still staring down at her, clearly waiting for a response.

"Yes," Ro admitted softly. "They were in my drawer this morning. I'm sure of it."

If she hadn't told him, Megan probably would have. Of course, she still wanted to strangle her best friend for ratting her out to her brother.

Though deep down, Ro knew Meg's betrayal had stemmed from a place of love.

"Why didn't you tell me that before?" Brody continued with his interrogation.

She swallowed, her cheeks burning with embarrassment. "Because it's my underwear. It's...private."

"It's creepy, is what it is." Megan sidled up beside them, the three of them now gathered in the open space between her living room and kitchen.

An arched brow was Brody's only response.

"I agree. If someone really did take them, then you're right." Ro swallowed again, her arms crossing in front. "It *is* creepy. But you're also still missing the point."

"Which is?"

"Clayton didn't do this."

Dark, aggravated eyes searched hers as the man before her asked, "Why are you so sure he's innocent?"

"Why are you so sure he's guilty?"

"I'm not sure of anything yet." Brody shook his head. "And you shouldn't be, either."

"I'm sure you've got better things to do than worry about my missing *hot pink* panties."

Invading her personal space to the point she had to crank her head back to keep their intense connection from breaking. Her heart kicked wildly against her ribs as he leaned in closer.

"Not worried about your panties, Princess." A muscle beneath his beard bulged with a clench of his strong jaw. "I'm worried about *you*."

Princess?

Ro blinked, shock parting her lips with a silent, frozen breath. That he was concerned for her safety wasn't what struck her speechless. They'd been friends for ages, and given what he did for a living, the man was a protector by design.

But as she stood there, staring up in to those angry, magnetic eyes of his, she couldn't help but feel his reaction to her current situation was about something else. Perhaps something...

More?

No. That couldn't be right. This was Brody, for crying out loud.

He was here because his sister called him. He was pissed because Ro hadn't. And his only stake in this game was wanting to make sure his *friend* was okay, which brought her back to her original argument against calling him in the first place.

"Your job is to protect government officials and keep

watch over super important people," she reminded the big lug. "In case you've forgotten, I'm neither of those things."

"Bullshit." Brody's deep, deep voice reverberated across the small stretch of air between them. "You're important, Ro." His throat worked with a hard swallow. "Really fucking important."

She was?

"I am?"

His burly chin lowered with a curt nod as he shocked her even more with a muttered, "More than you know."

Stone-cold anger was still present in his stare. How was it possible for this man to look and sound so furious while, at the same time, saying something so incredibly...sweet?

Not worried about your panties, Princess. I'm worried about you.

It was fair, she supposed. After all, wasn't she always a nervous wreck when he and the team left town on some super-secret mission that would almost certainly lead them head-first into danger?

Of course, she was.

While her feelings for the man may run deep on a set of tracks only she knew existed, Brody wasn't just someone she longed for in the dead of night when no one was around to judge.

He was her friend.

A good, loyal friend who was still staring down at her as if he were searching for something, though she had no idea what. But loyalty and friendship didn't change the fact that this sort of thing was a waste of time for someone like him.

"You're important to me, too." More than *he'd* ever know. "Which is why I'm not going to let you waste your time on something like this." Ro gave a nervous lick of her lips, her long hair subtly brushing against her upper arms with a shake of her head.

"You're never a waste of my time, Ro."

Did his voice soften just then? Maybe just a teensy, tiny bit?

Stop looking for something that isn't there and focus.

"Come on, Brody. This isn't the sort of thing you do, and you know it."

"I protect the innocent." His Adam's apple bobbed as he worked his throat. "Last I checked, that includes you."

If this man knew even half the things she wanted to do to him, he wouldn't be so quick to add her name to that list.

"I don't need protection. I just need to find my things."

"Uh...I think you might need both," Megan inserted herself back into the conversation. "Maybe Yorke isn't behind this, but someone obviously is. I mean, come on, Ro." Her friend's beautiful face fell with a look of concern. "Picture frames and earrings don't just walk off by themselves."

"Neither do panties."

Both women turned to Brody, who was as serious as he could be. But then...

"You couldn't help yourself, could you?" his sister accused. "You just had to go and say it again."

For the first time in what felt like forever, the former SEAL tore his focus away. But it was only for a second, just long enough for him to toss an aggravating wink in his sister's direction. And then he was looking straight back at Ro.

"I'll help you look for your things, but if we don't find them, we're calling the cops."

"The *cops?*" A rush of denial had Ro shaking her head and turning to Megan. "No. No way."

Might as well let him. You know he's going to anyway.

"Brody's right, Ro."

"No, he's not. Look..." She blew out a frustrated breath. "This whole thing has gotten blown way out of proportion. Meg, I'm sorry I worried you. I never should have called you." A quick turn to Brody. "And I'm sorry you raced all the way over here for nothing. But I'm sure that's all this is, right? Nothing. I probably just misplaced those things, and I'm going to find them as soon as I stop looking for them."

An unladylike snort found its way out of Megan's throat, her brows turning sharply inward as she threw her hands to her popped hips and scowled. "You've been in this house, what? Four months?"

"So?"

"So when was the last time you moved that picture of you and your dad? Because I have a very vivid memory of you putting it on your nightstand the day I helped you unpack. And it's been in that exact same spot every other time I've been here."

Though her focus was on Megan, Ro could feel the weight of Brody's stare. She didn't want to answer the question, because if she did, that would mean it was real. That someone really had come into her home—her new home—and they'd taken things that made no sense.

Unless...

"Not to mention, you also said you felt like you were being watched today."

Oh, crap.

She'd been so obsessed with finding her things—while also trying to convince herself and Megan that there *hadn't* been a break-in, after all—she'd totally forgotten about that part. Or maybe her brain had purposely blocked it out.

Either way, the unintentional omission had Brody

swinging an incredulous look her way. "Someone was *watching* you?" Disbelief turned to rage. "What the actual fuck, Aurora?"

God, she hated how much that expression on his gorgeous face bothered her. Like she was a complete idiot who'd disappointed him in the biggest of ways.

But she loved it when he used her full name. No one else. Just Brody. Even when he was mad, like now.

He's never been this mad at you, Ro. Like...ever.

"I forgot, okay? I know that sounds totally made up, but I swear to you, it's the truth."

"You forgot." A statement, rather than a question.

Clearly Brody thought she was full of shit.

"Yes, I forgot." She defended herself as best she could. "In case you haven't noticed, I've had a lot on my mind since I got home."

His deep, humorless laugh and snarky shake of his head made Ro want to punch the frustrating man right in his sideways smirk.

Without another word, Brody pulled out his phone and turned away. Head down, he tapped the screen a few times and then put the device to his ear.

"Who are you calling?" she demanded.

So naturally, he ignored her.

Seriously? "So that's it? You're not even going to talk to me now?"

"Give him a minute, Ro." Megan walked over to where she was standing. With a gentle hand to her shoulder, her friend added softly, "You need to trust his instincts with stuff like this. Just like I did with Christian."

"It's King." Brody's deep voice reached them from across the room. "I need your help."

Knowing the man was going to do whatever he wanted,

regardless of what she said, Ro turned to her well-meaning friend. "I do trust him, Meg. I'd trust him with my life, if I thought it was needed. But this..." She shook her head. "The cops are going to laugh in my face when they take my statement. A break-in with nothing broken and the thief took nothing of any real monetary value."

"Your mom's earrings—"

"Might bring in a couple hundred bucks at a pawnshop. And that's *if* the guy's lucky."

Megan's gaze was still filled with worry. "You said someone was watching you."

"I said it felt like they were," Ro corrected. "I never actually saw anyone."

"Cops are on their way."

Both women turned to see Brody marching back toward them. He didn't stop until he was in front of her once again.

"Was that Detective Hansen?" Megan asked.

"Do you want to...look for my stuff while we wait?" she asked hesitantly, unsure of what one did in a situation like this.

"No."

Okaaay... "Then what should we do?"

"*We* aren't doing anything. You're going to sit your sexy ass down and walk me through your entire day. Start to fucking finish. And this time, I want you to tell me everything."

Fear crept into her veins as the realization of what had most likely happened finally began to sink in. Because a guy like Brody...he didn't go from zero to burn the freaking world down this fast unless...

Tabling the fact that he'd just said her ass was sexy, Ro walked over to her couch and sat down as ordered. Megan joined her on the cushion to her left while Brody chose to stand.

Over the next few minutes, she went through her day again. From the time she woke up to when she'd called Megan freaking out, she shared it all. Including the part about her panties.

When she was finished, Ro swallowed her rising fear enough to choke out a quiet, "You really think someone was here, don't you?"

"I do." There was no hesitation in Brody's answer. Looking as serious as she'd ever seen him, he added a grim, "I also know how important it is to listen to your gut. You felt like you were being followed today, and then you come home to your back door being unlocked and stuff missing. Your initial response was to call for help." His dark eyes slid to his sister's and back. "That was smart, but you should have called the police first."

She didn't bother pointing out that she hadn't called him at all. That was all Meg. And while she'd been ticked off when he'd first arrived and she'd realized her friend had gone and done the one thing Ro had specifically asked her not to...

I'm really glad he's here.

Because the same steadfast denial that had been so overwhelmingly strong a few short minutes earlier was gone. Replaced by a dark, foreboding cloud of acceptance she wished like hell would vanish, too.

"But why?" She searched Brody's worried face for an answer she knew he didn't possess. "They won't get much, if anything, from the stuff they took. I mean, I don't have a lot, but you'd think a thief would take the T.V.s and computers and stuff like that."

"Computers can be traced, and T.V.s are bulky as hell,"

the man who'd know pointed out. "Especially if this was a solo job. But I don't think this was about money."

No, deep down, she didn't think so, either. But if it wasn't about money...

"You think someone purposely targeted me?" Ro surmised.

"I do." He nodded. "I also think we need to get you to the hospital as soon as the cops leave."

"The *hospital?*" She looked at Megan who, from the expression on her face, shared her state of confusion. "I wasn't hurt, Brody. I wasn't even home when they were here."

Whoever they were.

"That's not why I want you to go."

"Then why?" It was his sister who asked.

But Brody's hardened gaze remained fixed on hers, his tight voice dropping to a low, carefully controlled tone as he answered, "Because I don't think you simply passed out drunk last night. I think you were drugged."

7

"It's positive."

Brody's fists curled into themselves at his sides, the ends of his well-trimmed nails digging deep into his palms. "You're sure?"

Dr. Kerrigan Rawlins swung her almond-shaped baby blue eyes his way, her long, sandy blonde ponytail swinging over one shoulder with the move. "Flunitrazepam was detected in the urine Miss Tennison gave."

Motherfucker.

Earlier, after Detective Hansen and his merry band of crime scene techs left Ro's, Brody had driven her straight to the hospital. Thankfully it was a slower-than-usual night in The University of Chicago Medical Center's emergency room. And since Ro was a suspected victim of a date rape drug, they'd gotten her back without much of a wait.

"You can call me Ro," she told the doctor woodenly. "And what's Fluna...whatever it was you just said?"

Rather than look at the professional in the room, he kept his focus on the woman sitting on that damn hospital bed.

Legs dangling over its side, the normally strong, confident Ro was anxious as hell.

Not that he could blame her.

Back at her house, after explaining to her and Meg why he'd come to suspect she'd been drugged, he'd also shared his knowledge that most date rape drugs were still detectable in urine for up to seventy-two hours.

A tidbit he'd learned years ago during an op involving a senator's daughter who'd been kidnapped and held for ransom. SEAL Team 1 had gone in, rescued her, and eliminated the foreign mercenaries who'd taken her.

Brody remembered his team leader reporting back a couple days later that the girl had been kept drugged the entire time. And when her blood tests came back, the drug they'd used...

Flunitrazepam.

The girl they'd rescued still had it in her system three days after her rescue. Like Ro, she couldn't remember a single thing about her time while under the influence. A blessing for the senator's daughter.

A curse for Ro.

"Flunitrazepam," Dr. Rawlins repeated for her patient. "It's a depressant that belongs in the benzodiazepine class. Rohypnol is the most recognized brand, but there are others like it that create the same or very similar effects."

Brody hated that this had happened to her, but he was damn glad he'd convinced her to get tested. He'd also convinced Megan to let Christian come to Ro's house and follow her home.

That part hadn't been easy, though.

Like Brody, his sister could be incredibly stubborn. Meg also loved her best friend very much and wanted to be there for Ro as much as she could. Including expressing her desire to accompany them to the E.R.

But he'd made it very clear that wasn't going to happen. Not because he was a controlling ass, but because he'd almost lost his sister a few months back.

It was possible this thing with Ro was an isolated incident, but Brody didn't think so. And until they knew for sure what they were dealing with, he wasn't taking chances where either one of the women were concerned.

A view his future brother-in-law wholeheartedly shared.

Because Brody didn't believe Ro was slipped the drug at random. Not when he also added in her feelings of being watched on top of the presumed break-in. And if that were the case—if Ro was some sick fuck's target—there was no way to know if the suspect was a stranger, someone she knew, or...

Someone looking for revenge.

Delta may be the newest R.I.S.C. group in operation, but their time together had been well spent. They'd already taken down multiple criminals and terrorist organizations, either by way of thwarting their plans and aiding in their capture or eliminating them completely.

But while successes like theirs saved lives, it also created enemies. So erring on the side of caution, Christian had driven to Ro's before following Megan back to their house.

Just in case.

"Someone really drugged me?" Ro wet her lips and brought her gaze around to his.

The fear and vulnerability in her eyes were like a giant fist squeezing his aching heart. His chest tightened, bile churning in his gut as he thought of the awful, horrible things that could've happened had she left that bar alone.

"Yeah, Princess." Regret filled his tone, his back teeth

crushing together with a tight, almost painful swallow. "They really did."

Tears formed, causing her pretty blue eyes to shimmer beneath the room's fluorescent light. The sight of those unfallen tears made him want to tear through the city of Chicago to find the son of a bitch responsible.

Clayton Yorke.

The name popped into Brody's head almost instantly. It was one he'd be passing along to Liam—the team's tech analyst—as soon as he had the chance to make the call.

"I thought..." Ro spoke up again, her hands fidgeting nervously in her lap. "I thought I just hadn't had enough to eat." She pulled her bottom lip between her teeth. "I can't believe...I mean, I never even realized..."

"None of us did," Brody reminded her.

You should have known.

"Aurora, are you familiar with the symptoms of ingesting a drug like flunitrazepam?"

"I'm assuming amnesia is in there somewhere, since I can't remember the last hour I spent at the bar, the ride home, crashing on the couch..." A pinkish hue filled her cheeks as she sent him a quick, sideways glance.

Brody knew she was embarrassed about having been so out of it in front of him the night before. Was probably still wondering if she'd removed her top while he'd been watching, since they never got to finish that particular conversation.

You need to tell her. Ro's your friend, and she deserves to know the truth.

Dread filled his gut, because yeah. He did need to come clean about last night. Including his part in it.

"Amnesia is one of the most common side effects, yes. But as you know, the victims in these cases don't realize they can't remember until the next day. I'm talking about the way you feel when the drug first begins taking effect." When Ro stayed quiet, the thirty-something doctor began listing off the other symptoms. "Weakness, fatigue, slurred speech, loss of motor coordination, visual impairment... Any of those sound like anything you've experienced in the past?"

"Sounds like when I've had too much to drink."

"Exactly." The kind woman put a hand to Ro's shoulder. "Please understand, nothing about this was your fault, Aurora. Or yours." Rawlins turned her blue gaze to Brody's. "Unfortunately, I see this sort of thing a lot. Always different women. Different bars. Different drugs." Her disgust toward the assholes who did this sort of thing was obvious. "But in each of those cases—and with yours—the *only* ones at fault are the sick bastards who get off on assaulting women incapable of fighting back."

There was a bite to her words that made Brody wonder if maybe she had more history with this sort of thing than just from her patients. But that wasn't his business, and his focus needed to stay on Ro. She was what mattered here.

The only thing that mattered.

Speaking of Ro...

He took in her tense form. For the first time since arriving at the E.R., the tension in her gorgeous face seemed to lessen slightly. For that alone, Brody decided he really liked Dr. Kerrigan Rawlins. But the other woman's words did little to appease his own guilt.

Because *he* should have known something wasn't right with Ro last night. The signs were all there. But his head had still been so wrapped up with thoughts of wanting to beat Clayton Yorke's ass, he hadn't seen them.

Not when she'd started to sway and slur. Not when she'd nearly fallen asleep in his truck on the drive to her house.

He hadn't even suspected something more than alcohol was involved when she'd taken off her shirt and kissed him.

Jesus.

The woman had unknowingly been roofied, and instead of recognizing the signs, he'd fucking *kissed* her.

I'm so sorry.

"For what?" Ro slid off the bed and reached for the olive green jacket she'd worn here. "Were *you* the one who slipped something into my drink?"

Shit. He hadn't meant to apologize out loud. Not here, and not in front of a doctor they'd only just met. But he had, and then she'd said—

"Are you seriously asking me that right now?" He shot her an incredulous frown.

"No." She started putting the jacket on, first one sleeve and then the other. "I'm pointing out that you didn't drug me; therefore you have nothing to apologize for. I'm just glad you drove me home when you did."

Me, too, Princess. But you're wrong about the other. I have a lot to apologize for.

"The good news is," Dr. Rawlins spoke up again, "you don't seem to be feeling any further effects from the drug, and by this point, you shouldn't. In fact, it'll completely clear your system within a few days."

"So that's it?" Ro reached back and pulled her long hair free from inside the jacket's collar. Looking to him for verification. "I can go home?"

She'd been doing that a lot since they'd first arrived at the hospital. Looking to him when she asked a question, rather than the doctor. As if she instinctually expected him to have all the answers.

As if she trusted him completely.

I wonder if she even realizes she's doing it.

Unfortunately for them both, Brody didn't have all the answers. Or any, for that matter. Yet. But he was damn sure going to do everything in his power to find them.

Just as soon as he knew Ro was safe.

"I have the discharge papers right here." Dr. Rawlins handed her patient a set of stapled papers.

Tapping the screen of the electronic tablet the hospital used in place of the old, paper charts, she quickly reviewed the orders aloud from start to finish. The rote tone of the woman's voice as she read made it obvious she'd said those exact same words on many occasions.

"Do either of you have any questions for me?" The pretty blonde looked first to Ro and then Brody. When they both shook their heads, she nodded with a smile. "Like I said, you should feel completely normal from here on out, but if anything changes, my direct extension is at the bottom."

"Thank you." Ro gave the kind doctor a smile that didn't reach her eyes.

Your smiles should always reach those gorgeous eyes of yours, Princess.

"I'd say anytime, but it's my sincere hope I never see you as a patient in my E.R. again."

Understanding the intent behind Rawlins' words, Brody thanked the other woman as well before she turned to leave the room. Alone with Ro again, he pulled his truck keys from his pocket and blew out a breath.

"You ready to go?"

"God, yes." Without hesitation, she slid her purse over her shoulder and started for the door. "I hate hospitals."

"I know."

Surprise flickered in her weary gaze, those incredible

eyes of hers widening slightly from his comment. It was true. He did know she hated hospitals.

Because he remembered.

When they were younger, Ro and her dad had spent days—sometimes weeks—holed up in her mother's hospital room where she'd still been fighting the ruthless disease. He'd gone by a couple times with his parents and Meg, but his sister had been the one to spend hours on end there.

Keeping her best friend company and trying to help so Ro wouldn't completely fall apart.

Brody remembered Meg coming home in tears more than once because she knew Ro was devastated at the thought of losing her mom. A loss he and Meg would also suffer a few years later.

Only they hadn't just lost their mom. They'd lost both parents.

In the blink of an eye, Ro, Brody, and Meg had all had their worlds turned upside down from losing those they'd loved. And now…

What if I lost her, too?

Refusing to entertain the thought, Brody reached for the papers in Ro's hands. "I've got these."

He folded them vertically and slid them into his jacket pocket. Without thinking better of it, he then took her hand in his and headed for the door.

Despite the situation, he nearly smiled, his chest growing warm when she didn't pull away. But then…

"Wait." Ro kept her hold on him but refused to move.

He turned back, scanning the room. "What's wrong? Did you forget something?"

"No, I just…" A quick lick of her lips. "I just wanted to say thank you. For insisting we come here, and for coming to the house when Meg called…"

"Even though you told her not to?"

The corners of her mouth started to curve upward slightly, but then those lips he longed to kiss again fell. "I didn't want to bother you or cause any unnecessary worry."

At this, Brody turned himself so he was facing her fully. In a single stride, he was inches away from where she stood.

"You're never a bother to me, Aurora. Fucking ever. And if you're in trouble..." He leaned in closer to make sure she was paying attention. "I will always come for you."

She blinked, the solemn vow clearly taking her off guard.

You and me both, Princess.

Refusing to analyze the visceral reaction her comment about not wanting to bother him had created, he turned around, opened the door, and led her out into the hallway. Thirty minutes later, they were back inside Ro's house.

After checking every room, closet, door, and window, Brody called Liam to let him know what needed to be done. While he did that, Ro called Meg to share what they'd learned at the hospital.

Sitting at her kitchen table, Ro put her phone onto the smooth white surface before her and rested her head in her hands. "What a day."

The weary sigh that followed reached inside his chest and twisted his heart.

He'd always had a protective streak when it came to women falling victim to some asshole who thought he had the right to hurt those he saw as weak. But Ro wasn't weak.

She was strong. Resilient. He'd seen it time and again, first with the loss of her mom and later, when her dad finally drank himself to death to escape the pain of losing the love of his life.

That was the first time Brody could remember noticing

the woman's strength and determination. And she'd barely been a woman back then.

"What do you need?" He stood a few feet away, wishing like hell he could take away every last ounce of fear and uncertainty she was feeling.

"For the last twenty-four hours to never have happened." She looked up at him. "Or at least to be able to remember them."

"I'm sorry this happened to you."

"Me, too." She rewarded him with a ghost of a smile. "But it's done and over with, and I just have to remind myself that I was one of the lucky ones. I mean, it could've been so much worse." She pushed herself to her feet and straightened her spine as she faced him. "Honestly, I'd just as soon forget any of this ever happened. Which is ironic, since I've spent all damn day trying to remember everything that happened."

The spark of fire and smartass he saw in her was a soothing balm to his worried soul. "The important thing is you're okay."

It's the only thing.

Brody worked to school his expression. Doing his damnedest not to react to his most recent—and equally confusing—thought where this woman was concerned, he started to ask if she was hungry when his own stomach released a loud, angry growl.

Putting a palm to his midsection, he let out a chuckle. "Sorry about that."

"You're sorry for being hungry?" She looked at him like he was nuts. Pulling out a chair, she said, "Here. Sit. I'll make us both some supper."

"You're not cooking for me, Ro."

"Why not?" She was already making her way past him to

the floor-to-ceiling cabinet attached to the wall across from where he stood. "You're hungry; I haven't eaten since breakfast, and I'll have you know..." She turned around, holding a loaf of bread and a red and white can. "I make a mean grilled cheese and tomato soup."

Her spirit seemed to have miraculously lifted, but as Brody studied that entrancing gaze of hers, he saw it. The anxious energy she was trying valiantly to expel.

And just like that, he understood.

She needs something to do. A distraction to take her mind off everything.

Brody flashed what he hoped was a light-hearted grin. "Grilled cheese and tomato soup sounds perfect. Thanks." Going over to the chair she'd pulled out just for him, he fought his instincts to help and sat. "Oh, and that was Liam on the phone earlier. He's going to access the club's security footage to see if we can catch whoever it was that put that shit into your drink."

"Is that legal?" She looked over at him from the stove.

A shrug of his shoulder was all he gave, but it was enough.

"Right. Forget I asked," she commented dryly.

From his seat, Brody watched as Ro got to work making the quick and comforting meal. She was so graceful in her movements. Even the way she buttered the bread before placing it carefully in the hot skillet was mesmerizing.

And as he watched her hands as they prepared their food, Brody couldn't help but remember the way they'd clutched onto him the night before during the kiss that had damn near knocked him on his ass.

A kiss she has no idea ever happened.

With his elbow leaning on the table, he ran a tight hand over his bearded jaw. God, he didn't want to tell her. She was already embarrassed as it was. And it wasn't like anyone got hurt by what she'd done.

What they'd both done.

He could just not tell her, since he was the only person on earth who even knew the kiss happened. So if he just kept his big trap shut...

This is about more than her embarrassment. This is about your friendship and her trust in you. You keep this from her, and she somehow does remember it later, there will even worse hell to pay.

He'd tell her. He *would*. Just...after dinner.

"Figured I should probably steer clear of alcohol for a bit, so I went with iced water." She set two clear glasses filled with water and floating ice on the table. "But I have beer if you'd rather have that."

"Water's fine. Thanks." He grabbed the nearest glass.

"Okay, so..." She returned to the counter to grab the food. "It's not fancy, but it's hot and edible. At least, I'm pretty sure it is." A steaming bowl of soup and a saucer holding two golden-crusted sandwiches—both cut into triangles—appeared on the table in front of him.

"Thanks, Ro. This looks great." It really did. "Wow. You didn't have to make me two."

"From the hangry sound I heard a few minutes ago, I'm pretty sure your stomach would disagree. Besides I figure with all that muscle mass of yours, you probably need the extra protein."

Her movements stuttered slightly, so slight she probably thought he hadn't noticed. But he had.

It seemed as if he noticed *everything* about her now. Ever since last night. Ever since...

That kiss.

Picking up one of the four triangles on his plate, he took

a bite big enough to cut the piece in half. Hot, melted cheese oozed from between the slices of toasted bread and landed on his tongue. Dipping the remnants into his bowl, he finished the first half in the next bite.

With another plate and bowl in her hands, Ro joined him at the table. From the seat across from him, she took a bite of her own sandwich. And then...

She moaned.

An innocent response to the cheesy, buttery goodness, but damn if it didn't immediately make him think of sex. Brody felt his dick start to swell, and he was suddenly very thankful his crotch was hidden from her view.

"Good?" he choked out, praying she didn't notice the strain in his voice.

"So good. Or maybe I'm just really hungry." Another bite.

Another fucking moan.

She's your friend. She's your friend. She's. Just. A. Friend!

But even as he forced the silent words through his mind, Brody felt as if they were a lie. Which was ridiculous because he and Ro *were* just friends. One drug-induced kiss didn't change that.

No, but a second, sober one might.

"I know what you're thinking."

Brody choked on the sip of water he'd just taken, damn near spitting it out all over the table...and Ro. Coughing and sputtering, he covered his mouth with the inside of his elbow as he cleared the inhaled water from his lungs as best he could.

"Are you okay?" Concern filled Ro's face as she rushed to grab a dishtowel to wipe up the mess.

"I'm good." Another hard cough. "Just went down the wrong way. Sorry."

"You don't have to apologize for choking," she chuckled. "Just glad it was water, and you weren't choking on the food. I'd hate to have to drive *you* to the hospital."

Brody could practically see the thoughts her lighthearted comment brought forth. The smile he'd loved seeing again had started to fall, and she broke eye contact and looked away. Before she did, however, he'd caught sight of the renewed fire there already beginning to fade.

Fuck that.

Shoving himself to his feet, he reached out, covering the hand still wiping down the table with his own. "Stop."

She stopped.

"Look at me."

She looked at him.

Goddamn, she's beautiful.

Brody shook the ill-timed thought away. This moment wasn't about him and his rogue hormones. This was about Ro.

"You're safe." With him, she'd always be safe. "You know that, right?"

She responded with a tiny nod, even as a single tear drew a silver streak down one of her flawless cheeks. His heart twisted into knots at the sight, and he didn't hesitate to pull her in for a comforting hug.

"Come here." He was thankful as hell when she wrapped her arms around his waist and rested her cheek against his chest.

Ro's muscles tensed, her chest unmoving with her efforts to hold back her emotions.

Ah, baby.

"It's okay to let go, Princess." He felt a hitch in her breath. "What happened to you is a very scary thing."

"I'm n-not crying because I'm scared. I'm crying because I'm p-pissed."

There she is.

Despite her tears and his own rage at what she'd been through, Brody's lips twitched with the urge to curl into a smile. "Me, too, Princess," he soothed. "Me, too."

Pulling back just enough, her watery gaze lifted to his. "That's like the third time you've called me that today." A slight dip of her dark brows. "Why 'Princess'?"

His heart kicked against his ribs. Not from the question, but from the way it felt to hold her this way. To have her back in his arms, her warm body pressed against his as she stared up at him with eyes he suddenly wanted to lose himself in.

"Brody?"

Shit. He still hadn't answered her yet.

"Because you remind me of Snow White."

A flash of heat filtered through the leftover tears. "I do?"

He nodded, his gaze falling over her features as he began listing them off. "Dark hair, flawless skin the color of snow...." His focus landed on her luscious mouth. "Ruby red lips..."

Lips that had just parted with a soft inhale.

In what appeared to be a subconscious move, the tip of her tongue peeked out, running along the narrow seam. In a flash, Brody's mind conjured up the image of that tongue running along other parts. *His* parts.

One very specific, painfully throbbing part in particular.

"I can quit calling you that if it bothers you."

"No." Her answer came in a rush. "I mean, I..." Another nervous lick of her lips. "I don't mind."

His heart kicked. "No?"

With his arms still around her, Brody's eyes fell back to

her lips. *Holy fuck*, it was hard not to take her mouth again. But there was the business of last night that needed to be dealt with first.

Out of respect for Ro as a friend and whatever else she may become.

"Ro, there's something I need to tell you," he rumbled. "It's...about last night."

Trepidation flooded over her. "What about last night?"

Just tell her.

"At Meg's shop this morning, you asked if you'd waited until I fell asleep before taking off your shirt—"

"It's okay." Her lids fell shut with an expelled breath. "I kinda figured I wasn't that lucky." She opened one squinted eye. "Sorry about that."

"No need to apologize." He absentmindedly caressed her back with his thumb. "Just think you deserve to know what happened. Especially given the circumstances."

"Well I guess if that's the worst thing I did..." She blushed with a nervous chuckle. "I mean, you've seen me in a bikini like a million times before. A bra's not much different.

Yeah, he had seen her in a bikini, and now he was kicking his own ass for not paying better attention all those times. But she was wrong about the bra.

All that white lace...those dark, rosy shadows only half-hidden...Ro's bra wasn't just different than her swimsuits. It was better.

So much better.

"That *is* the worst thing I did, right?" Her hopeful expression made telling her the truth that much harder.

"Nothing you did was bad, Ro." It was the God's honest truth.

Seeing her shirtless...feeling her lips and tongue

dancing with his... It had all been really fucking good. So good, in fact, Brody had been able to think of little else since.

"Tell me," she demanded with a pointed look. When he hesitated, she warned him with a low, drawn out, "Brody..."

"You, uh..." He started but then backtracked a bit. "Just try to remember, you were unknowingly under the influence of an illegal drug, and—"

"For the love of God and all that's holy, will you please just tell me what I—"

"You kissed me."

A sudden and total silence filled the air around them, to the point Brody was surprised she couldn't hear his racing heart. Shock-filled eyes blinked back at him several times as she processed his blurted confession.

"I...w-what did you just...I mean, I really..." Ro sniffed and swallowed, stuttering over her own words. "I-I really...*kissed* you? Where?"

"In your living room."

A dramatic roll of her eyes made his palm twitch with the urge to swat her sexy ass. Not something he'd ever really been into, but for some reason, *this* woman apparently brought it out in him.

"Not where in the house, dummy. I mean where, as in... where on your *body*."

He fought another smile because this was the Ro he knew and—

Liked. The Ro I know and like. That's *what I was about to think. Nothing more.*

Ignoring the blatant lie he'd just tried telling himself, Brody put Ro out of her misery and told her the truth.

"The lips."

"The *lips?*" Those eyes grew even wider half-a-second

before she dropped her forehead to his chest with a muffled, "Ohmygod, just kill me now."

A deep chuckle rumbled through him as he gave her back a few gentle pats. "It's okay, Ro."

"No, it's not."

"It really is."

"It's really *not!*"

"Look at me." When she didn't obey the first time, Brody gave her a dose of her own previous medicine. "Aurora..."

He'd purposely used her full first name, knowing she almost always responded to it.

With a slow, tentative movement, Ro finally brought her mortified gaze back up to his. "What?"

Holding her close, he grew serious because he needed her to see that he was. About this, he was as serious as a man could get. "What you did, that wasn't your fault. But I..." Brody pushed aside his guilt and shame and told her, "I'm the one who owes you an apology."

"You?" Genuine confusion left her brows turned down and her blue eyes searching his. "Why? What do you have to apologize for? I'm the one who kissed you, so why—"

"Because I kissed you back."

8

Six days later...

"Wow. Your boobs and ass look amazing in that dress."

Ro looked at herself in the mirror and smiled. "You think?" She turned to check for herself. "And I still wish you could be there tonight."

She studied her reflection again, admittedly loving the way she looked in her new dress. And Meg was right. Her boobs and ass *did* look amazing.

"I know, but you know how Christian and my brother both are. Overprotective doesn't even scratch the surface with those two. Especially after what happened with the whole murder-for-hire plot I managed to get wrapped up in. But tonight is going to be fabulous and go off without a hitch, so please don't worry about any of that. You have to promise me you'll have a good time, and you won't worry about all the rest."

"I promise to have a good time," she conceded. "And I'm not worried about the other. Not anymore."

She really wasn't.

Despite Delta Team's efforts to the contrary—as well as Detective Hansen's unit in the CPD—there wasn't a single piece of evidence, video or otherwise, that could even lead them in the right direction. After a week of dead-ends, Ro had finally written it off as two unfortunate, but unrelated, incidents.

As far as she was concerned, she was more than ready to put it all behind her. Brody and the others, however, weren't so quick to throw in the towel. Heck, he'd barely agreed that tonight would be his last night under her roof.

He had a life and work he needed to focus on. Real work with real cases and clients with real problems.

"But back to more important things..." Megan came to stand by her side "Yes, I think you look like a million bucks. I also think you're going to have every guy at the party wiping the drool from their mouths."

Ro's smile widened a touch. Thanks to a last-minute change of mind, she'd gone with the royal blue number rather than the black, more conservative dress she'd originally considered buying.

Thank goodness for same-day delivery.

It was true, she'd specifically picked the sexier style hoping to gain the attention of a man tonight. But not just any man. No, this particular dress was purchased for the sexy, stubborn former SEAL waiting downstairs this very minute.

Brody's laughing face filled her mind's eye, and Ro had to work not to outwardly react. She still hadn't told Megan she'd kissed the woman's brother.

Not exactly the easiest conversation to start.

She'd picked up the phone a dozen times over the past week to tell her. But then Ro would chicken out, inwardly excusing her cowardly behavior by the fact that she hadn't wanted to tell Megan something like that over the phone.

And since Brody had insisted on being her live-in shadow this past week, it wasn't like she'd had a lot of time alone for such a private discussion.

You could tell her now.

Ro couldn't spill that kind of tea with one foot out the door. She nearly smiled, thinking of how it would go...

Thanks for coming over early to help me get ready for tonight's party, Meg. Oh, by the way, I stuck my tongue down your brother's throat last weekend. See ya later!

Rather than picture what Megan's shocked face would look like if a moment like that actually occurred, her mind created another imagined image. One of her, standing shirtless in her living room while she devoured Brody's mouth the way she'd always dreamed of.

For Brody, that moment had truly existed. But for Ro, it was simply a figment of her imagination.

Because fate was a snarky, backstabbing bitch who apparently thought it would be funny to grant Ro her greatest wish...and then rip the memory away forever.

"Hey, you okay?" Megan's voice tore her from her thoughts. "You look a little flushed."

"Huh?" Ro zeroed back in on the mirrored image before her. As expected, her cheeks were noticeably rosier than they'd appeared minutes before. "Oh. Yeah. Probably just a little hot from rushing around, that's all."

You're not red because you were hurrying. That blush in your cheeks is from thinking about him.

Her inner voice was right. It was the same crawling heat she'd felt off and on every day this past week.

Every time she entered a room, and Brody was there. Or

when she'd look up to find him smiling back at her or flashing one of those panty-dropping winks her way.

Even the way he'd looked at her when he'd shared the embarrassing tale of their forgotten kiss had made her blush. And the shocking revelation he'd revealed during his unexpected confession...

I kissed you back.

Those words had rolled through Ro's brain on a near-constant loop since he'd uttered them. At first, she'd taken the comment as a joke.

A flippant remark meant to lighten the weighted mood. It was easy enough to believe, she supposed. Especially considering neither of them had broached the subject since.

In fact, in the days following Brody's massive bomb drop, they'd pretty much been avoiding each other at all costs.

He'd kept his distance with her, most likely because he still felt like he'd taken advantage of her inebriated state when he'd kissed her. But like Ro had told him, she'd acted, and he'd merely *re*acted, and got caught up in the moment.

Just like any other single, hot-blooded man would have. And probably most women, if the situation had been reversed.

Ro had also been quick to remind the stubborn man he'd also been the one to put a *stop* to things before they could get too far. His words, not hers.

She'd kissed him; he'd stopped her, and then, according to Brody, she'd passed out cold in his arms. So yeah. She'd been playing the avoidance game, too. A feat that was pretty much impossible for them both since he'd insisted on staying at her place at least until after tonight's launch party.

Just as a precaution.

That's what he'd told her, anyway. But Ro could tell

Brody was more worried about her safety than he'd let on. The proof of that was in the brand new, state-of-the-art security system he and the other Delta men had installed the day after the break-in.

However there'd been something other than worry and guilt in those eyes over the past few days. Though she had no evidentiary proof, Ro had all but convinced herself that the new, tiny flickers she'd seen staring back at her were what she'd wished upon every star in the sky to see.

Desire.

It was well-hidden, or so the man probably thought. But she'd seen it with her own two eyes on more than one occasion. The first was during their conversation in the kitchen over grilled cheese and soup. And, unless Ro was mistaken, she'd seen it in several stolen glances since.

She'd been watching for it, of course. Every chance she got. A glimpse here, a sideways glance there. Yes, she'd taken advantage of them all.

And unless she was totally off her rocker—a diagnosis still under review—she was pretty sure Brody King, at the very least, found her physically attractive.

Hence the ruched, off-the-shoulder dress that showed just the right amount of cleavage, hugged every God-given curve, and stopped two inches above the knee. Appropriate for the party's requested cocktail attire, yet sexy enough to catch a certain fella's eye.

Hopefully.

But even as the word flittered through her mind, a familiar trepidation began to settle in. It was the same feeling Ro had gotten every time she'd thought about putting herself out there. A seed of uncertainty her father's heartbreaking demise had long ago planted.

And now that she was finally starting to think it was

time...now that she was ready to take a chance on something she felt in her heart would be wonderfully and amazingly real...

What if I mess it up?

"What about your hair?" Megan asked. "Were you going to put it up, or are you planning on leaving it down?"

Ro shook the nerves away and looked at the long locks hanging over one shoulder. "I was thinking I'd leave it like this. What do you think?"

"Down's good. And not that I don't absolutely love the dress you have on—because I do, and if you even think about changing I'll kill you—but I thought you said you'd picked out a black dress for tonight."

Ro grinned. "I did. But then I saw this one and changed my mind at the last minute."

With a slight tilt of her head, her best friend studied her closely. "Any particular reason for the sudden change in style?"

Ro's heart kicked against her ribs. "Like what?"

"Oh, I don't know. I just thought maybe there was a certain guy you were hoping to impress tonight."

"I sincerely hope you're not talking about Clayton Yorke. Because I made myself very clear on that front during Monday's meeting."

A meeting that was switched from in-person to virtual per Brody's order. At first, Ro had put up a fight, but it hadn't taken long for him to convince her otherwise.

His threat to attend said meeting with her just so he could "beat the guy's ass into the ground" had pretty much sealed the deal.

While Ro was far from happy with Clayton's behavior at the bar—and the months leading up to that, really—she didn't want to see the man beaten within an inch of his life. Knowing Brody firmly believed Clayton was the one who'd not only drugged her, but had also stolen the things from her house, Ro knew that's exactly what he would've done.

And since he was the security expert—and she was still leery about all the other—she'd switched her final meeting with the billionaire heir to online. Naturally Brody had insisted on being in the room with her for the duration of the video call.

She'd allowed it, but on the promise he'd remain silent and away from the camera's view.

Though she'd never admit it to him, Ro was secretly glad he'd been there. If for no other reason than to serve as a witness to the not-so-professional ass chewing she'd given Clayton for his unacceptable behavior at the bar that night.

As well as the few times prior to that.

By the time the conversation was over, Chicago's Most Eligible Bachelor had been more than happy to let her out of her contract early—with a glowing letter of recommendation and without recourse—effective immediately following tonight's party.

Ro had also made it very clear to Clayton that if she ever heard so much as a whisper of a rumor that he'd treated any other woman the way he had her, she'd report his actions to every news outlet and social media platform in existence. And when she was done with that, she'd file a civil suit against him for sexual harassment.

Brody had smiled at her, then. A warm, half-crooked grin from across the room. One that had left her lungs breathless and her panties wet.

And the look he'd had in those dark, soul-stealing eyes...

He wanted me.

It may have been fleeting, and he may not have even

realized it, but it was there. Ro had been on the receiving end of looks like that before and had recognized it instantly.

In that moment, with Clayton Yorke's chagrined face filling her computer screen, Brody King had wanted her the way she'd always dreamed of. But then Clayton had said something, and the intense connection was lost.

Ever since, the two had been following a choreographed dance consisting of walking on eggshells, awkward conversations about the weather, the fact that Delta's brainiac computer guy had come up empty with the bar's security footage, and the disappointing knowledge that the cops had also hit a dead end.

But Ro was done hiding from an enemy who wasn't coming, and she was done tiptoeing around her feelings for Brody. She wanted him. There was no denying that. And she was pretty sure he wanted her, too.

Maybe.

If he didn't, fine. Well not *fine*, but she'd survive. Lord knows, she'd made it through worse heartache than an unrequited love.

She could find a way to get over him, too.

Hopefully, after tonight, I won't have to.

"I'm not talking about Clayton Yorke," Megan spoke up again.

Ro blinked, mentally slapping herself for having become lost in her own thoughts. Meeting her friend's knowing gaze in the mirror, Megan greeted her with a decidedly arched brow.

"Well...good." She ignored the look. "Because after tonight, my dealings with that man are through."

"Really?"

"Yep. I've told you a thousand times I have no interest in Clayton."

"What about Brody?"

Her heart slammed against her ribs a millisecond before her pulse began to race. She'd only just decided to tell Brody she had feelings for him that went beyond friendship. Maybe.

Telling Megan, however, was *not* on tonight's agenda.

One King sibling at a time, please.

Ro's stomach fluttered with an unsettled feeling of dread. Meg couldn't know. There was no way she could know. Not unless...

Had Brody already told his sister about the kiss? No, he would never do that. He'd stood in her kitchen that night and swore to never tell another living soul.

And he was nothing if not a man of his word.

"W-what about Brody?" she asked much too innocently.

Megan turned to face her directly, rather than talking through the mirror. "Seriously? Ro, how long have we been friends?"

"Since we were five, but what does that have to do with your brother?"

"It's more about the fact that you clearly don't trust me."

The woman could have told her she was pregnant with a litter of puppies, and Ro wouldn't have been as stunned as she was right then. "Don't trust... Megan, what the hell are you talking about? I trust you with my life. Always have."

"Life, schmife." Her friend waved the truthful sentiment away. "I'm talking about the fact that, for whatever reason, you don't feel like you can tell me you're in love with my brother."

Ro's world came to a grinding halt. "W-what? I-I don't... I'm not...what are you—"

"Girl, please. You've been head over stilettos for that

man for years. What I don't understand is why you felt you had to hide it from me."

Ro opened her mouth to vehemently deny the accusation again but pressed her lips together before they could utter another lie. Megan was right. She was her closest friend and confidant.

And since the jig was already up...

Without a word, she turned and walked over to her jewelry chest. Using her search for a few finishing touches as an excuse not to look her friend in the eyes, Ro took several long, deep breaths before confessing her most treasured secret.

"It started as an adolescent crush." She spoke softly. "That's why I didn't tell you back then. We were just kids, and I was embarrassed. Even though I was pretty sure it was normal to crush on your friends' older brothers. I just thought it was something I'd grow out of."

She waited but continued when she realized Megan was giving her the time she needed to get it all out on her own terms.

"By the time we got to middle school, I thought I'd never get over him. But then you told me about how, after high school graduation, he was going off to boot camp. I thought...this is it! I was *finally* going to forget all about Brody Freaking King. And since your brother wanted to become a Navy SEAL more than anything else in the world, and the training for that would take, like, forever, I figured... by the time he finished and came back home, I'd have finally moved on."

"But you didn't." Megan's soft voice reached her ears from behind.

Ro picked up a pair of cheap costume earrings, hating that she didn't have her mother's to wear for the occasion instead. "I came close once," she admitted. "I even got to where I'd sometimes go days without thinking about him. But then my dad's funeral came."

"Ah, Ro."

"I remember standing at that damn podium, fighting my way through a eulogy that had taken the entire night before to write..." She swallowed. "I was talking about the kind of man my dad had once been. A strong, selfless man. So caring and loyal. Willing to stand up for what he believed in and ready to defend the honor of others. And I remember, as I was saying those things to a bunch of people I didn't even know, I realized those same, amazing qualities my dad used to possess were the things I loved so much about your brother. Not because I had daddy issues." She cringed at that. "But because those qualities were what made my dad such a good man. And they made Brody a good man, too."

Ro paused to swallow down the painful knot of emotion blocking her throat. The jewelry in her hands blurred with unshed tears, but she blinked them away before they could fall.

"I remember stopping then, trembling as I fought to keep it together. Just long enough to get to the end. That's what I started praying for. I was standing at the front of a church, praying for the strength to make it through the rest of my speech...the rest of the day...and then I saw it." The memory was as clear as if it had happened that very morning. "This larger-than-life-shadow standing between the church's big double doors that had been left open at the end of the aisle. At first, I thought my grief-stricken mind was seeing things. But then the shadow started to move, and the light coming through the stained glass window hit the man's face just so, and that's when I realized...it was him."

"Brody."

She faced her friend with a nod. It took Ro a few seconds, but when she finally looked Megan in the eyes, she didn't find a single drop of anger, resentment, or betrayal there. Only the love of a sister.

"He was still wearing his fatigues." She smiled sadly. "He told me later that his SEAL Team had just gotten back from a three-month deployment. Somewhere overseas that he couldn't tell me about. But instead of going home and getting the rest he'd obviously needed, your crazy, stupidly sweet brother had hopped on the first red-eye flight to Chicago he could find, just so he could be there."

"For you."

She nodded again, going to her bed and sitting on its edge. "That was it. That was the moment I fell completely and hopelessly in love with your brother." Her lungs filled and expelled a deep, cleansing breath. "And I don't think I've ever really stopped loving him."

"Oh, Ro." The mattress dipped from Megan's weight as the other woman sat down beside her. Putting an arm around Ro's shoulders, her sweet friend pulled her in for a side-hug. "Why didn't you ever pursue things with Brody? You had to know I wouldn't care. I mean, it's not like you and I made some stupid promise like my idiot fiancé did with my brother."

Ro chuckled at that. It was still astonishing to her that Christian had kept his distance from the woman he loved for years, all because he'd made some ridiculous promise to Brody back when they were all kids.

Boys go to Jupiter to get more...

"I didn't think you'd care." She licked her glossy lips.

"Then why hold back?"

"For one, I was pretty sure Brody had zero interest in me back then. And two..." Ro let her voice trail off, the second half of her list of excuses much more painful to admit.

"And two?"

"My dad." A quiet admission. "You were there. You saw what happened to him. My mom's death destroyed him. The doctors all said the alcohol destroyed his liver. And yeah, the bottle may have been the bullet, but..." Her voice cracked, but she cleared it and moved on. "His broken heart is what pulled the trigger."

"You're not your father, Ro."

"You don't know that. Hell *I* don't know that. My dad loved my mom with every cell in his body, and when she died, the man he used to be died with her. And I'm just like him, Meg."

She slapped a palm to her chest, the conversation diminishing her earlier resolve to come clean with Brody about her true feelings.

"No, you're not."

"Really? Because I already lose sleep when Delta Team is away on some super-secret mission that will almost certainly put your brother in harm's way. If Brody and I did get involved, and something happened to him..." Her voice threatened to buckle again, but she managed to swallow down the thick knot of emotions and finished what needed to be said. "If I finally had the chance to be with your brother, and I lost him...Megan, I don't think that's a loss I could survive."

A long stretch of silence passed before her friend spoke up again. Ro had expected words of support and understanding. Maybe even an apology, not that anything Meg had said or done warranted one. But neither of those was the response she received.

Instead, her bestie laid it all out there, calling Ro on her bullshit the way a true friend should.

"So that's it?" Megan shot her a look. "You'd rather live the rest of your life, wondering 'what if' than take a chance and see where things with you and my brother could go?"

"I just told you." Ro pushed herself to her heeled feet. "I won't end up like my dad." She *couldn't*.

"Okay."

The other woman's white flag waved a little too easily. With a frown, Ro looked over to where Megan was still sitting. "Okay?"

"Sure." Her friend stood and made her way across the room. "I just have one more question for you. If you can give me a good, solid answer, I'll drop the subject of you and Brody forever. Scout's honor."

"You were never a scout."

"Whatever, you know what I mean."

Ro's gaze narrowed with suspicion. "What happens if I can't give you a good, solid answer? Which, by the way, sounds far too subjective for this little deal you're trying to make with me."

"You've known me long enough to know I'm both objective and fair. And if you can't give me a satisfactory answer, then...you have to ask my brother out on a date."

"You're insane."

"What's the matter?" Meg taunted. "Afraid you're going to lose?"

A low snorting sound bubbled up. "No."

"Then agree to the bet."

"Fine." Ro blew out a frustrated breath. "What's the question?"

Pausing dramatically, Megan gave her an assessing once-over, as if to study her choice of fashion. When the sly woman asked her final question, Ro understood why.

"If you're so certain you and Brody are doomed from the start...if you're so afraid of taking that leap and seeing if there's something real between you two...then why, after spending a week under the same roof as the man, did you change your mind and rush-order a sexy as hell dress...in my brother's favorite color?"

9

FUCKING GORGEOUS.

Brody stood next to Ro, unable to take his eyes off her as she spoke with two of Clayton Yorke's elite guests. Truth be told, he'd been struggling to look at anything else all night.

Hair down, the thick, dark waves fell in a silken waterfall over one of her bare shoulders. Unlike so many of the other women in attendance tonight, Ro had kept her makeup simple and light.

The less-is-more look gave her an air of casual elegance that shined in the sea of false lashes and artificially filled lips. But that dress...

If blue wasn't already my favorite color, it sure as hell would be now.

The tight, fitted off-the-shoulder dress showcased Ro's delicate neckline, teasing him with just a hint of cleavage that made him wish for more. Soft and stretchy, the gathered material hugged the woman's curves in a way that made him jealous of the damn thing.

Even her damn collar bones made his fingers itch with the urge to touch.

She takes my breath away.

It wasn't an exaggeration or some dramatic declaration. When he'd first caught sight of her back at the house, Brody had *literally* lost the ability to breath.

He'd been standing in her living room, talking to Christian about the logistics of tonight and last minute adds to the guest list when he'd lost his own words mid-sentence. Ro had come down those stairs looking like his deepest, most desired fantasy come to life, and everything had just...stopped.

She'd looked at him. He'd stared back at her. And for that brief, unexplainable moment in time, it was as if they'd been the only two people in the room.

Seconds later, Meg had joined them, saying something to her fiancé as she'd walked past. Just like that, the unexpected spell had been broken.

Even now, after having been glued to Ro's hip for the past hour-plus, while she perused the crowd at Yorke's ridiculously extravagant party, Brody had to force his lungs to pull in a breath every time he glanced her way.

It didn't matter that she'd been quieter than normal on the ride here, or that he'd spent the last week vowing to keep her at arm's length and in the friend zone. Nor did Brody care about the trove of Chicago's most eligible single females—all clad in barely-there dresses and heels that defied all sense of logic—currently making their rounds through the crowd of plastic and money.

Whether in passing or from clear across the room, the brazen, lingering looks and come-hither smiles he'd received did nothing for him. He looked at those other women and felt...nothing.

No spark of attraction. No desire.

Nothing.

Tall or short. Blonde or...blonder...it didn't matter. There was only one woman who'd caught Brody's eye tonight, and she was standing right beside him.

"Here's my card." Ro held out the small square of colorful cardstock to the couple who'd shown interest in hiring her to redesign their charity's website. "My socials are on the back, and there's also a QR code to my website. From there, you can see my digital portfolio, which shows samples of work I've done for others, including Mr. Yorke."

The smile she flashed the well-dressed husband and wife duo wasn't at all like the ones he'd seen her throw Yorke's way when they'd first arrived. This one was real, and it was all Ro.

Wide and genuine, seeing it warmed his heart in ways he didn't understand. The most beautiful smile he'd ever seen, he decided. And Brody couldn't help but wonder how he'd never noticed it before now.

How did I not notice...her?

The answer to those unspoken questions was simple. Before this past week, Brody hadn't seen Ro as anything more than Megan's best friend because he hadn't bothered to *look*.

He was damn sure looking now, though. And fuck all if he knew what to do about it.

"We will definitely be in touch, Miss Tennison." The wife slid Ro's card into her small, sparkly clutch purse. "The work you've done for Clayton speaks for itself."

"Yes, it's all very impressive," the sharply dressed gentleman added.

"Thank you so much. And please, call me Ro."

"Ro." The wife grinned. "A name as adorable as its owner. I like it."

Brody watched and waited, already knowing what came next.

Three...two...

A crimson hue crept into Ro's porcelain cheeks.

There it is.

Something else he'd noticed, as of late...compliments made the talented woman blush. Not that he'd given her a lot the last few days.

Ro had spent most of the past week holed up in her home office while he and the team focused on her case. A case that, so far, had turned out to be a dead end.

Between his frustrations with that and his burgeoning feelings for Ro, Brody had thought it best to keep their interactions to a minimum. Apparently Ro thought the same.

Though she'd instantly let him off the hook for his confessed behavior that night in her kitchen, Ro had also been noticeably distant. They'd slept under the same roof, but he'd barely seen her.

While he spent his days working on stuff for Delta Team and looking into her break-in and drugging, she'd been working on projects for various clients and last-minute to-dos for Yorke. While Brody either ate in the kitchen or living room, Ro took most of her meals to her desk and ate while she worked.

He stayed up late. She went to bed early. He woke early. She was already in her office with her door shut.

At first, Brody was convinced she was secretly pissed at him for having kissed her back. God knows, he still felt like an ass for not having more self-control that night. But she hadn't *seemed* upset with him when he'd finally confessed it all.

She'd been blushing up a storm and falling all over

herself with unnecessary apologies to show even a hint of anger or resentment toward him.

There'd been multiple times during his stay at her house when Brody had started to ask her about it, but truth be told, her vanishing acts had been a relief most days. Not because he didn't want to be around her...but because he did.

Around her.

On her.

Under her.

Hell, just plain wanted *her*. And he had no fucking clue what to do with that.

"We'll be sure to reach out so we can set up a time to chat." The wife held out her hand for Ro.

The two women shook on it, followed by the same shared gesture with the husband. When the couple finally moved on, Ro turned to him with a smile that lit up the entire room.

"Did you hear that? They want *me* to redesign their charity's website!"

Her joy was so contagious, Brody couldn't help but smile right along with her. "That's great, Ro. I'm proud of you."

"Thanks." She beamed. "I'm proud of me, too."

His chest swelled. This was the Ro he was used to seeing. Not the quiet, withdrawn woman he'd been rooming with this past week. No, his Ro was confident and full of life. Ready and willing to take on the world.

Except she isn't yours, dumbass.

The reminder should have created a sense of relief, but only because he shouldn't think of her that way. And yet, knowing she wasn't his—knowing he *couldn't* have her the way he had in last night's dick-swelling dream—created an ache in Brody's soul he couldn't begin to explain.

So he ignored it and focused on the real reason he was here. To keep Ro safe.

She has to be safe.

He checked his watch again, mainly to have an excuse to look somewhere other than her entrancing stare. "It's about time for your big introduction. You ready?"

"No." She scoffed, as if the answer should have been obvious. "But at least I just have to stand there and smile. Can you imagine if I had to give an actual *speech*? I'd make the biggest fool out of myself, I'm sure."

"Your speech would be flawless, and every person in this room would be hanging on your every word."

Her gaze widened, the tiny hitch of breath that had escaped Ro's lungs reaching him over the steady hum of nearby conversations. A slight flush colored the skin of her face and exposed neck.

It wasn't the same bashful blush he'd seen minutes before. No, this was something altogether different. An unmistakable heat that left her lips parting and the blues in her eyes darkening to the color of midnight.

Ro's tongue darted out with a lick of her full lips. Looking uncharacteristically nervous, she opened and closed her mouth twice, almost as if she were afraid of what she was trying to say.

"Brody, there's um... There's something I wanted to ask you. I was going to wait until later, but..." Another quick swipe that made him want to slam his mouth to hers. "I was wondering if maybe...and feel free to say no." She gave a nervous chuckle. "But I was wondering if maybe you'd want to—"

"There's my star!"

They both turned to see Clayton Yorke approaching through the parted crowd.

Impeccable timing, asshole.

"I hope you're ready, Aurora." The other man's squinty stare didn't so much as twitch in Brody's direction. "It's your time to shine."

"Oh, u-uh..." Ro's blinking gaze bounced between him and Yorke. "Yeah. I mean, yes. Of course."

His fists curled at his sides, his frustration two-fold. First and foremost, Brody wanted to throat punch the entitled prick for interrupting Ro before she could finish asking whatever it was she'd been trying to ask. And two...

I want her real smile to come back.

Because the one she'd just flashed her uppity client's way was anything but.

Forcing his fingers to relax, Brody reminded himself that Ro would no longer be working with Yorke after tonight. He'd been damn proud when he'd stood in her office while she—very professionally—ripped the guy a new asshole.

He'd also been hard as a fucking lead iron pipe. Just like he was now.

"There's nothing to it," the other man assured her. "Really. You'll follow me up on stage...and don't worry. My assistant will tell you when to go and where to stand. Once we're up there, I'll go to the mic, thank everyone for coming, say a few words, and then I'll introduce you and the others who played an instrumental part in the company's rebranding."

"Then she's off the stage, right?" Brody needed to be sure.

Since the break-in, there hadn't been so much as a hint of danger where Ro was concerned. But minus their daily trips to and from Cup of Joe, as well as a couple quick and efficient grocery runs, this party was the first time in a week she'd been out in public for more than a few minutes at a time.

He was fine as long as she was next to him. But the idea of her being up on that stage, well out of his reach and exposed to a million different vantage points throughout the room...

Brody's gut suddenly began to churn with dread.

Turning to Ro, he opened his mouth to tell her not to do it. To beg her not to go up on that stage, but then—

"How 'bout this party, huh?"

The crowd erupted in cheers and applause as a woman he'd seen Yorke talking to earlier took the stage. As the clapping died down and the woman began to continue with her speech, Ro's client looked at her and smiled.

Shit.

"That's our cue. Follow me."

Clayton started for the west side of the stage, and once again, the crowd around them parted as if the man were the Second Coming. Barely resisting an eye roll, Brody fell in line behind Ro, keeping mere inches between them to prevent a possible separation.

Bringing his left hand to his ear, he pressed the tiny receiver hidden there to reactivate his mic. "We're on the move," he informed the rest of his team.

"Copy that," Christian responded immediately.

The rest of the team checked in as well.

Upon Brody's request, all five of the other Delta men were in attendance. Each one had been strategically scattered throughout the expansive event center. It was the one, non-negotiable condition of Ro's attendance at tonight's soirée.

Either Delta Team was in charge of the party's security, or she didn't go. Period.

Ro had agreed surprisingly fast, and Yorke hadn't so much as flinched at the demand. The guy had even gone so far as to voluntarily offer up the names on his guest list, as well as those from his own personal staff who were in attendance.

He, Christian, Rocky, and the others had dressed for the occasion, making it easy to blend in with the rest of the crowd. But what the other guests didn't know—what they couldn't possibly see—was that Brody and the rest of Delta were armed to the teeth beneath their well-pressed suits and ties.

Beneath his polished exterior, Brody had a Glock 19 pistol tucked in his side holster, a Sig Sauer P226 9mm in an S.O.B.—or small-of-back holster—and a KelTec P3AT pistol at his ankle.

All three weapons had their mags full and one in the chamber. And in case those weren't enough, Brody had also strapped on his trusted Hogue tactical knife with a button flipper and spear point blade.

Christian, Rocky, Cade, Liam, and Jagger were just as prepared as him.

Only thing better would be if we could walk out those doors right now and forget all about Clayton Fucking Yorke.

The thought had Brody stealing a quick, indiscernible glance at the woman walking before him. His heart kicked and his dick twitched. From the front, Ro looked indescribably beautiful in that dress.

But seeing her from this angle...

Holy. Hell.

"Okay, then." Yorke's annoying voice tore Brody from his thoughts. "You're welcome to wait with the other guests, if you'd like."

He lifted his gaze slowly, refusing to let the other man

think he gave two shits about being caught checking out Ro's sexy ass. Keeping his voice flat, he told the asshat, "I'm good here, thanks."

Those narrow eyes slid to Ro's. Yorke's scruff-framed lips curved into a smirk Brody wanted to wipe clean off. "You know, Aurora, if your boyfriend is that concerned about you, he could always join you on stage." He turned his gaze back to Brody's. "Oh wait. I forgot. You told me you two were just friends."

"We are," Ro jumped in nervously.

Brody wasn't nervous. He was fed up.

Stepping just inside Yorke's personal space, he put on his own fake as fuck smile and kept his voice low enough only Ro and her shithead client could hear. "Friend, boyfriend, bodyguard...I'll be whatever *Ro* needs me to be."

Another sharp inhale from beside him said she'd heard what he'd said loud and clear. As for Yorke...

"Message received." That camera-ready grin never wavered. To Ro, Yorke held out his arm with a polished, "Shall we?"

Brody swung his gaze to Ro, who was staring up at him with an almost hopeful expression. And as she curled her fingers around the other man's elbow, she let her eyes linger on his a moment longer, even after the two had begun making their way toward the steps.

"Boyfriend?" Christian's voice filled his ear. "There something you want to share with the rest of the class, King?"

"Nope."

That was it. That was all he gave. Lucky for him, his friend didn't push.

Christian would, though. Later. Of that, Brody had no doubt. But right now, they were all in mission-mode, and given the uneasy feeling swirling around inside his gut, he was damn thankful to know they were here.

Brody surveilled the low-lit room with an expert eye before returning his focus to Ro. Yorke had just taken the stage to another, louder eruption of applause, but his eyes were locked on the woman waiting at the bottom of the stairs.

"I don't like this," he rumbled to his team.

Rocky's voice struck with a curious, "Which part?"

"All of it."

"Relax, King." Liam came next. "I ran backgrounds on all the names on Yorke's list, plus the caterers and staff, plus Yorke's personal staff. Oh, and the DJ. Can't forget him."

"He's right, Bro," Cade backed his teammate up. "I personally checked the I.D. of everyone who walked through those doors, staff included. Plus, I've been standing guard at the main entrance since the start of this thing, and the only thing I've seen that concerns me is the alarming number of plastic surgeries gone wrong."

"Same with the back door," Jagger piggybacked off of that. "Well, not so much the surgeries gone wrong, but... yeah. I'd say your girl's safe, King."

"She's not my girl."

"Ah, me doth think the gentleman protests too much," Rocky teased.

"Jesus, can we please stay focused?" He barked. "Ro's about to go on stage."

"King's right." Christian got serious. "I get that this is probably overkill on our part, especially since there haven't been any further attempts to approach or harm Ro or her house. But we all know how fast shit can turn sideways so stay alert and at the ready."

My thoughts exactly.

"And saving the best for last, I'd like to introduce the woman who has been instrumental in making this entire rebrand possible." Yorke's annoying voice boomed out over the crowd. "Please welcome my amazing graphic designer, Aurora Tennison."

Showtime.

The crowd celebrated Ro's on-stage appearance with roars of cheers and a thunder of clapping. Brody watched from his place on the floor, his focus locked onto her as she carefully made her way up the short flight of stairs.

Practically floating across the stage, his first thought was that Ro was a natural in front of the crowd. His second...

So fucking beautiful.

Though he hated to do it, Brody returned to his duty of scanning the room. The others were probably right. Chances were he and his overactive protective instincts had turned this whole thing into something it wasn't.

He'd even started to wonder if he'd exaggerated the potential danger as an excuse to stay close to her. But Brody knew to his core he'd never do something like that to Ro or any other woman. Which meant the threat he'd assumed had stemmed from factual events.

And *that* meant he needed to be on his A-game until he could get her away from this place and back home. Safe and sound, just the way he needed her to be.

Yorke said something more about Ro's incredible talent with design and colors before asking for a final round of applause for all her hard work and dedication to his cause.

Brody looked at her once again, his heart flipping when he caught sight of that adorable as fuck blush filling her cheeks. Even from here, he could see the pinkish hues, and damn if it did something to him he couldn't explain.

With a few parting words, Yorke thanked his guests

again before ordering everyone to "eat all the food and get as drunk as humanly possible". The entire place exploded with cheers, followed by the start of some very loud, very upbeat music filling the room's booming speakers.

He watched as Ro turned to leave the stage with the others. Her eyes immediately began to search, stopping the second they landed on him.

God, he loved that she knew to look for him. That she knew he was here and would keep her safe. And the smile she was sending his way now...

It was different than the one she'd given Yorke and the guests she'd spoken with earlier. This one was warmer. Almost a tad flirty?

Whatever it was, Brody felt it reach inside his chest and squeeze his heart to the point he thought it would burst. And it was in that moment he decided...

I'm going to do it. I'm going to ask Ro out on a date.

Despite the mess it very well may cause, he knew he'd always regret it if he didn't at least try. So as soon as they got back to her place—the very second they were alone—he was going to take that crazy leap.

What's the worst that could happen?

There was a laundry list of things that could go wrong, he knew. The worst being losing Ro as a friend. But as her heeled toes hit that first step with those insanely blue eyes still locked onto his, that imaginary list—and the concerns that came with it—seemed to vanish.

Brody started to make his way over to her. Ro reached the bottom of the steps and headed toward him.

Having followed her down the stairs, Yorke appeared anxious, almost distracted as he glanced down at his watch. But then the man disappeared behind the stage—to where, Brody didn't know, nor did he care.

Ro's obligation to this evening's event, as well as Clayton Yorke and his newly rebranded company were complete. Which meant he could finally get her the hell home.

"So...how did I look up there?" She called out to him over the deafening pop song.

"Like a princess," he hollered back.

Her lips curved even more, and damn, if he didn't feel a primal sense of pride knowing he'd put that smile there. He also loved that it was meant only for him.

Definitely worth the risk.

The thought drove through Brody's head with only a few feet left to go. With plans to take her hand in his and lead her straight out the door, he was giving the immediate area a final once-over when it happened.

Ro was walking toward him with that sexy as fuck smile still spread across her face. Another guest—some jackass who was paying more attention to their phone than where they were walking—accidentally shoulder-checked her.

Momentarily losing her footing, Ro nearly toppled over, but righted herself just in time. Brody rushed to get to her, but she simply laughed it off as if it were nothing. And then...

No!

Brody heard the telltale zip of the bullet as it flew through the narrow space still separating him and Ro. Her body jerked from the impact, and she fell to the floor before he could catch her.

"Ro!"

Reaching into his jacket, he pulled out his Glock and threw himself over her fallen form. Determined to use his body—and the bullet resistant vest he had on beneath his dress shirt—as a barricade between her and any additional bullets, Brody kept his eyes up and his trigger finger ready.

"Shooter!" he shouted in his coms. "Shot came from the north!"

"On it!" Jagger responded first.

Christian's voice came over the coms next as the team's leader took charge and began shouting orders. All around him, the crowd had become a free-for-all of screams and panic. Yorke's guests running wildly in their search for the nearest exit.

But Brody's focus was on Ro...and the growing pool of blood on the floor beneath her.

10

"I'm going to fucking kill him."

Ro's eyes flew from her injured arm to Brody's blackened stare. The murderous fury burning there turned her veins to ice. "Please don't say stuff like that."

"Why not?" The vein in his forehead popped with rage. "It's the truth."

Ro searched for even a hint that the man stewing before her was joking. He wasn't.

From the time she'd regained consciousness in the back of the team's SUV, to the minute they'd walked through Brody's front door, to now, there was only one item on the angry man's agenda...

Find Clayton Yorke and kill him.

Only Clayton hadn't been the one to shoot her. Ro could *feel* it deep in her gut.

Detective Hansen and his partner—a woman whose name she couldn't seem to think of at the moment—had come by the hospital to take down her statement, as well as Brody's and the rest of the team's.

She hadn't been any help, of course. Being thrown to the ground from a bullet's impact and then knocking herself unconscious had pretty much ruined her chances of offering anything useful.

And until the cops finished processing the scene and questioning Clayton and the other witnesses...

"It would be pretty stupid of him to shoot me in a room full of witnesses two minutes after he'd just been on stage with me," Ro pointed out.

"Seems like a brilliant plan to me," Brody quipped. "What better way to draw suspicion off yourself than to commit the crime in a way that would guarantee he'd be a suspect?"

"Like a killer calling in the crime and claiming to have found the body," Christian added in.

Both she and Brody slid their attention to the team's leader—and medic—while the other man wrapped a wide strip of transparent film dressing around the bandaged wound on her upper left arm.

"Exactly." Brody motioned a hand toward his supportive friend.

Turning to her, Christian switched subjects long enough to educate her on what he was doing. "This film is waterproof. Not something they typically give in the E.R., but I wanted to cover the original bandage completely, so you'll be able to take a shower without worrying about the wound getting wet. Just make sure you don't do a lot of quick movements or heavy lifting with that arm for a few days and follow the care instructions the hospital gave you."

"Thank you."

She offered her friend a tiny smile but hissed in a breath between her teeth when his fingers pressed a little too closely to where the bullet had entered—and exited—the fleshy part a couple inches below her shoulder.

With her free hand, Ro fisted a section of thick comforter beside her. *Brody's* comforter. On Brody's bed. In Brody's house.

Because that's where the enraged man had insisted the team bring them once she'd been released from the E.R. Two trips in a week's time. Not exactly a record she intended to break.

God, I hate hospitals.

"Sorry." Christian adjusted his hold.

"It's okay," she mumbled softly.

"The fuck it is." Brody tossed a scowl her way. "There's not a goddamn thing about this that's okay."

Pacing the length of his bedroom, the man looked like he was ready to start an all-out war, and Ro wasn't sure how to stop him. She also didn't know how to get him to see that what happened wasn't his fault.

"Clayton didn't do this," she reiterated her earlier point. "Even if he'd wanted to, the guy had just walked off stage when it happened."

"Exactly." Those eyes of his burned into hers. "He disappears somewhere backstage, and seconds later, someone takes a shot at you. A shot that came from that very same direction."

"What?" Her eyes widened, dread filling the pit of her stomach. "I didn't...you never told me that part."

"I'm sorry. Guess I've been a little busy, what with making sure you're okay after being fucking *shot*."

"You heard the doctor, Brody. It's literally just a flesh wound."

Still hurt like hell, but at least no bones or major arteries had been struck. If that had happened, she'd be in a whole other world of hurt.

Or worse.

"She's right, brother," Christian backed her up. "I'm as pissed as you about this whole thing, but it *is* just a flesh wound."

"She shouldn't have a wound at *all!*" The man's angry voice echoed off his bedroom walls. To her, he added, "And you weren't just shot, Aurora. You were also unconscious for four-and-a-half minutes."

"Yeah, because I hit my head on the floor when I fell, not because I got a through-and-through in the fatty part of my arm."

That's what the doctor had told her, anyway. And she didn't even have a concussion, so...

Storming over to where she sat, Brody stood directly in front of her. All hard lines and furrowed brows, his fiery gaze made him appear madder than she could ever remember seeing him.

"This is serious, Ro." He announced this as if she wasn't already aware. "If that idiot hadn't bumped into you at the last second, you'd be dead. You get that, right?"

She stared up at him with a tilted head and a sarcastic, "Yeah, I'm pretty sure I was there for that part."

Unlike the night of Cade's birthday party, Ro remembered every single thing about the moments leading up to tonight's shooting...

The rustling nerves she'd felt standing up on that stage. The prayers she didn't fall on the way up—or down—those stairs. The pride she'd felt at seeing things through and finishing the job.

Not for Clayton. For herself.

But mostly, when Ro thought back to the seconds before that so-called idiot bumped into her, she pictured the man staring back at her as if he were about to start spitting nails. Because in that moment, he hadn't been Brody King, former Navy SEAL-turned-Delta Team operator. He was just...

Brody.

The man who'd spent the last several days focused solely on protecting her and keeping her safe. A man whose jaw had nearly dropped when he'd first seen her in her dress.

A dress now stained with blood.

Guess he won't be taking this off me tonight, after all.

Stupidly that's what she'd envisioned when she'd made the online purchase. It's what she'd dreamed of after trying it on to ensure it fit, and it's what Ro had hoped for when she'd slipped it on earlier tonight.

But now...

"You should be good to go." Christian began gathering up the trash and supplies from the med kit he always kept in his truck. Noticing the awkward back and forth glances between her and Brody, the other man added a low, almost hesitant, "I'm, uh...I'm just gonna give you two a minute to talk." To her, he said, "I'll call Megan and give her an update. I know she's pissed I wouldn't let her drive here after I called from the hospital, but I feel better knowing she's locked in tight at home."

"Thanks. And me, too. I'm glad you sent Cade to sit with her until you get home." Ro's chest tightened. "I'm also glad you convinced her not to go to the party. If she'd been there, she probably would have been next to me when..." Her voice cracked just thinking about it. "You almost *were* right next to me."

That last part was meant for Brody, whose face had blurred behind a wall of unshed tears. Not only because tonight had been terrifying, but because he could've been the one to get shot.

He could've been killed trying to protect me.

It was the one silver lining in being the shooter's target. There had only been one shot. One bullet. And one person hit.

Me.

Her lids fluttered with several quick blinks, but despite her efforts to stave off the sudden onslaught of moisture, a few tears still managed to escape. Beneath his breath, Brody mumbled a curse before disappearing into his en suite bathroom.

Seconds later, he was back and squatting before her.

"Here." His softened voice was in stark contrast to the harsh lines still present on his hardened face. A strong hand offered several tissues.

"Thanks." Ro sniffled as she took them, looking down as she patted her cheeks dry. "Sorry."

"Don't."

The sharp order had her head rising and her eyes searching his. The intensity there left her heart racing and her lips speechless.

"You don't apologize for this." His pupils flared with fury. "Not ever."

Instinctually, Ro knew his anger wasn't directed at her but rather the person who'd pulled the trigger.

"I'll be downstairs with the guys when you're ready," Christian mentioned again.

A slight tip of Brody's chin was his only response.

Sending her a parting *good luck* expression, Delta's

leader walked out of Brody's bedroom, shutting the door quietly behind him as he went.

"How do you feel?" Brody's deep rumble pulled her attention away from the door. His expression had softened slightly. Voice, too.

"My arm's throbbing, and I have a headache. But it's nothing some ibuprofen won't cure."

"What about the other?"

The question confused her. "The other?"

A knowing look fell over him, then. One she supposed only people who'd been on the receiving end of a killer's bullet could possess.

"Truth?" She licked her lips, catching a stray, salty tear in the process. "I'm terrified."

"Good."

His unexpected response had her physically recoiling. "*Good?*"

The confusing man stood just long enough to take a seat beside her. The mattress dipped beneath Brody's weight, the heat from his body like a warm, comfortable blanket against her chilled skin.

I'm so cold. Why am I so cold?

"You remember me telling you Rocky, Jagger, and Liam stayed back at the scene while Christian and I took you to the hospital, right?"

Her head dipped with half a nod. "I was shot this time, not drugged."

The flippant comment was meant to be a joke. A light-hearted comment to ease the molasses-thick tension filling the room.

But Brody didn't laugh. He didn't so much as crack a smirk. Instead he slowly lifted a hand—a *trembling* hand—to her face.

Cupping her cheek in the gentlest of holds, he told her, "If you're scared, you're more likely to be careful. And I need you to be careful, Princess." An audible swallow. "I need you safe."

Reaching up, Ro wrapped her fingers as far around his thick wrist as they would go. Her thumb absentmindedly brushed across his warm, naturally tanned skin.

"I *am* safe, Brody," she whispered. "Because I'm with you."

With him, she always felt safe.

But the stubborn man was already shaking his head before she was finished talking. "If that were true, you wouldn't have a bullet hole in your arm."

Yes, well, that was something she'd deal with later. On her own time, when she was alone so no one could watch as she curled into a ball and ugly cried. Until then...

"If you're going to take the blame for someone else shooting me, then you'd better point that finger at me, too."

"You?" That hand dropped with a sudden shove to his feet. "There's not even a *fraction* of what happened tonight that's your fault."

"Isn't there?" She stood, careful not to jostle her arm too much in the process.

"No! There isn't." Spinning back around to face her, the same fingers that had touched her so gently seconds before raked angrily through Brody's thick, dark hair. "I'm the one who promised to keep you safe. And *I'm* the one who was so distracted I missed a goddamn *shooter!* How could you even begin to think any of this was your fault?"

"You tried to talk me into staying home, remember? All week, you did your damnedest to convince me to call Clayton and tell him I couldn't make it. You do remember those conversations, don't you?"

More like tiffs she'd eventually won, though now she wished like hell she'd listened.

"Doesn't matter." Brody started to walk away as soon as she got close.

Ro shot out her good hand and stopped him. "It *does* matter!" she challenged back.

He didn't attempt to move away again, thankfully, but he also wasn't looking at her. She needed him to look at her. Needed him to see the truth of her words in her eyes.

I need him to see...me.

"Look at me." A whispered plea that went unanswered. "Brody, please..."

In a hesitant move, those dark eyes finally came back around to hers. The pain there broke her heart, and suddenly Ro wanted nothing more than to take it all away.

Before she could talk herself out of it, she lifted onto her bare tiptoes and pressed her lips to his rugged cheek. She could feel his entire body stiffen, a reaction she'd wholeheartedly expected.

And that was okay because this kiss wasn't about physical need. It was about the love of a friend and her desire to comfort.

"What was that for?" he whispered softly.

"To thank you." She held his gaze, praying for the words needed to make him see. "Christian told me you threw yourself on top of me after I was hit. You put yourself directly into harm's way for me."

"That's my job."

"Actually, it isn't," Ro adamantly denied his claim. Standing so close she could feel his warm breaths on her face, she told him under no uncertain terms, "I'm not a Delta Team client, nor am I your sister."

"No.' He practically growled. "You're sure as hell not."

It was the hardest she'd ever had to work to school an expression. "Right." A flash of a smile so he wouldn't see just how deeply his words had cut. "Exactly. So there really isn't any reason for you to—"

"I keep seeing you fall." The interruption was quiet, almost as if he were talking to himself more than her. "In my head, I keep hearing the whiz of that bullet, and I knew. There was no way I could get to you in time."

Oh, Brody.

"But you *did* get to me."

"Not fast enough." His haunted gaze fell onto the fresh bandage secured around her upper arm.

"Brody—"

"You went down, and you weren't moving. There was so much blood, and I thought..." His Adam's apple bobbed with an audible swallow. "I thought I'd lost you."

"You didn't lose me, Brody. I'm right here." Ro lifted a hand and placed it on his chest. "I'm here, and I'm not going anywhere. Not unless..."

His gaze seemed to sharpen then as it locked up tight with hers. "Unless?"

Ro's heart raced with the force of a hundred thoroughbreds, and her nerves were about as shot as they could get. Her timing was crap, and she was probably making the biggest mistake of her life, but she'd almost died tonight, damn it.

It was like Brody said. If that man hadn't bumped into her when he did, she'd be dead. *Dead.* As in never coming back. And what would she have to show for it?

Two dead parents, a mortgage she still wasn't convinced was a good investment, a love of coffee, and a blossoming career that was just starting to gain traction.

Bet no one would have to stay up all night to write that eulogy.

So yeah, she was shooting her shot. If she missed, so be it. At least she wouldn't die never knowing.

Inching closer, Ro carefully lifted her other hand. With both palms resting against his warm, sculpted chest, she drew in a steely breath. Dropping her carefully crafted walls just enough, she finally allowed him to see the desire she'd felt all this time.

Desire she felt only for him.

"I'm not under the influence of anything stronger than aspirin right now." She continued staring up at him. "I say this, because I need you to know I'm fully aware and in control of my faculties. That's important for you to know."

"Because?"

"Because I have something I need to tell you, and I really need you to understand it has nothing to do with what happened tonight."

"Okay..."

"I mean, it does, I guess. But only because tonight made me realize how much I could've missed out on had that bullet done its job."

A muscle in his jaw twitched, and she could tell by the look on his face he was reliving that moment in his head.

"You said it yourself; I could've died tonight." Ro's throat became thick with emotion and nerves. "God, I could've died tonight without having ever known..."

"Known what?" Brody's encouraging whisper seemed to fill the air around them.

This was it. If there was ever a time to risk it all, *this* was it. Worst case, she could use the excuse of a head injury or the shock of having been shot to explain her craziness away.

Or, if she got really desperate, Ro figured she could always cry amnesia again.

Only this time would be so different because Ro knew...

Good or bad, no matter how Brody reacted to the secret she was about to reveal, she'd remember every breath of this moment forever.

"What it feels like to kiss you." There. She'd said it.

Now all she could do was hold her breath and wait.

11

Ro could feel Brody's heart pounding away beneath the touch of her hand. Its hard and fast staccato of a beat matched almost perfectly with the wild thumping inside her own chest.

He didn't pull her into his arms and devour her like she'd seen in the movies. He also didn't move away.

"You're hurt, Ro."

"It's just a scratch."

"You've been through something traumatic, and you're not thinking clearly."

"Now you're going to tell me what I'm thinking?" Ro frowned. "Didn't I *just* say I was in complete control of my faculties?" Smartass that she was, she tilted her head to the side and pretended to think a moment. "Yes. Yes, I do believe those were my exact words."

"Aurora."

"Brody."

Several seconds passed as the standoff continued, each staring deep into the other's unwavering gazes without moving a muscle or saying a word. For a moment, Ro considered dropping the subject and giving the man his space. After all, he wasn't exactly jumping for joy over her blatant advance.

He's also not pushing you away or running in the opposite direction.

No, no, he wasn't. And since she'd already put herself out there...

May as well go for broke.

"I want you, Brody." Ro moved in even closer. "I have for as long as I can remember. Apparently Meg's known pretty much that whole time, even though I never said anything to her or anyone else. And there's a laundry list of reasons I kept my feelings a secret before now, but..." A soft, breathy chuckle released from her chest. "After what happened, everything on that list suddenly seems so insignificant."

She stopped there, because really...what more was there to say?

Taken off guard by the confession, Brody's eyes grew wide with surprise. "You...want me?"

"My whole life."

And now he knew everything. Well, *almost* everything.

"You never..." A frown lowered his dark brows. "Why didn't you say something sooner?"

One corner of her mouth quirked up. "Laundry list, remember? And I'm telling you now. Only question is, does anything I just said even matter?"

Brody flinched, his brows knitting together with confusion and a bunch of other stuff she wished she could decipher. His lips parted, his jaw falling with intended words that never came.

Aaand...there's your answer.

This man didn't want her. Of course, he didn't. And she was the idiot who thought opening herself up was a good idea.

At least now you know.

"It's okay, Brody. Really." She shook her head with a forced smile to show there were no hard feelings. "You don't have to say anything."

Hurt feelings, perhaps. Crushed dreams she'd have to find a way to forget. But she would…eventually. Because her inner voice was right.

She'd put herself out there, and though he hadn't reacted the way she'd hoped, she now knew and could finally move on. How she would do that, Ro had no earthly idea. But she'd figure it out.

And…eventually…she'd be okay.

Because that's what she did. If Aurora Tennison fell, she simply picked herself back up, brushed off the dirt, and forged on. She'd done that twice before, first with her mom's death and then her dad's.

She could do this, too.

Not because her heart didn't feel as if it were breaking into a million pieces, but because Megan had been right before. Just because her dad couldn't get past losing the woman he'd loved didn't mean Ro had to let her broken heart rule the rest of her days.

I won't end up like him.

She wouldn't. No matter what this or any other man felt —or didn't feel—for her. Because she was Aurora Freaking Tennison. And she was a survivor.

Dropping her hands from his chest, Ro backed away. She started to turn, to go where she wasn't sure. But a gentle hand to her good wrist stopped her.

"You're wrong."

The guttural declaration had her swinging her head back around. Had he seriously just told her she was wrong? No, no, she wasn't wrong. Ro thought she was spot freaking on, actually.

She'd just laid her heart on the line for him, and he hadn't said a word in return. Seemed pretty cut and dry to her.

"It's fine, Brody. Really. Let's just forget this ever happened and move on."

"What if that's not what I want?"

Her chest tightened, and it took everything Ro had to keep her chin from trembling. "You don't..." She cleared the crackling from her throat. "You don't want to move on?"

A single, slow, purposeful shake of his head. "I don't want to forget."

The tightening in her chest shifted and morphed, swirling into a cyclone of fear and longing. A burgeoning storm of emotions she was finding more and more difficult to keep hidden.

"Brody?"

With the gentlest of tugs, he pulled her back to him. Moving willingly, Ro didn't even consider putting up a resistance.

Her steps came to a halt when the tips of her painted toes touched the tips of his shiny dress shoes. A hand rose to her face, first one and then another. Ro's pulse spiked, every ounce of air in her lungs freezing instantly from his electrifying touch.

Despite Ro being five-eight, Brody's six-four frame towered over her, that firm, intense stare of his becoming fixed on hers. Inhaling deeply through his nose, his slowly exhaled breath struck her forehead like a warm, summer breeze.

"I have to be honest, Princess." His low rumble made her lower belly tingle and sent shivers down her spine. "Before last week, I never thought of you…of us…like this. But…"

Oh, she really, *really* liked that "but".

"Yes?" Ro stared up at him, praying this was headed where she thought it was.

God, it was hard to breathe. Impossible, even. And if he didn't spit out whatever it was he was trying to say in the next two seconds, she very well may pass out from lack of oxygen.

Wouldn't be the first time you passed out in his arms.

"Now I can't seem to think of anything else."

The breath she'd been holding escaped in a rush. Afraid this was nothing more than a dream, Ro almost didn't bother asking her next question. But if this was real, if the man she'd been pining for her entire adult life—and longer—really *was* saying what she thought he was saying…

I have to know.

"What, um…" She gave a nervous lick of her lips. "What changed?"

Brody's hard expression softened, a slightly crooked smile dancing on his bearded lips that made her crave. "You kissed me."

Her heart thundered in her chest as she shot back a half-teasing, "If you say so."

"You don't believe me?"

Ro inched impossibly closer, her breasts pressing up against his blood-stained shirt. Dark, crimson stains he'd gotten while scooping her into his arms and racing them both to safety.

But she didn't see the blood, then. She didn't see anything but…

Him.

The man who'd risked his own life tonight in an effort to save hers. A man who was holding her close and whose eyes had just glinted with an unmistakable need.

He feels it, too.

"I believe you," she whispered honestly. "I just hate that I can't remember it."

His thick, masculine throat worked with an audible swallow, but those fiery eyes stayed with hers. "We could fix that, you know." Another swallow. "Can't make you remember that night, but we could—"

"Try it again?" Ro finished for him, praying they were on the same page. "I mean, it's only fair, really."

A single dark brow lifted high. "Fair?"

"Sure. Think about it. You know what it's like to kiss me." Her gaze dropped to his tempting mouth. "To taste me. But I…I have no idea what it feels like to kiss you."

"Hmm. I see your point." He filled his lungs before releasing what appeared to be a very serious sigh. "Well, I guess there's really only one thing left for us to do."

Ohmygod. Was this really happening? Was the one man who'd managed to make her dream of a future really going to—

Brody pressed his lips to hers.

Soft and warm, his feathery whiskers created the most tantalizing friction that sent her pulse racing. Ro opened for him, the tentative meeting of their tongues lasting only a second before…

Passion exploded as he began to devour her in the way she'd always imagined. Only this wasn't like in her dreams. This was better.

So much better.

Brody tasted and teased as she nibbled and licked. Careful of her bandaged arm and the bump she'd gotten earlier when she'd fallen, he guided her head in a slight tilt for a better angle, allowing them both to dive in for more.

A primal growl reverberated from somewhere deep inside him as he devoured her in a way she'd never experienced before. Almost as if she were his favorite meal, and he was a starving man.

Ro released a small whimper of pleasure as she fisted the front of his soiled shirt. And as they continued to feast on one another with reckless abandon, she reveled in the fact that she was finally, *finally* tasting what her heart had longed for all these years.

But then...

She felt him start to pull away slowly, and though the last thing she wanted was for the most incredible kiss of her existence to end, Ro let him break the breath stealing connection without a fight.

Brody's heaving breaths matched her own, and while he'd ended the kiss, those strong, callused hands kept their gentle hold on the sides of her face. Though his dark beard made it difficult, she could almost make out the flush of arousal filling the skin underneath.

She'd most definitely felt the other, more *obvious* sign that he was as turned on as her. Kind of hard to miss something so big and...*hard*...as the impressive bulge that had been pressing against her lower belly from the start of the kiss to the end.

Even now, she was so tempted to let her gaze drop to the source of her not-so-hidden desires. But the blazing heat staring back at her made it impossible to look away.

"Think you'll remember that?" A low, rough rumble.

"For as long as I live."

At first, she worried her whispered confession was too

much. Perhaps a tad too desperate. But then something magical happened...

Brody smiled.

This wasn't some twitch of his lips or a sort-of-smirk. It was a full-blown, eye-reaching, face-lighting, ear-to-ear smile.

And it was all for her.

So beautiful.

"Me, too, Princess." His thumb brushed against her cheek. "Me, too."

Ro opened her mouth to ask the dreaded but necessary *what does this mean* when a knock sounded from the bedroom door.

"Hey, Brody?" Christian's voice traveled from the hallway on the other side. "Don't mean to rush you, but Hansen just called. We're good to go whenever you are."

Crap. She'd been so caught up in the unexpected—and amazing—moment, she'd completely forgotten the guys were still here.

"Be out in a second," Brody hollered back.

Not bothering to hide her disappointment, Ro stared up at him with a frown. "You're leaving?" *Now?*

"Just for a little bit." Another feather-light touch from his thumb. "Don't worry. My security system's as tight as they come, and Rocky's going to stay here so you won't be alone."

She hadn't been worried about that because she hadn't been *thinking* about that. But now that he mentioned it...

"Where are you going?"

"The guys and I just need to take care of something. I won't be gone long, though. Promise."

The guys and him...

Remembering what he'd said earlier, Ro shot Brody a

pointed look. In her heart, she already knew the answer to her next question—or at least, hoped she did. But that didn't keep her from asking it.

"You're not really going to...kill Clayton. Are you?"

"Depends."

It depends?

Ro knew the man who'd just kissed her senseless was a killer. But Brody had only ever taken the lives of men who deserved it. Terrorists who killed, raped, and tortured at whim without so much as an ounce of remorse.

She'd never asked him about it, of course. And though she never knew specifics about any of his missions—either with the SEALs or with Delta—she knew enough. About the work those guys did and the kind of man Brody King was.

And the one thing she knew—the one thing Ro was unequivocally certain of—was that the man standing before her now would do whatever he felt necessary to keep those he cared about safe.

"Depends on...what?" she asked, praying she'd see a teasing smirk or hear a bubble of laughter.

Instead Brody very matter-of-factly responded with, "His answers."

"Brody—"

"Relax, Princess. We're not going to Yorke's place to kill him." Brody slid his hands free, but not before dropping a playful tap to the tip of her nose and added, "Unless he gives us a reason.

"Can you please be serious about this?"

"I am being serious." The look on his face supported the claim. "You heard Christian. He said Hansen called, and we're good to go. He was talking about Detective Hansen. We were waiting for him to let us know when the cops were finished questioning Yorke. Apparently they are. Now it's our turn."

"The cops are letting you interfere with an official investigation?"

"Not interfere," he corrected. "Assist. Look, Hansen and Christian go way back. That's why he was the first call Hunt made when that son of a bitch broke into Meg's place and tried to kill her." A haunted look fell over him, then, but he blinked it away and continued. "Delta Team has a...we'll call it an *off the books* agreement with the CPD. Specifically the Violent Crimes Unit, which Hansen leads. The cops had their turn. Now it's ours."

"But anything he tells you...won't it be inadmissible?"

From what she'd seen on the true crime shows she liked to watch, it sure seemed as if a confession made under duress wouldn't be allowed in a court of law. And Ro didn't even pretend to think Clayton wouldn't be under duress once Brody and the guys got a hold of him.

"Sure. But there are ways around that."

Ro drew in a deep, cleansing breath. Releasing it slowly, she reminded herself that Brody and the others were good, decent men. Men who'd lay their own lives down for strangers if they felt there was someone in need of saving.

But she didn't want Brody risking himself for her. She didn't want any of them getting hurt. Especially not because—

"Hey." He brought a hand back to her face. A gentle touch that feathered across her skin like a dream. "We're just going there to talk."

"But you said—"

"I know what I said. And I meant every word." Brody held his gaze to hers. "Yorke turns out to be the one who tried to kill you, he's finished."

"He didn't do this."

"We'll see."

"You can't kill someone for me, Brody. Even if it *was* him, you can't just murder someone in cold blood. I don't want that. Not ever. And even if I did, that's not *you*. You're not..." She paused, giving a quick lick of her suddenly dry lips. "You're not capable of something like that."

"Ah, Princess." Those dark eyes left hers but only so they could soak her in. "If you truly believe that, then you don't know me as well as you think you do."

Ro was struck speechless by that remark, unsure of what to even think, let alone say. So she said nothing.

"Do you have any idea how scared I was tonight?" Brody asked after the longest ten seconds of silence ever.

She gave a silent shake of her head.

"You were walking toward me with that breathtaking smile, and I thought, 'My God. She's the most beautiful thing I've ever seen.' And then..." His voice cracked, but he cleared it and moved on. "A second later, you were lying on the floor, unconscious and bleeding because some asshole shot you."

"I'm sorry I scared you. And I know you're pissed, but—"

"Pissed?" A humorless laugh. "No, pissed was me seeing Yorke put his hands on you in that bar. Carrying your limp, bleeding body out of a building where someone just tried to kill you? *That* makes me want vengeance, Princess." He leaned in close. "Fucking. Lethal. Vengeance."

"Brody?"

The deadly look in his eyes softened as they took her in once more. "It really is true what they say, you know? Sometimes we don't see what's right in front of us"—Brody's gaze fell on her bandaged arm—"until it's already gone. But I see you, Ro. I finally see you, and I'll be damned if I lose you now."

Ro was dumbstruck by the conflicting thoughts and emotions whirling around inside her head. On the one hand, the thought that he could even joke about murdering someone on her behalf was mortifying.

On the other, she felt an overwhelming sense of elation that he cared about her so deeply he would kill to keep her safe. But Ro was also terrified he'd have no choice but to resort to violence in order to end the nightmare she'd been inexplicably thrown into.

But on the other, *other* hand, she was still reeling from the fact that the one and only man she'd ever loved had just wildly and thoroughly kissed her. And, by his own admission, he thought she was the most beautiful thing he'd ever seen.

So many emotions, so little time...

Brody leaned in one final time for another soft, sweet kiss. "Try to get some rest." Another peck. "You can take my bed. I'll be back before you know it."

"But—"

"Rocky will be here if you need anything." He turned to leave. "Clean towels are in the linen cabinet by the shower, and there should be an extra toothbrush in one of the drawers. You need anything else, let Rocky know, and he'll either order it, or we can pick it up on our way back."

He talked about stopping by the store after paying a visit to the man he suspected had tried to kill her as if this were just another Saturday night. Of course, given what he did for a living....

"Be careful!" she hollered out after him. "And...maybe at least *try* not to kill anyone while you're gone."

He's not really going to hurt Clayton. He wouldn't...

Brody opened the door but stopped to look at her from over his shoulder. With a smirk lifting one corner of his mouth, he avoided her request altogether and said, "Sleep tight, Princess."

A quick wink that sent her heart flipping, and then...

He was gone.

12

"So...you and Ro, huh?"

Brody's head swung to the man sitting in the passenger seat as he maneuvered the team's SUV through Chicago's late-night, weekend traffic. "Me and Ro, what?"

Christian's brown eyes met his in a stare that challenged the bullshit Brody had just tossed his way. "You think your sister's the only one who's seen it?"

His heart gave a hard kick against his ribs. "Seen what?"

"Come on, King," Jagger spoke up from the back seat. "You know Hunt's like a dog with a fucking bone. May as well just fess up now and be done with it."

"Fess up to *what?*" He flipped on his turn signal and waited for a car to pass before slipping into the left lane. "What the hell is it you assholes think I've done?"

Liam snorted. "Not it, my friend. More like *who.*"

"I don't know what you guys *think* you know, but you're way the fuck off base with this one."

"Seriously?" Christian's gaze burned into Brody's peripheral. "Dude, you've been glued to the woman's side for the past week. And the way you were hovering over her while I was putting the clear adhesive on her bandage..."

"Well, let's see. In the past week, *the woman's* been drugged, had shit go missing from her house—personal shit no random burglar would've taken—and tonight she was fucking shot." *I could have lost her.* "She's Meg's best friend, for Christ's sake. Hell yes, I'm going to hover."

And he'd damn well *keep* sticking to her sexy ass like glue until the son of a bitch who'd put her in his sights was caught or killed. Preferably the latter.

Brody's fists tightened around the wheel. Despite washing his hands three times, traces of blood were still visible around his cuticles and beneath his nails.

His nails. Shirt. Jacket. Pants.

Ro's blood was all over him, the macabre stains adding fuel to the already raging inferno flaming inside him.

"You sure that's all Ro is?" Liam chimed his nosey ass back in. "Your sister's best friend?"

Meeting the technical analyst's knowing gaze in the rearview, Brody clenched his back teeth together as he added a truthful, "I haven't slept with Ro. And to answer your questions, she's my friend, too. Clear enough?"

"Friend. Sure." Liam settled back against the black leather bench seat. Sitting behind Christian, the other man added a muttered, "If you say so."

"You got something on your mind, Cutler, spit it the hell out." Because he wasn't in the mood for juvenile games.

Not tonight.

Not after I almost lost the one woman I never knew I needed.

"Nope. I got nothin'." A beat passed and then, "Just that Ro's a smart, self-sufficient, attractive, single woman."

She was all those things and more.

"Your point?"

"No point. More of an observation, really. I mean, we've all seen the way she stares at you when she thinks no one is looking."

"Bullshit." The denial was out of Brody's mouth before he could stop it. Almost immediately, Ro's earlier words began rolling through his brain.

I want you, Brody. I have for as long as I can remember.

"Nah, he's right." Jagger rejoined the uncomfortable conversation. "I've seen it with my own two eyes. And you know I have perfect vision, right?

Before he could respond to the former Air Force Combat Controller, Christian spoke up from the passenger's seat, once more.

"I have to admit, I never really noticed it until Meg pointed it out. But once she did, and I started paying closer attention—"

"Meg?" Brody frowned.

As soon as he uttered his sister's name, he remembered Ro had said something about how Meg had revealed to her she'd known about the secret crush Ro had been harboring for him. Apparently his sister felt the need to share her suspicions with *his* best friend.

Of course, she did.

"Oh, yeah." Christian chuckled beside him. "She mentioned it to me not long after she and I got together. According to Meg, she picked up on Ro's feelings for you years ago but never said anything because she was trying to give Ro time to bring it up herself."

Liam's golden-brown eyes found his in the mirror's reflective surface. "Guess the only question left is...what are you planning on doing about it?"

Christ, it was like being stuck in a vehicle with bunch of gossiping teenage girls.

"There's nothing *to* do, okay?" He continued with the denial as he maneuvered through the city streets.

Nothing I'm going to tell you assholes about, anyway.

"Really?" Jagger shifted in the seat behind Brody, his voice lifting into an almost hopeful tone. "I mean, that's cool. But hey, if you're not gonna go there, then you wouldn't mind if I sampled some of the woman's sweet—"

"Finish that sentence." Brody's sharp warning cut the man off. With his eyes locked onto Jagger's reflection, he added a low, "I dare you."

Not one to scare easily, the other brown-eyed man lifted his mouth into a sideways smirk as he uttered a knowing, "That's what I thought."

Cursing beneath his breath, Brody pulled the SUV into the gated parking garage attached to Yorke's upscale high rise apartment building. "We're here, so can we please just focus on what we came to do and drop the junior high lunchroom gossip bullshit?"

A casual shrug from Liam. "If that's what you want."

"It's what I want," Brody growled between his clenched teeth.

"Consider it dropped," Liam agreed…just before he mumbled a low, "For. Now."

Fuck me.

Brody pulled up to the building's security guard post stationed at the parking garage entrance. Thanks to a preemptive call by one Detective Hansen, once Brody showed his I.D.—driver's license and official R.I.S.C. badge—the gate was lifted, and they were allowed to enter.

Entering through the main lobby, he wasn't surprised by the elaborate greeting the high-end space provided.

Wall-to-ceiling windows lined the two sides of the building facing the adjoining streets outside. Marble tile flooring lay beneath three massive chandeliers, their linear tubes and illuminated crystals lighting up the open space with the kind of elegance rich bastards like Yorke probably drooled over.

Brody didn't care about marble or crystals. He only cared about finding the person who pulled that fucking trigger. And the number one suspect on his list—the only name he had to go on—lived in the building's two-story, forty-five-grand-a-month penthouse suite.

Something Liam had discovered during his tertiary look into the smug S.O.B.

"Oh!" the metrosexual-looking man behind the enormous reception desk at the lobby's front chirped. "Can I... help you gentlemen?"

Wearing a skinny gray suit that looked two sizes too small, an electric blue shirt that made Brody blink, and blond hair that looked like it had enough gel in it for ten men, he gave Brody and the others a blatantly disapproving once-over.

"We need to speak with Clayton Yorke."

Skinny's narrow gray eyes lifted to Brody's. "I'm sorry. Mr. Yorke is not accepting visitors, at this time. Perhaps you'd like to schedule an appointment."

A suggestion, rather than a question.

This guy can take his suggestion and shove it up his skinny-suit-wearing ass.

"Call him," Brody ordered the man as if he had every right to. "Tell him Brody King is here to see him."

"Sir, I just told you—"

"I heard what you said, but here's the thing." He rested his elbows on the desk and leaned in. "I'm sure you've heard about the shooting that took place at Yorke's fancy party tonight, yes?"

The skinny man nodded.

"Excellent. Now my friends and I"—he motioned to the other men standing nearby—"work for R.I.S.C. Delta Team, a private security company here in town. Perhaps you've heard of us?" Brody held up his R.I.S.C. badge for good measure.

A sliver of unease filtered in the younger man's eyes as he gave a second, jerkier nod.

Ah, so he does know who we are.

"My team was working security for Mr. Yorke's party, and we're here following up with the ongoing investigation. Feel free to call Detective Hansen with the CPD's Violent Crimes Unit if you'd like."

Christian pulled a card from his wallet and slid it across the desk's smooth surface. "There's his direct line."

Brody's lips threatened to twitch. Damn, he loved that guy.

"Th-that won't be necessary," the noticeably less cocky *gentleman* stated. "If you'll just give me a moment..."

The team waited while the phone call was made. Less than five minutes later, they'd been given a personal escort—courtesy of the building's own security—and were in the elevator and on their way to see Yorke.

"You couldn't take two seconds to change?" Jagger eyed the blood stains on the front of Brody's suit.

"Not all of us can be fashionistas like you, Brooks."

The comment was meant to be an annoyed jab, but the stylish man simply stared back at Brody with a knowing smirk. "Don't hate me because I'm beautiful, brother."

Several deep snorts filled the confined space. And though he didn't make a peep, the middle-aged man wearing the stereotypical black suit and tie—complete with a coiled earpiece—did allow the corners of his mouth to lift with a slight curve.

But Brody wasn't smiling. He was too busy planning.

A loud ding announced their arrival on the thirty-second floor. The top floor, reserved for the most expensive penthouse suite in the city.

"I wonder if the guy realizes he could own an eight-million-dollar home with acreage for what he pays for this place," Liam commented to no one in particular.

An incredulous expression twisted Cade's clean-cut face as they followed the guard through the opened doors and down a long, equally elaborate hallway. "What the hell would a guy like Yorke do with acreage? Doesn't exactly strike me as a fishin' or huntin' type."

"Right?" Christian snickered. "Wait, I got it. Clayton Yorke, a pair of denim overalls, on a riding lawnmower."

"Prick's probably never even seen one," Brody grumbled.

"Here we are." Their polite escort pressed the doorbell and waited.

Expecting a butler or servant to appear, Brody was surprised when Clayton Yorke himself answered the door.

"Thank you, Harold." He handed the security guard a hundred dollar bill.

"Thank *you*, Mr. Yorke." To Brody and the others, the man whose name was apparently Harry gave a curt nod. "Gentlemen."

"Thanks, Harry!" Jagger waved at the man's back as he disappeared into the awaiting elevator. "It's been a blast!"

"Seriously?" Cade shot their teammate a look.

"What?"

"Do you have to be a twenty-four-seven smart ass?"

Jagger stared back at Cade with a flattened expression. "Have to? No. *Want* to…"

"How is Aurora?" Yorke looked and sounded genuinely worried as he stepped to the side and held the door for the team.

This guy wouldn't know genuine if it reached up and punched him in those perfect teeth.

"She has a bullet hole in her arm." Brody marched past the son of a bitch. "How the fuck do you *think* she's doing?"

Shutting the door behind the team, Yorke followed them further into his apartment. "I-I asked Detective Hansen about her status, but no one would tell me anything."

Christian kept his expression unmoving when he told the other man, "Not exactly common practice for the cops to share the personal information of a victim with the man they suspect of being the one to shoot her."

Brody stepped directly in front of the man. Doing his best to honor Ro's request and not kill the son of a bitch, he made something very, very clear. "Aurora's *status* is none of your goddamn business. In fact..." He got right in the billionaire's face. "Nothing about Ro is your business. Not now. Not fucking ever. Understood?"

A visibly trembling Yorke swallowed twice before saying, "I-I had nothing to do with what happened tonight. You have to believe me."

"Wrong." Brody's fists curled at his sides. "The only thing we *have* to do is find the asshole who tried to kill Ro. And I can't help but wonder if I'm looking right at him."

"What?" Yorke's eyes widened with a look of bewilderment. "N-no! I just told you, I had—"

"Nothing to do with the shooting," Jagger cut the other man off. "Yeah, we got that part. Problem is, most killers don't typically confess to their crimes. Not right away, at least. So, you'll forgive us if we don't simply take your word."

"I'm telling you the *truth!*" The idiot glanced at the entire team as if he were looking for one of them to come to his defense. "Why would I try to kill the person who helped make tonight such a success? Or...at least, it *was* a success. Until..."

"Until some bastard with a gun shot her two minutes after you disappeared behind the stage. Which, by the way, is where the shot originated from. I'm assuming Hansen shared that little tidbit with you?"

"Yes." Clayton gave a solemn nod. "He told me."

"And?"

"And I'm home, aren't I?"

"Your point?"

"You think they would've let me go if the detective thought he had a reason to charge me with Aurora's attempted murder?"

"Guy with your kind of money?" Liam snorted. "Yes. We absolutely believe they would have let you go."

"Just because they don't have the evidence needed to back up a charge doesn't mean you're innocent," Brody added.

"I *am* innocent."

"We'll see."

"What's your problem, King?"

"You. You're my problem. And people *like* you are my problem. You walk around this city with your nose stuck so high in the air, you can't see the rest of us. But we see you, dickhead. Crystal fucking clear."

"Now you're the one who's wrong." That arrogance was back. "You see what I *let* you see."

"Explain," Brody barked the order.

"It's nothing. Just...forget it."

"Not a chance. You got something you think will help in your defense, we're all ears. How about this? Let's start with what the hell you were doing backstage when that shot rang out."

"Like I told the detectives, I was conducting business."

"What kind of business?"

Something flashed behind those entitled eyes, but then, "That's none of your concern."

"Not my..." Brody let loose with a humorless laugh. "See, now...that's where you're wrong. Someone I care very much about was nearly killed right in front of me tonight. So yeah, Clayton. It *is* my concern. In fact, everything about tonight concerns me. So I'll ask you again. What the fuck were you doing behind that stage?"

"I was...speaking with someone."

"Who?"

"None of your business."

He looked to Christian and the others. "Did I not just go over this with him? No? Okay." With an exaggerated sigh, Brody pulled his phone from his pants' pocket.

"W-who are you calling?"

"Detective Hansen."

"You're calling the cops?" Yorke's brows shot up. "Why?"

"You don't want to tell me the person's name you were speaking with at the time of the shooting, I'm sure Hansen will be more than happy to oblige."

Truth be told, Brody was livid Christian's detective friend hadn't passed that information along before now. Three breaths later, however, he understood why that was.

"You can ask him, but the detective won't be able to tell you."

"Why not?"

"Because he doesn't know."

"You keeping secrets from the police, Clay?" Jagger made

a clicking sound with his tongue. "Not smart, my man. Not smart at all."

"Perhaps that's true, but I can assure you, the private conversation I had was just that. Private. It had nothing to do with the party, and it most definitely was not related to what happened to Aurora. Which is why I didn't mention it to the detectives."

"I don't know, Brody." Christian shot him a serious look. "Pretty sure omitting pertinent information from an official witness statement would be considered interfering with a police investigation. Of course, that would be up to the police and prosecutor to decide. Don't you agree?"

"As a matter of fact, I do." Brody tapped the phone's screen—a locked screen he'd purposely kept out of Yorke's line of sight—and put the device to his ear.

He knew the second he saw the first bead of sweat form on the entitled prick's exfoliated forehead his bluff was going to work.

"I'm telling you, there's no need to involve the police with this."

Brody kept his unwavering stare locked on Yorke's. "A woman is almost murdered at a party you hosted minutes after being seen with you on stage, and you just happened to sneak off to have a supposed private conversation with someone you refuse to name. You don't think that's something the cops would be interested in knowing?"

Christian went on to add, "A conversation that, by your own admission, you purposely left out in your statement to the police."

"Please. I'm telling you the truth."

"What did you tell the cops?" Liam spoke up from Brody's right.

"What do you mean?"

"I'm assuming they asked where you were at the time of the shooting. What lie did you tell them so they wouldn't know about this alleged mystery person you were meeting with?"

Those eyes bounced back and forth between Liam and Brody. "I-I told them I was taking care of an issue with the caterers."

"So you *did* lie." Brody kept staring.

"Y-yes. But to the cops, not to you. And I know what you're thinking, but—"

"You don't have the slightest fucking clue what I'm thinking."

York paused a beat before speaking again. And the words he chose were the exact wrong ones to say.

"I think I'd like you to leave." An audible swallow. "Now."

"Not until I have that name."

"You're not the police, and you have no authority over me." The rich bastard jutted his chin as if he'd finally grown a spine. "So either you leave, or I'll—"

"What?" Brody challenged. "Call the cops? Be my guest." He held out his phone for the other man to use. "Just make sure you ask for Detective Hansen, 'cause he's gonna want to be here when I tell him why I refused to leave."

"Go to hell."

Brody didn't think about what he did next. He just fucking did it.

Pulling his concealed pistol from the shoulder holster beneath his jacket, he brought the weapon up with one hand as he fisted the shithead's shirt with the other. Almost simultaneously, he shoved the bastard against the nearest wall.

"W-what are you...ohmygod!"

Brody kept the barrel of his Glock19 pointed smack dab in the middle of the man's forehead. Lowering his voice to a deadly calm, his cold gaze met Yorke's terrified stare with a promise he meant to keep.

"I'm going to ask you one more time, and then things are going to get very bad for you. Now I want that name."

"Please. Y-you don't understand."

"Name."

"Y-you have no idea what you're asking me to—"

"Tell me the goddamn name!" Brody wasn't just pointing his gun at Yorke's forehead, then. He was pushing the end of the barrel against the fucker's skull. "I will not ask again."

Yorke's normally polished appearance crumbled. His entire body quivered with fear beneath Brody's bruising hold. Tears began pouring from the corners of his eyes, and unless his sense of smell was deceiving him, Brody was fairly certain the guy had just pissed his pants.

"T-Tommy." Yorke finally gave it up. "T-Tommy Carrigan."

"Carrigan?" Cade joined in the fun. "As in—"

"The Chicago C-Carrigans." A jerky nod of Yorke's head. "Y-yes."

The Carrigan name was well known around the city and had been for generations.

"Liam?"

"On it." Liam used the tablet he'd brought with him to do a quick search. Seconds later, he flipped it around so Yorke could see the screen. "This him?"

Another uneven nod.

Brody spared a quick glance at the image on the small screen before returning his focus back to Yorke. "We ask this guy if he was with you at the time of the shooting, he's gonna say yes?"

"I-If I tell him it's okay, h-he will."

"If you tell him..." Brody huffed out a breath. "You control what this guy does or doesn't say?"

"With this...yes."

"You don't get to script your own alibi, Clay." Jagger sighed. "That's not exactly how this thing works."

"I'm not scripting, I-I'm...p-protecting."

"This ought to be good," Jagger rolled his eyes as if he were bored.

But Brody was already asking, "Who are you protecting? Carrigan?"

"And myself."

"From the cops?"

A sadness filled the other man's eyes. "From everyone."

"Enough of this bullshit." Brody pushed the gun a smidge harder against the guy's forehead.

"It's not bullshit. I swear! I-I'll call Tommy right now. H-he'll tell you everything!"

"As long as you say it's okay."

"Jesus Christ, man. I'm not a goddamn killer, okay? I didn't even realize what had happened until Ro was already down, and whoever did it was gone!"

"You expect us to believe you were so enthralled in your secret backstage meeting with Tommy Carrigan that you didn't notice an active shooter situation until it was over? What could the two of you have *possibly* been discussing that was so important it took you away from your own party?"

"P-please."

"What were you talking about?"

"We weren't talking!"

"Then what the fuck *were* you doing?"

"Having sex!" Yorke's shouted confession echoed off the

walls around them. "Tommy and I were..." A defeated sigh. "We met in the supply closet behind the stage to have sex."

The entire penthouse grew silent. Brody blinked but didn't speak. And for the next several seconds, no one uttered a single sound.

Nearly laughing at the idiot's lie, he kept the weapon steady. "You expect us to believe you're gay?" he challenged. "You do realize I have a gun pointed at your head."

"I'm aware, y-yes." The man was literally shivering in his socked feet. "But I swear, what I said was the truth."

"Bullshit." This came from Cade. "I've seen the women you parade around town."

"Different one every week," Liam quipped.

Brody kept his eyes on Yorke, searching for the first sign of deception as he added, "And I saw the way you were with Ro that night at the bar."

"Jesus, man. That night was all a show!" Yorke's shoulders fell with a pathetic sigh. "Every goddamn night is a show."

"Explain."

"I'm the only child—the only *name-bearing* child—of the great and powerful Yorkes. You think my family...you think my *father* would accept a homosexual as a son? Especially since I'm his only chance of carrying on the family name?"

"Dude, it's not Nineteen Fifty-Two," Jagger pointed out. "Nobody cares if you're gay."

"Yeah, well, you've never met my father. "A slight tremble of the man's chin. "He cares. He cares a great deal."

"So what happens if he finds out you're gay?" Cade asked.

"What do you think? I'll be cut out, that's what!"

"Your parents would seriously take you out of the will just because you like dudes?" Christian arched a brow.

"In a heartbeat." The beat-down man didn't hesitate in his response. "*That's* why I make sure to be seen with a different woman every week. And that's why I sometimes act the way I sometimes did with Aurora. I just needed her to think...I needed whoever was *watching* us to think that I was what the world expects me to be."

"Billiondaire playboy?" Jagger guessed.

Yorke slid a weary look in the other man's direction. "Chicago's most eligible bachelor."

The man practically spat the title out as if it were a curse.

If he's telling the truth, it probably is.

But that was a big fucking *if*. And since Yorke had already confessed to lying about who he was with—and what he was supposedly doing—at the time of the shooting, Brody wasn't about to take him at his word.

As if reading his mind, Yorke's next comment was, "You don't have to take my word for it. I have...proof."

"Really?" Jagger grinned, his voice rising higher than normal with the man's exaggerated excitement. "Well, *this* should be interesting."

"Where's this so-called proof?" Brody demanded.

"Remove the gun from my head, I'll show you."

"Fuck you." He kept that gun right where it was. "Tell us what it is and where to find it, and we'll do the rest."

Yorke's lips pursed, but after a beat of hesitation he realized he was in no position to negotiate. "There's a false bottom in the second drawer of my nightstand. Inside it is a safe."

"What's in the safe?"

"Several things, actually." The other man thought better of his smartassed answer almost immediately. "There's a phone."

"Burner?"

Yorke nodded. "Tommy got them for us to use a couple years ago, right after we started seeing each other."

"What's on it?"

"Texts. Pictures. A few voicemails I've saved." He drew in a stuttered breath. "Everything you'll need to know I'm telling you the truth."

"I'll go," Christian offered.

Falling in line behind him was Cade. "I'll go with you."

Both men listened closely as Yorke spouted off the passcode to open the safe.

"Can you please put the gun down now?" Yorke begged. "Come on, man. Look at me. Even if I wanted to, it's not like I'd have a chance against the five of you."

"I'll put the gun down once they're back with the phone and can confirm your claims."

A few minutes later, Christian and Cade returned.

"Found it." Christian tossed the phone to Liam, who caught it with ease. "Right where he said it would be."

Powering it up, Liam entered the password as Yorke spouted it off. Once the device was unlocked, Brody and the others watched and waited.

His gun never left Yorke's head the entire time.

"Holy shit." Liam's gaze found Brody's. "He wasn't lying." Several swipes and taps later, he walked over and held the phone up for Brody to see for himself. "There are texts on here going back two years. Pictures, too."

He studied the images and words, his gut tightening when he realized his teammate was right. Yorke was clearly in an intimate relationship with the man Liam confirmed as Tommy Carrigan. And, from what he'd just seen, it had been going on for quite some time.

"I'm sure, if you haven't already, you'll be looking over

the event center's security footage," Yorke spoke directly to Liam. "If you watch closely, you should be able to see Tommy slip backstage at the same time I walked on stage. That was the plan, you see. When he saw me go up for my speech, that was his cue to go into the storage room and wait."

"You penciled in storage room sex during your own party?" Jagger shot the man a look.

"Judge if you want." Yorke's backbone returned. "It's not like Tommy and I have a lot of opportunities to meet up, so we have to take advantage when we can."

The man had a point. But while the evidence of his and Carrigan's secret affair appeared to be solid, Brody wasn't quite ready to let him off the hook. And until Liam had a chance to look over that footage...

"We're taking the phone," he informed the man still shoved against the wall. "We'll check out the footage, and we will be having a conversation with your boyfriend."

A flash of fear raced across Yorke's face. "Please. You can't expose Tommy. His family's just like mine. They'll never understa—"

"I don't give two shits who you sleep with," Brody growled. "All I care about is making sure Ro is safe."

Those words resonated through him, and suddenly Brody realized just how true they really were. He cared about others, of course. Megan. Christian and the guys. But Ro was different. She was...more.

He hadn't planned it. *Sure* as hell hadn't seen it coming. But planned or not...unwitting or not...something inside him changed the second Ro pressed those luscious lips to his.

Like a blind man miraculously given the ability to see, he'd suddenly realized the piece of himself he never knew was missing had been standing right in front of him all along. No longer was Aurora Tennison simply a friend. She was...more.

She's everything.

And as he stood there with his weapon shoved against another man's head, Brody knew. He'd kill without blinking an eye if that's what it took to protect her.

"I'm not a threat to Aurora," Yorke vowed. "And...no matter what you decide to do with the information I've given you tonight...I really do hope you find the person who hurt her."

"Oh, I'll find him," Brody gave his own solemn vow. "If it's the last thing I do."

He finally lowered that gun and slid it back into his holster, releasing Yorke with a shove. More than ready to get back to the woman he'd left standing by his bed, he left Yorke with one final warning.

"If you're telling us the truth, your secret will remain just that. You have my word."

"Th-thank you."

"*But*...I find out you're lying to me about this, and it really was *you* who hurt my Ro...I will come back here." He leaned in closer. "And I will kill you."

"Thanks for the hospitality, Clay." Jagger sent Yorke a wave as he, Cade, and Liam turned to leave. "It's been fun. Hopefully we can do it again real soon."

Brody waited a breath before pulling back and turning away. And as he and Christian followed the others out, he wondered just how soon that would be.

13

Ro woke to the sound of rushing water. Feeling like she'd washed her eyeballs with sandpaper, she blinked away the remnants of her earlier tears and looked around. Confusion struck, but then...

Brody's. I'm at Brody's house.

She settled back onto the pillow beneath her. His pillow. In his bed.

Drawing in a deep breath, his masculine scent surrounded her, offering a sense of comfort and safety she'd only felt when he was near. The sound of running water came to a sudden halt, and it was only then that Ro realized where it had been coming from.

The shower.

She turned toward Brody's master bathroom. Her chest tightened when she found its door closed, a small sliver of light shining through from underneath.

He's back.

Her gaze lowered to the digital clock on his bedside table. Three hours had passed since he and the others had left in search of Clayton, but he was back. And in the shower.

Naked.

Careful of her sore and aching arm, Ro slowly pushed herself up in bed. Brushing several strands of wayward hair from her face, she leaned her back against Brody's smooth wooden headboard and waited.

As she did, she couldn't help but wonder what had transpired between him and her former client. Former since Clayton had already agreed to let her out of her previously agreed upon contract after tonight's party.

And since she'd been shot at said party...

I still don't think Clayton did it.

Ro wasn't sure why she felt so strongly about it, but that didn't diminish the gut feeling she'd had from the start of this whole thing. Maybe she was wrong, but something told her Clayton wasn't their man.

She'd shared that with Rocky earlier. The poor guy had been tasked with babysitting her, and while she felt bad about him missing out on going with the rest of his team, Ro would be lying if she said she didn't appreciate his presence.

Though their interactions after Brody left was minimal, knowing someone with Rocky's training and experience was there, watching over her... It was the only reason she'd been able to even consider falling asleep.

It still hadn't come easily, however. The long, hot shower and even longer crying jag had probably helped. Ro was just thankful Brody hadn't been around to see it.

The door to the bathroom opened, and a cloud of steam was set free. Brody's imposing figure filled the doorway, but he froze when he realized she was awake.

"Hey." Those dark eyes found hers in the shadowed room. "Sorry if I woke you. Figured I should probably clean up after..." He looked at her injured arm. "How do you feel? Are you hurting?"

"It's sore and throbs a little," she answered honestly. Although the view certainly helped to take her mind off the pain. "I took something for the pain a couple hours ago, so it's not bad."

"What about your head?" Brody stepped further into the room.

The closer he got the harder Ro found it to breathe.

Wearing a pair of gray sweatpants and no shirt, Brody looked like every woman's alpha male dream come to life. Tall. Dark. Naturally tanned. And a body so perfectly sculpted it could have been made from stone.

Her gaze fell to the dark tattoo made of four triangles on the inside of his right forearm.

The larger triangle was solid black, and there was a smaller one upside down below it. Drawn over the center of the larger one were two other triangles—both upside down, and both simple outlines.

Ro remembered when he'd come home after BUD/S with it, and she'd asked what it meant. He'd said it was something to do with the elements, and it symbolized that he, as a SEAL, would move heaven and earth to protect the innocent the best way he knew how.

That's my Brody. Always trying to save the world.

She'd always loved that tattoo...and the man it belonged to.

"Ro?"

Her eyes flew up to his, and she knew she'd been caught gawking. But after everything that had happened—including the kiss that had left her heart swollen and her body wanting more—Ro couldn't bring herself to care.

"Sorry, what?"

A knowing glance met hers, and if she wasn't mistaken, there'd been the slightest of twitches lifting one corner of his mouth. "I asked about your head."

It's all wrapped up in you. "It's fine. A little sore, but nothing I can't handle." Afraid to ask how things had gone with Clayton, Ro chickened out and instead asked, "Is Rocky still here?"

Brody shook his head as he walked slowly across the room toward his closet. "He left after I got back."

Just ask him.

"Did you...see Clayton?"

Ro held her breath and waited.

"We did." Brody pulled out a thick, folded blanket from the closet before shutting the door.

"And?"

"And..." He set the blanket down near the foot of the bed. "You were right. At least, it seems as if you were."

"So...you *didn't* kill Clayton?"

His broad, noticeably bare shoulders shook with a breathy chuckle. "No, Princess. Clayton Yorke is still very much alive, although I'm not sure how *well* he's doing, at the moment."

"What do you mean?"

Making his way around the foot of the bed, Brody came over to where she was. He sat down, his body filling the space between her and the mattress's edge.

"It seems you're not the only one who's been keeping secrets."

Heat crawled into her neck, knowing he was referring to what she'd revealed earlier. But knowing he was just as attracted to her as she was to him, Ro put it aside to focus on the here and now.

"Clayton?"

A gentle nod. "Not sure it'll ever go public, but it turns out that revolving bedroom door of his doesn't exist."

Yeah, he told her the man's secret because she'd fucking earned the right to know the truth. To know Yorke may just be innocent, as she'd been claiming.

"What do you mean?"

Ro sat quietly and listened as Brody shared the unbelievable truth-bomb Clayton had confessed to him and the others. It was almost impossible to reconcile a man who'd come on to her so frequently—often blatantly—with the one Brody had described him being tonight.

Scared. Weak.

Gay.

That was a bomb she most definitely had *not* seen coming. She had absolutely no problem—or judgement—with the lifestyle. It was just such a shockingly stark contrast to the playboy persona he'd led her and the rest of the world to believe.

All of a sudden, the gut feeling that had driven her away from him as a suspect made perfect sense.

"How long do you think it will take Liam to access the event center's security footage?" Ro asked in the quiet of the night.

"He texted just as I was coming out of the shower. Video footage supports Yorke's story."

"So Liam could see this Tommy guy go backstage like Clayton said?"

"Unfortunately, yeah."

"Why is that unfortunate? I thought proving Clayton's innocence would be a good thing."

"Being gay and meeting Carrigan backstage before the shot was fired doesn't prove he wasn't the one behind the gun,' Brody pointed out. "But it does raise a lot of questions that, unfortunately, we don't have the answers to. Namely if Yorke really isn't our guy, then—"

"We have no idea who is."

"Exactly."

A stretch of silence passed before a promising thought struck. "Hang on. If the footage caught Clayton's secret boyfriend sneaking behind the stage, then wouldn't it have also picked up the real shooter?"

"That's the hope." A slight tilt of his handsome head. "But right now, we have no idea when the shooter arrived, how long he was waiting back there before pulling the trigger..." His deep voice trailed off. "It'll take a day or two for Cutler to go over it all, but I promise you, once he's finished, he'll have combed through every inch of every angle from every camera mounted in that place. If the shooter's on there, he'll find him."

"And in the meantime, I get to sit here, knowing someone out there wants me dead."

Shivers that had nothing to do with the beautifully shirtless man sitting inches away raced through her.

Scooting even closer, Brody shifted his body to face her more fully. In a move she was starting to love, he reached up and cupped one side of her face.

"We're going to catch this guy," he promised, as if there were no other option.

Because there wasn't. Not if she wanted to live.

Leaning into his touch, Ro told him truthfully, "I believe you. I just wish I knew why this was happening."

"Me, too, Princess." A feathered brush of his thumb across her cheek.

"So what now?"

"What do you mean?"

"I mean...what am I supposed to do in the meantime?"

"You stay here." His throat worked. "With me."

The offer warmed her heart, and while part of her wanted nothing more than to stay this close to him forever...

"I can't just move in here, Brody."

"Why not?"

"Because I'll be in the way."

"You're never in my way, Princess."

Ro's insides tingled, her thoughts threatening to wander to things that were much more pleasant than gunshot wounds and unidentified killers. But she forced all that away and focused on the important conversation she and the sexy former SEAL were currently engaged in.

"I'm serious, Brody. You can't be out there, doing what you guys do, if you're stuck here babysitting me the whole time."

"This is what we do, Ro. Trust me, I've got this." He stared into her eyes so deeply it was as if he could see the very depths of her soul. "I've got you."

Her pulse quickened. "But you...only have one bed."

"True."

She slid a glance toward the blanket still folded at her feet. "You can't spend every night on your own couch."

"Didn't plan on it."

The rumbled words had her focus swinging back up to him. At first, she thought maybe...but then she shook her head with the embarrassing realization. "Right. Because I'll be the one on the couch." *Slick, Ro. Way to play it cool.* "That makes a lot more sense, anyway. I mean, you're a lot taller than me, and I'm perfectly fine taking the couch, so—"

"Are you?"

The question had her searching his dark gaze for clarification. "Am I...what?"

"Perfectly fine taking the couch."

Her breaths grew shallow, and Ro inwardly cursed her overzealous hormones. Because the way he'd asked that just then almost made it sound as though...

"I, uh..." She swallowed as her heart pounded in her chest. "I don't mind."

"Well I do." He leaned in closer, that hand of his sliding lower to the side of her neck. "You want the couch, it's yours." Brody brushed the tip of his nose against hers. "Or..."

She liked *or*. In fact, *or* was her newest, most favorite friend in the whole entire world. Because that tiny, two-letter word brought with it a promise. One that would give her the very thing she wanted most of all.

"Yes."

"You could sleep in here," he breathed the tantalizing offer. "With me."

"That wasn't me searching for clarification, Brody." Ro mimicked his position by raising a hand to his face and resting her palm against his rugged cheek. "I was saying yes."

A slow, panty-dropping smile lifted his lips in a way that made her heart stop, and her toes curl beneath the sheets. And then...

"You need to be sure, Aurora," he said her full name in a way that made everything else around them disappear. "Because once we start this..." A shake of his head. "I honestly don't know if I'll be able to stop."

Oh. My. God.

"I've waited for you my whole life. The last thing I'm ever going to want is for you to stop."

"Ah, Princess."

"Make love to me, Brody." Ro brushed her lips against his. "Please."

It was all she needed to say.

Leaning in, he captured her mouth with his. Soft. Slow. Lingering. Their lips moved together, an unhurried dance of longing and discovery.

Brody's hand caressed the side of her neck, his fingers raking gently into her hair. Like he had earlier, guiding her head into a slight tilt. Deepening the kiss, Ro felt the mattress lift with a rise to his feet.

Never taking his mouth from hers, the talented man removed the covers from her lower half and brought himself onto the bed next to her. Though he didn't address it verbally, Ro could tell every move of his was made with a conscious effort to avoid the bandaged area of her arm.

My protector.

Brody's lips moved from her mouth to her throat, his kisses leaving a blazing trail of fire in their wake. Ro arched her back, her breath coming in short, ragged gasps as his hands roamed over her.

Dressed in nothing but a shirt she'd found hanging in his closet—and the thong she'd worn beneath her ruined dress, since they'd come straight here from the hospital—she felt exposed and a tad vulnerable.

But this was Brody, and with him, Ro knew she was safe.

"Please, Brody." She arched her lower body toward the warm, callused hand she felt wandering down along her curves. "Make me forget," she begged. "Make me forget everything else but you."

A low, hungry growl rumbled from his chest to hers, and his gentle touch turning almost possessive as his hands explored her. Shivers ran the length of her spine. The sensation created this time by pleasure, rather than fear.

His hot, wet mouth returned to hers. Ro's fingers traced the hard lines of his back, her nails scraping lightly across his skin as she remained mindful of her wound. The intensity of their connection was so strong it threatened to overwhelm.

Brody's hand slipped beneath her shirt, and Ro shuddered. She moaned when he filled his palm with her breast, and when he began rolling her nipple between his forefinger and thumb, she thought she'd died and gone to Heaven.

"Mmmm..." Another soft, unintentional moan.

He continued teasing and playing, first with one breast and then the other. And when he was finished with that...

"Need to taste you."

The deep rasp reached her ears a heartbeat before Brody's weight lifted from hers. Ro opened her mouth, her intention to protest, but then she realized *his* intention and decided to help him along.

With oh-so-careful moves, the two worked together to remove the shirt she'd been wearing, leaving her in nothing but the tiny scrap of a thong.

Brody tossed the shirt to the side, his almost blackened gaze drinking her in as if she were his favorite beverage. "Fucking beautiful."

She barely had time to process the words before his mouth was on her. The wet heat of his mouth engulfed her as Brody gave exquisite attention to one of her distended nipples. Using his tongue to pleasure and tease, he took his time...and his fill.

"Ah!" Ro threw her head back with a cry. Her hands went to his hair, her fists clutching the short, thick locks as best they could.

Moans and whispers of his name filled the room as Brody continued the incredible torture. Just when Ro didn't think she could take anymore, he released her with a soft pop before giving the other breast the same, glorious attention.

Feasting on her mouth once more, Brody's tongue dominated hers as he guided her back down to the mattress. When the passionate kiss was no longer enough, he pulled away and looked down at her with a hungry, heated stare.

"More." He moved down the length of her body, his fingers dipping between the skin at her hip and the miniscule strap of elastic holding her black satin thong in place.

The caveman-type speech made her smile. She'd never seen this side of Brody before. Almost frantic with desire and need.

No, the Brody King she knew was always in control. *Always.* But the man who'd just ripped that thong right off her—literally—was all ragged breaths, rough movements, and deep, almost desperate growls.

A man filled with a sort of animalistic need.

That's exactly how Ro felt just then. Wild. Feral. Like an animal in heat.

And for the first time in her life, she was filled to the rim with such need she thought she might *die* from the magnificent pressure building up from deep within.

But Brody wouldn't let her die. Figuratively or otherwise. Not if he had the power to stop it. And right now, in this moment, he was the most powerful man in Ro's world.

"Beautiful," he whispered into the night.

Her bare chest rose and fell with heavy, shallow breaths as she watched and waited with an anticipation like none before it. Reaching out, the amazingly wonderful man slid his hands down the length of her thighs. A teasing, feathery touch that left her entire body trembling.

"Please," she begged shamelessly. "I need—"

"I know." A deep declaration.

With a gentle push, Brody used those same hands to push her legs apart. He started to lean down, and in her foggy state of exotic bliss, it took Ro a full two seconds to understand his intended plan.

Oh...my...

His mouth was on her, his desperate, greedy indulgence bringing her closer to God with every lick of his talented tongue. Fast and slow. Starving and savoring. Brody feasted on her as if she'd been created solely for his pleasure.

Ro gasped and panted. Her fingers digging into the top of Brody's head as her need for him grew exponentially. And as he continued making love to her with his mouth, Ro lifted her head to brazenly watch the erotic scene unfold.

Talk about beautiful.

The bathroom light was still on, its soft glow filtering into the room with just enough of a glow she could see him —and what he was doing—clearly.

Eyes closed, Brody's head was between her splayed thighs. His taut, muscular arms held her close as he slowly ran the tip of his tongue along the length of her slit.

Ro gasped, her pelvis lifting from the bed in search of more. Lapping and laving, he consumed her with surprising grace. The soft whiskers from his beard created the most deliciously tantalizing sensation that was nearly her undoing.

She'd only had two lovers before him. In both cases, the sex had been less than memorable. But this...

With him, I'll never get enough.

Moving upward, Brody found her clit. Swollen and stiff, she knew her body was exposing the soul-deep desperation she felt for this man. But Ro didn't care.

The only thing she could think about...the only thing

she could *feel*...was the incredible pleasure he created. And then he added his hands.

"Oh!" Ro's internal muscles flexed as Brody slid first one, and then another into her drenched core. Thick, powerful fingers that were pumping in and out at an achingly slow pace.

"So wet," he growled against her most sensitive skin. "So hot."

"Brody..."

His tongue worked her clit with perfection, putting the exact right amount of pressure as he licked and loved the swollen bundle of nerves. At the same time, his hand worked in and out...in and out...the thrusting motion even and steady.

Until it wasn't.

When the pressure became too much, when the need became all-consuming, Ro begged him one final time.

"Please." A moaned plea. "I need..."

Her voice trailed before she could finish, and this time...*this* time...her carnal prayers were answered.

Brody increased the pressure. With both his tongue and his fingers, he picked up the pace. Ro could feel her entire core quivering with her impending release, the sounds of wet sex filling the otherwise silent room.

And as she lay there, moaning and writhing beneath his touch, she had no doubt this man had already ruined her for all the others.

"I'm close," Ro announced as he pumped his hand with vigor. "God, I'm so... Oh, yeah..." Another thrust. "Just like that..." A flick of his tongue. "Oh, god... I'm going to... *Brody!*"

She came harder than she ever had in her life. Breath stolen, Ro's entire body seized from the all-consuming orgasm. Working its way from outward, the powerful lightning bolts spread throughout her like an electrifying explosion of pleasure.

Minutes, maybe hours later, Ro opened her sated eyes to see a decidedly smug Brody smiling down at her. With the weight of his body resting on one elbow, he brushed some hair from her face.

"That was incredible." Fire lit up the darkness in his eyes.

"You're telling...me." Her chest heaved with forceful breaths as the otherworldly climax finished working its way through her system.

Brody's deep chuckle shook against her. "It might be too soon to tell, but I'm pretty sure we just ruined our friendship."

"That's okay." She continued her efforts to slow her breathing. "We weren't really all that close, anyway."

He threw his head back, a bark of laughter filling the entire room.

Talk about beautiful.

Wanting to give him as much pleasure as he'd bestowed up on her, Ro used her good hand to nudge Brody over onto his back.

"What are you—"

"Shh..." She pressed her lips to his. After kissing him thoroughly, she pulled back just to see his eyes. And as she stared down at the man who had forever changed her, she smiled with a whispered, "My turn."

14

My dick is going to explode.

Brody was almost certain of it. He was so hard, so *full*, the damn thing felt like it was seconds away from splitting itself right in two if he didn't find the release he was craving. And yet...as he laid with his back on the mattress and Ro's head between his legs, stopping her was the very last thing on his mind.

Hot, wet, and velvety smooth, she ran the tip of her tongue along his steely length. The slow pace at which the vixen moved was both Heaven and Hell. An exhilarating, torturous rollercoaster of pleasure he wanted to ride forever.

Brody hissed in a sharp breath when the tip of her tongue brushed across a particularly sensitive spot.

Reaching down, he filled his hands with her long, silken hair as Ro moved up one side and down the other. He moaned loudly, wondering somewhere in the back of his mind if death by pleasure existed.

If not, I may just be its first victim.

Wet, molten heat surrounded him as Ro sucked him as far into her mouth as he could physically go. His throbbing tip hit the back of her throat a fraction of a second before she began to pull back again.

Up and down. Up and down. Her lips felt like fiery velvet as they sucked him with perfection.

"Jesus, Ro." Brody panted.

Those lips sucked him harder, her teasing tongue licking and taunting him in ways he never wanted to forget. But as she began to move faster, suck harder, he knew her needed to stop.

Not because he wasn't enjoying what she was doing, but because he wanted to be inside her when he came. And if he didn't stop her really fucking soon...

"Nope." Brody used both hands to gently pull her off and away.

He had to be careful with her. *Always* with her. But he had to be especially careful now since she was injured.

Not just injured. She has a fucking bullet hole in her arm.

Yeah, she sure as hell did. Which meant this was the very last thing they should be doing. But when he'd walked out of his bathroom and seen her sitting up in his bed with her hair disheveled from sleep and his shirt covering her delectable body, he'd only had one thought...

Mine.

And when she'd begged him to make love to her, well. He wasn't a saint, and a man could only be so strong.

"Hey!" Ro looked up at him as she sat on her knees between his thighs. "Why'd you stop me? I wasn't finished."

"No, but I was."

"Oh." A wry grin lifted one corner of her red and swollen lips. "I see."

"Do you?"

Did she truly see him? Was it even possible for her to

truly see what she was doing to him? What she'd already done?

She's stolen something from me I don't ever want back.

Rather than answer him with words, the sexy temptress began crawling her way up the length of his body. Stopping mid-way, she straddled his hips, her toned thighs holding him in a place he never wanted to leave.

He watched as she reached between their bodies, his breath hitching from the feel of her soft, warm fingers wrapping tightly around his swollen cock. She lifted herself up, positioned him at her drenched entrance, and then...

"Wait!" His hand shot down to stop her. "Condom."

"I get the shot to regulate things," she told him bluntly. "I haven't been with anyone in an embarrassingly long time, but if you think we need one—"

"Nine months," he blurted. Clearing his throat, Brody attempted a second, much smoother, explanation. "That's how long it's been for me. Nine months. And I've always used protection."

It had never been a question for him. But now...with *her*...

"It's your call, big guy." She stroked him up and down slowly. "I trust you."

His heart swelled with an emotion he couldn't quite put into words, and suddenly his dick wasn't the only thing that felt like it would explode.

Laying there, staring at the most incredible surprise of his life, Brody no longer questioned what he was feeling for this woman. He didn't second-guess or wonder whether they were making a giant ass mistake.

This was Ro. Sweet, sexy, sassy Ro. And while it may defy all logic, in that moment, Brody knew she was his...and he was hers.

Keeping his eyes locked with hers, he reached down and wrapped his hand around hers. Understanding flickered behind her sapphire gaze, and she didn't resist in the least when he guided himself back to her welcoming entrance.

"You sure?" She watched him closely.

Giving her a slight nod against his pillow, Brody rasped out a whispered, "I trust you, too."

That was all it took.

With their gazes fixed, Ro lowered herself over him. Inch by agonizing inch, she took him into her molten core. He'd felt how tight she was around his fingers minutes earlier. Had expected the feeling of being inside her would be incredible.

Brody did not, however, expect to lose the ability to breathe.

Holy fuuuuck.

Feeling her body come together with his without anything in between was a connection unlike any he'd known. And that's when she began to move.

Like a piston, she slid her body up and down. Slowly at first, a sensual dance so perfect it was as if they'd spent years perfecting it.

That's what being with Ro was like. Perfect. Amazing. Wonderful.

Right.

Ro began to move faster. He lifted his pelvis off the mattress. Over and over, they became lost in their search to bring each other to the edge. Brody's hands held her hips in a bruising grip as he guided her through the powerful thrusts.

Time ceased to exist, the outside world vanishing in a swirl of inviting sensations and consuming emotions as he became drunk off her sensual heat. Ro's body trembled above his, her thighs quivering with what he knew was another impending explosion of pleasure.

Feeling his own telltale signs that he was precariously close to the edge, Brody slid a hand to where their bodies met. Ro cried out, her head falling back as he worked her swollen clit.

"That's it, Princess." Rough. Gravelly.

She moved her hips up and down with vigor. He met her thrust for thrust while his fingers continued rubbing the spot he knew would get her there.

Bodies slapping together, the sounds of their love-making created an erotic soundtrack Brody would spend his entire life savings to hear again and again. And when he felt her muscles stiffen and clench around him, he knew she was almost there.

"Let go, baby. Just...let...*go!*"

They came together, their orgasms striking at the exact same moment in time. Ro cried out his name as she began to fly above him. A rush of hot liquid covered his convulsing dick as he emptied himself inside her welcoming womb over and over again.

Brody didn't just come. He *erupted*. Still he managed to hold her steady as they rode wave after wave of the ecstasy crashing over them both.

When the trembling ceased and their movements slowed, Ro's limp form fell lazily over his. His chest heaved, his racing heart kicking his chest as hers pounded against him at the same heightened pace.

Holding her warmth in his tight embrace, Brody managed to pant out a facetious, "And this is where I die."

Ro giggled, the sound as adorable as the woman creating it. "Oh, yeah." A breathless agreement. "I'm definitely...a goner."

She lifted her head, bringing those sated, heavy-lidded eyes to his. Brody's lungs froze half-a-second before his chest swelled with a sense of primal male pride.

He'd done that. *He'd* put that look on her face. And as he lay there, soaking in the breathtaking view, Brody realized it was a look he wanted to give her every day for the rest of his life.

The rest of your life, huh? You sure about that?

Ro put her mouth on his, the sweet, sensual kiss the only answer he needed. Hell yes, he was sure. He just needed to figure out a way to tell her.

"I'm going to hop in the shower." She pressed her lips to his once more. "Wanna join me?"

Why yes. Yes, he did.

Hours later, Brody was lying fast asleep with Ro curled up in his arms when a blaring alarm pierced the otherwise silent air. Recognizing it as his home's security system, he shot straight up and grabbed the pistol he always kept on his nightstand.

Pointing it outward, he scanned their immediate area. Thankfully there was no threat in sight.

"Wha...what's going on?" Ro sat up in a sleepy haze. Brushing some hair from her blinking eyes as she looked first at him and then the gun. "Brody, what's—"

"It's the alarm." He threw the blankets off his legs and jumped to his feet. Remembering he was naked, Brody set the pistol down long enough to pull on the sweats Ro had yanked off of him the night before. "Call Christian. Tell him to get the team here as fast as he can."

"The team?" She was already pulling on his old shirt. Wincing as she worked her injured arm into its sleeve, Ro swung her terrified gaze to the door. "Do you think it's him? The person who shot me?"

"Don't know." It was a lie. Hell yes, he thought it was their guy.

No way the timing's a coincidence.

"Shouldn't we call the police first?"

"Alarm system already has."

"I want to come with you."

"Absolutely not."

"Brody, please. What if there's more than one of them? Y-you could be walking into some sort of trap. Or what if—"

He was across the room and cupping her face before she could finish the thought. "This is what I do, Princess. Now I need you to trust me. Can you do that?"

"I do trust you," she insisted.

"Good." He gave her a hard, fast kiss. "Call Christian and lock the door behind me. Do not answer it for anyone other than me or one of the team. Got it?"

She nodded shakily. "Please be careful. I can't..." Ro palmed one of his cheeks. "I can't lose you, too."

His chest tightened, knowing she was thinking of the loss of her parents. "You won't." He gave her another quick kiss—because he couldn't walk away from her without one—and then Brody spun on his bare heels and left the room.

Clearing the immediate space, he kept the lights off to conceal his presence. With the deafening alarm still blaring, it was impossible to hear his intruder's movements, which made the situation even more volatile.

Brody's pulse raced, but with anger rather than fear. This wasn't some glitch, nor was it some stray cat that had tripped his alarm. The system didn't work that way.

He knew because he'd helped design and install the damn thing.

If that alarm was tripped, it was because someone had breached the security of his home. Given everything that had been happening with Ro, he had to assume the shooter had come to finish the job.

Not. Fucking. Happening.

Keeping his focus sharp and his weapon at the ready, Brody moved with speed and efficiency, clearing each room as he came to it...

The spare bedroom he used for storage. Full, separate bathroom. Hallway closet.

When he was finished checking those areas, he began a slow, cautious descent downstairs. At the bottom, he checked the front door, surprised when he found it shut and locked, just as he'd left it after Rocky had left earlier.

He shifted his body so his back was to the wall behind him. Reaching up, he entered the alarm code by memory, effectively cutting off the ear-piercing sound. The space was instantly quiet, the shift from loud to nothing a stark difference.

Knowing there was only one other way inside, Brody used slow, silent steps to first clear the living room and nearby half-bathroom. He checked the kitchen next before moving down a short hallway leading to the back corner of the house.

He crept down the narrow space, a mixture of adrenaline and relief rushing through him when he got to the small mud room and found it empty. Like the front door, the back one was also closed and secure.

What the hell?

The unexpected find was more than a little confusing. Systems like his didn't just go off for no reason. And yet, it had.

Brody took precious seconds to stop and think, his mind

racing back through the alarm's design. Unable to come up with a valid excuse for the unpleasant wake-up call, he decided to go back through the house one last time, just to be on the safe side.

You've checked every room, dipshit. There's no one here but you and Ro.

But even as the thought drove past, Brody's stomach was falling, and his heart was leaping into his throat. He'd cleared the house, sure. Except...

My bedroom.

Brody spun around and took off. It wasn't likely that an intruder somehow made it inside the house before the alarm went off, but he damn sure wasn't going to risk Ro's life on assumptions.

He raced out of the mudroom and through his kitchen. His gut churned with fear for the woman he'd fallen hard and fast for, but she was okay. She had to be okay.

For him, there was no other option.

Brody made it out of the kitchen and into his living room, his entire focus on getting upstairs. On getting to *Ro*. Because his gut was screaming now that something was very, very wrong.

He was three feet from the bottom of the stairs when the front door facing those same stairs exploded in a cloud of dust, blinding light, and splintered wood. On reflex, Brody turned away to protect himself from the flying debris.

But just as he did, the front door that just had been blown from its hinges flew straight at him. The unforgiving wood struck from behind, the door smacking him in the head on impact.

Brody was out cold before he ever hit the floor.

Ro didn't just hear the explosion, she'd *felt* it. And it left her even more terrified than when she'd discovered she'd been shot.

She wasn't in fear for herself. Well, she *was,* but even more than that, Ro was beyond scared for the man she'd spent half the night making love to.

Brody!

He'd left in search of the assumed threat, and now Ro couldn't help but think he'd walked head-first into danger.

"What the hell was that?" Christian's worried voice came through the phone.

"I-I don't know." Her voice quivered with fear. "I think something just exploded downstairs."

The house had shaken beneath her bare feet, and she'd heard what she could only describe as a loud boom.

"I'm still fifteen minutes out, but Rocky's less than ten," her best friend's fiancé informed her. "I already texted him while we've been talking, and he's on his way to you now."

That was all well and good, but...

"I don't think I have ten minutes, Christian. And Brody's—"

"King can handle himself. Right now, I need you to focus on getting your ass out of that house. You said you're in his bedroom, right?"

"What?" The ringing in her ears made his voice sound muffled. "Yeah. Brody told me to lock the door and wait for him here."

"Change of plans. I need you to go to the window."

She spun around and looked. "Which one?"

Brody had two windows in his bedroom. One facing the backyard, the other offering a view of the next door neighbor's house several yards—and two privacy fences—away.

"The one in the back. Over the patio."

Understanding began to sink in. "I can't leave Brody."

"Damn it, Aurora! Brody would tell you the exact same thing I am. Now don't fucking argue with me, just go!"

She hesitated two seconds longer before springing into action. Running over to the window in question, Ro used her left shoulder to hold the phone to her ear. A flash of pain came from the wound in her arm, but she ignored it and pushed open the window.

"Ro?"

"I'm still...here." Her voice was strained as she worked the screen up the frame's narrow track next. "Okay." She blew out a breath. "Window's open."

Looking down, her heart nearly beat straight out of her chest. She was going to have to jump. With an injured arm... and without panties.

"Good girl." Christian's deep voice cut through once more. "Now I want you to carefully climb out the window and lower yourself down onto the patio roof. Then you run as fast as you can to the nearest neighbor and wait for help. Can you do that?"

Could she? Absolutely. Did she want to...

"I can do it." She was already bending and twisting herself through the open window.

The fact that she didn't have anything on under Brody's extra-large t-shirt came back to the forefront of her mind. Luckily the need to survive overshadowed whatever modesty she may have been feeling.

The window's frame scraped and pinched the bare skin covering her thighs, but Ro ignored the tiny pricks of pain—and the renewed throbbing in her bandaged arm—and continued making her escape.

"Christian, I can't do this and hold the phone. I'm going to put it in my mouth while I climb down."

"Do what you've got to do, sweetheart. Rocky should be there in five. Maybe less."

Five minutes.

What had forever seemed like a blip on the scales of time suddenly felt like an eternity. So yes...less would definitely be best.

"I'll let you know when I make it to the bottom."

Keeping the phone call active, Ro shoved her cell phone between her lips and gripped the sill as if her life depended on it. Because, well...it did.

The sharp edge of the frame's metal track dug into her palms, but Ro didn't dare loosen her hold. Sending up a quick prayer that she wasn't about to break something—or, you know...fall to her death—she began to lower herself down.

Son of a bitch, that hurts!

Her injured arm screamed in protest, and Ro was pretty sure the growing warmth there meant she'd re-opened her wound. But she'd deal with that later. Assuming there *was* a later.

Stretched as far as she could go, Ro looked down to see how close she'd come. *Damn it.* There were still at least three feet between her dangling toes and the roof below.

A three-foot drop or face an intruder that probably wants you dead. Hmmm...let me think.

Ro sent up a quick prayer—for both herself and Brody. Glancing down again, she gauged an estimated landing spot, and...

She let go.

Momentarily weightless, her stomach flew into her throat as gravity pulled her down to the shingled roof below. She landed with a thud, her knees buckling beneath her on impact.

Ro grunted, the jolt sending her down onto her hands and knees and the phone flying from her lips. She reached out to try to catch it, but only managed to barely touch the phone's slick edge before it fell off the patio roof to the concrete below.

No!

Ignoring the scrapes she could feel from the shingles' rough surface, she wasted no time scrambling to the southwest corner of the roof. It was a calculated risk, but she figured her chances of avoiding further injury were best if she could shimmy herself down the roof's support post.

Feeling much better about the distance between her and the ground, she made quick work of lowering herself over the roof's edge and wrapping herself around the wooden post. One leg at a time, followed by more of the same with her arms.

Ro could feel the blood oozing out from the clear adhesive wrap Christian had placed over the bandage earlier, but she paid it—nor the pain—no mind and continued her escape. Hair blew into her mouth from the chilly fall breeze, but she simply spit it out and kept moving.

Seconds later, she was on the ground and running toward the phone. She picked it up, her heart sinking when she saw the shattered screen. A few tries later, it was clear the thing was dead.

Ro tossed it into the grass and started to run, following the cute pathway Brody had fashioned that led around to the front of the house. She was halfway to the privacy gate when she stopped.

Her gaze flew to the house. Brody was in there right now. He was in there, alone with whoever had come to do them harm, and she was just...leaving him to fend for himself?

She started to go back with the thought of sneaking into

the house from the back door and seeing if there was something she could do to help. But then Christian's earlier words rang through her head, giving her pause...

Brody would tell you the same fucking thing I am. Now don't argue, just go!

Meg's fiancé was right. Like Brody said, this is what he does. The last thing he needed was for her to go barging back inside to help, only to distract him. Or worse, get him killed.

Ro turned around once more and ran. She made it to the gate and flung the safety latch free. Relieved that she was actually going to get away, she'd just started to pull the gate open when a gloved hand appeared from behind, covering her mouth and preventing her screams from being heard.

No!

Her throat burned, her neck muscles straining with her muffled cries for help. She kicked and hit and clawed at the man pulling her away from the gate.

Pulling her away from safety.

The heels of her feet scraped against the unforgiving pathway as she desperately tried to keep her attacker from covering more ground. But the man was big—bigger than Brody—and unflinchingly strong.

The eyes. Go for the eyes!

Reaching behind her, Ro blindly clawed at the man's face, her fingers meeting what felt like some type of mesh-like face mask. She didn't let that stop her.

The man jerked his head back, out of her reach as he continued to pull her roughly toward the back of the house. Ro knew she probably looked like a wild woman, but right then, she genuinely prayed someone got there in time to see her.

Sirens blared in the distance, the sound Ro's first sign of

hope since she'd reached that damn gate. But the sound was also a warning. An announcement to the intruder that authorities were on their way.

Almost instantly, the beefy man shifted gears. Swinging her around, he forced a still-fighting Ro closer to the side of the house. With no door or even a window in that part, her frantic mind raced to decipher the asshole's plan.

The gloved hand slid away from her mouth. Ro sucked in a breath with the intention of screaming but cried out when the man fisted the hair on the back of her head. Her hands flew back to the source of the burning pain, her fingers working hysterically to pull the large male's fingers away.

She was still struggling to get free when her attacker slammed her forehead into the side of Brody's house. Once. Twice. Explosions of pain erupted, stealing Ro's ability to keep fighting.

And by the third and final strike, the terror she'd been feeling vanished. As did the world around her.

15

"Aurora!" Brody's eyes flew open, his wild gaze searching frantically as he shot up from where he'd been laying.

"Whoa, whoa, whoa." Rocky's blurred image came into view. "Take it easy, brother. You're hurt."

He didn't give a shit if he was hurt. He needed to get to Ro. He needed—

Someone shone a bright as fuck light in his eyes a beat before Brody heard, "Definitely concussed."

The light went away, and it was only then that he realized he was surrounded.

Still on the floor where he'd landed after the world around him exploded all to hell, he found Rocky by his side. Next to him was a man and woman he'd never seen before —paramedics who'd apparently been called in to treat him.

"I'm fine." He squinted as that damn light found his eyes again.

His head felt like someone had taken an industrial sized sledgehammer to it, and he very well may throw up in the next minute or so. But he was alive and breathing and still had full use of his extremities.

Like I said. I'm fine.

"You just got your ass blown to hell." Christian appeared in his demolished doorway. "You're not fine."

"Where's Ro?"

"Perimeter's clear." Jagger and Cade were the next to join in the fun.

From somewhere behind him, Liam's voice came next with, "Security cams got the asshole from several angles, but the fucking mask he had on makes facial rec impossible."

"What about a vehicle?" Christian asked the other man. "You able to get a plate, or—"

"Where the fuck is Ro?"

Brody's booming voice echoed off the living room walls, and everyone in the place stopped to look his way. Cops. Medics. His team. They were all staring down at him, but no one was saying a word.

A thought struck, then. One with the power to destroy him.

Ah, Jesus. God, please no.

"Ro's, uh…" Rocky stuttered in his response, the man's gray-blue eyes giving away too much.

"No." Brody shook his head, not giving a damn about how badly it throbbed. "She's not…" God, he couldn't even say it. "Ro's not—"

"She's not dead," Christian put that thought out of his head in a hurry. "She's just…"

"Not here."

Brody looked up to see Detective Hansen standing over him.

Tall. Built. Square jaw. Thirty-something with light brown hair and even lighter green eyes.

He was a friend of Christian's and was quickly becoming a friend of his. But right now, Brody wanted to punch the asshole in the throat for not elaborating more about the woman Brody had come to love.

Yeah, he loved her. Heart and fucking soul. Which was why he was going out of his mind with worry.

"I'm sorry, Brody." Guilt clouded Rocky's features. "I got here as fast as I could, but...he took her."

His entire world stopped spinning.

It. Just. Stopped.

"Who?" He barely managed to choke out the demand.

"We don't know." It was Liam who answered that one. "Cameras show a man dressed in all black approaching the house from the back. He walked up to the kitchen window and tried to open it, which set off the alarm. Then he went around the walkway and up to the front door, where he fashioned a rolled breaching charge combined with a small amount of explosives."

"The camera's position makes it impossible to tell for sure," Rocky chimed back in. "But from the damage, I'd say C4."

"Jesus." Brody rolled himself to his knees. "Who the hell are we dealing with?"

"Uh...Sir?" The female paramedic addressed him before his team could answer. "You really shouldn't—"

"Where do I sign?"

"I'm sorry?"

Something pulled against his arm when he pushed himself to his feet. When he looked down, he found an I.V., which had apparently been administered while his ass was still out cold.

Brody yanked the catheter free from his vein and tossed the plastic tube onto the floor next to the rest of the medical supplies. "A.M.A." He shot the woman a pointed look. "Where do I sign?"

The young redhead blinked. "You want to sign out against medical advice?"

He gave a curt nod.

"Sir, I highly advise against that," the other paramedic offered his unsolicited advice.

"Yeah, King." Hansen took the guy's side. "You've been out a while. I'd listen to him if I were you."

"He's right." The woman's wary gaze found his once more. "Concussions are very serious, and you could risk—"

"I know the risks," he growled. "Just give me the papers so you and your partner can be free to go help someone who needs it."

He knew he sounded like a total dick, but social mores weren't exactly high on his current list of priorities.

Both medics and Hansen all looked as though they wanted to argue, but thankfully, they kept their mouths shut and did as he'd asked. Once the electronic form had been signed, they drove off in their ambulance and he was finally able to focus on what mattered.

"What do we know about Ro?"

God, he could barely breathe for the fear running through him. Last he'd seen her, she was in his bedroom—naked and looking like every wet dream he'd ever had. He'd kissed her before he left, and then...

"Maybe you should just show him."

Brody turned to Cade, who looked as miserable as the rest of them. With a slight lift of a shoulder, the just-turned-thirty-year-old sniper looked him in the eyes with an honest, "If she were mine, I'd want to know."

Ah, fuck. That didn't sound good.

"Know what?" He scanned the entire group, including Hansen. "I swear to Christ, if someone doesn't start talking right the fuck now—"

"Here." Liam brought his trusty tablet over to where Brody stood. "It's dark, and he wore a mask, so you can't make out the bastard's features, but...." The tech genius tapped the screen, and the frozen image that had been there came to life.

Fear turned his veins to ice as he watched Ro climb from his bedroom window, drop to the secondary roof, and then shimmy her way down the post. He also felt damn proud of how incredibly brave she'd been in her attempts to escape.

But as Liam switched to show a different camera's viewpoint—there were three in his backyard, alone—Brody's heart ripped all the way open as he stood there, watching while some meaty bastard grabbed her from behind.

Ro fought. She fought damn hard. But then...

Ah, God.

The man holding Ro against her will made an abrupt change of course, pulling her up next to the house, and then slamming her head against its side. Three fucking times, the bastard did that to her. Then he picked her up—limp and unconscious—and carried her toward the alley behind his house.

One of the cameras he'd installed was mounted on the back of his house, facing that direction. From there, he could see the man shoving Ro into the trunk of a dark, partially concealed car before driving away into the night.

Taking the woman who owned Brody's heart with him.

Liam lowered the tablet. Several began talking at once. Detective Hansen stepped in to take charge, but Brody wasn't listening to any of them.

He was too busy spinning around and punching a fist-sized hole in the nearest wall.

"Christ, man!" Christian stopped him from making a second hole. "Hey. Knock that shit off."

"She's gone." Brody struggled to free himself from the other man's hold. "I promised I'd keep her safe, and now she's fucking *gone!*"

He did break free, then. He also made that second hole.

A small cloud of dust formed, and bits of paint chips and drywall flew out and fell to the ground. Brody's chest heaved with forceful, heady breaths.

On the brink of hyperventilation, he tried—and failed—to regain control of his lungs. Brody could *feel* the staring eyes of those around him, their retinas burning into his skin.

He needed to leave. He needed to get out of there right the hell now. Because if he didn't, the next thing he punched might not be a wall.

Brody didn't say a word as he pushed and shoved his way through the small group surrounding him. Stepping up and over his blown-in door, he didn't give two shits that he was barefoot and shirtless. He didn't even notice the chilly autumn air.

His thoughts—his entire *being*—was too consumed by the fact that Ro had been taken right out from under his fucking nose. All his bolstering to Yorke about what he'd do to the person who'd dare to hurt Ro, and now look at him...

There was a knot the size of Texas on the back of his head, his knuckles were split open and bleeding, and he had to physically work not to show the others how fucking dizzy he really felt.

But the worst wound of all was the one he'd given to himself. An invisible, internal wound that ran far deeper than any cut or concussion could reach.

For the first time in his professional career—Navy or Delta Team—Brody had failed. He'd made a promise to protect...had looked Ro *square* in those beautiful eyes, and he'd sworn to keep her safe.

Now she was gone, and he had absolutely no idea where she was, who had taken her, or why. And without a place to start...

The flash of a very recent memory filled his mind's eye. Ro's face above his, her cheeks flushed with arousal as she rode him into ecstasy.

Another picture took its place. This one of Ro laughing while he tickled her in the shower.

Soon his entire mind became filled with memories. Recent, intimate ones. Older moments they'd shared as friends. Some memories returned from decades past, back when he'd first met a young, pigtailed brunette with a wide smile and eyes that seemed too big for her face.

Ro had eventually grown into those eyes. She'd grown into the most incredible, loving, intelligent, talented woman he knew. And now...

Now I've lost her to an enemy I know nothing about.

"Ah, God."

Brody's legs gave out from underneath him. He would have fallen flat on his ass, too, if not for the set of hands shooting out at the last second to catch him.

"Come on, brother." Christian guided him over to a nearby chair. "That's it. Just sit and breathe."

"I can't." He tried pushing himself back up. "Ro needs me. She's—"

"We're going to find her, but first we have to make sure you're okay."

"No." Another push to his feet brought him right back down on his ass.

"Goddamnit, Brody. Would you just stop?" Christian finally managed to hold him in place with a strong push on both shoulders. "Now I want to find Ro as badly as you. We *all* do. But you're not going to be any good to her if you pass out cold."

"You're wrong." Voice flat and wooden, he felt numb as he met his best friend's stare. "No one on this planet wants to find her as badly as me."

A look of understanding saturated the browns in his best friend's eyes. "I get it, brother. I do."

"You can't." He couldn't. "No one does."

"Really? You don't think I know exactly how you're feeling, right now?" Christian sounded pissed, then. "You don't think I can tell that you're beating yourself up, blaming yourself for what happened, even though there's not a damn thing you could've done to stop it? Maybe you've forgotten that I've lived through the part where someone wanted to kill the woman I love."

The angry glare Christian was sending his way—and the words he'd just spoken—showed Brody the error of his ways. The other man *did* know how he felt, in a way. Because Christian had been on the phone with Megan the night someone broke into her apartment and tried to kill her.

His friend had shared the story with him, after the fact. Brody could still see the haunted look that had come over Christian's face when he'd told him how terrified he'd been that he wouldn't get to Megan in time.

He had, of course. Thank God. But now Ro was the one in need of rescuing, and Brody was the one left behind to sit and wonder.

Was she okay? Was she hurt? What had that son of a bitch done to her? What's he doing to her right this very second?

"Don't do that."

He blinked. "Do what?"

"You let yourself fall down the rabbit hole of what-ifs

and who knows, you're going to drive yourself batshit. Now I agree with Hansen, I think your ass needs to be in the hospital—"

"I'm not going to the fucking hospital."

"—but I also know you'd skip out on us the first chance you got to try to go all Lone Ranger on our asses and find Ro yourself." Christian gave him a *tell me I'm wrong* look. "So how 'bout we skip a step, and you go get yourself cleaned up and changed. In the meantime, I'll check in with Hansen, and then we can figure out our next step. Together." He emphasized that word. "As a team."

"I have to find her, Christian." His words were barely audible. "I *have* to."

"We won't stop until we do."

A stretch of silence passed between the two friends as they shared a look that spoke volumes. Both men would do whatever it took to find the woman they cared about. A woman near and dear to Megan's heart.

The woman who had no idea she owned his completely.

I'll tell her, God. If you let her live, I swear to you, all that's holy, I will make sure Ro knows how much she's loved.

He'd tell her every day for the rest of his life if she'd let him. Something else he planned on sharing with the ivory-skinned beauty.

Brody may have spent his entire adult life avoiding relationships and strings, but things were different now. Because of Ro, he found himself wanting more. With her, he wanted...

Everything.

And the only way he was going to get it was if he got off his ass, got himself cleaned up, and he and his team made a plan.

Filled with a renewed sense of faith and determination,

Brody rose to his feet, walked himself upstairs, and he took the fastest shower known to man.

Once the soot and dirt and blood from a few scrapes he hadn't realized were there was washed away, he got dressed and went back downstairs to join the others. After Hansen finished taking his statement and the place had cleared out minus the team, Brody popped a couple aspirin and got to work.

Pulling his security feed up on the big flatscreen mounted high on his living room wall, Brody and the others began watching it from the beginning. Only this time, when he assessed the recordings, Brody studied them with an operative's eye.

He was still going through them, watching each angle over and over again in search of something—anything—that would lead them in some sort of direction, when a phone began to ring.

Knowing it wasn't his, he continued with the task at hand.

"Dude, is that you?" Rocky looked over at Cade.

The youngest on the team shook his head. "Not mine. Brooks?"

They all turned to Jagger who was already shaking his head as well. "Nope. Got mine right here." The Jack of all trades patted his back jeans' pocket.

"Well, it's not mine, and I know it's not King's," Christian shared with the group. "So that leaves—"

"Don't look at me." Liam held up a palm.

Rocky sent them all an incredulous look. "I'm the one who asked Cade if it was his, remember?"

Several muttered agreements later, and the phone was *still* ringing. Assuming either one of the paramedics had left it behind, or someone with the police, Brody and the others began following the sound.

It didn't take long for someone to uncover the source.

"Uh...Brody?" Rocky hollered at him from just inside the kitchen. "You're gonna want to come take a look at this."

Rushing over to where his teammate stood, Brody followed the man's line of sight to the open drawer in front of him. His chest tightened when he saw the bulging white envelope lying on top of his wooden silverware tray.

In the center, written in black marker, were the handwritten words *His Highness*.

His High...

Frowning, Brody opened the drawer below that one and grabbed a pair of metal tongs. Using those to keep from disturbing any possible prints, he carefully lifted the envelope out of the drawer and placed it on the counter.

Cade shot Rocky a look of concern. "You don't think that thing's gonna...blow. Do you?"

"My guess is, no." Rocky stood beside Brody.

"I agree." A nod from Jagger. "If the guy wanted you dead, he'd have killed you before he split with Ro."

Brody's gut churned with dread, just the sound of her name hurting from his need to find her.

"Unless it's a trap designed to kill us all at once."

Every man in the room turned to look at Liam, who stared back at them with a lackadaisical expression. "I'm just sayin'..."

It *would* be the perfect opportunity to blow them all to hell. But that wasn't what this was about.

His home. His woman. An envelope in his kitchen with that title...

Using the tongs to flip the envelope over, Brody dumped

its contents. A small black cell phone slid onto the counter. With it came an intricate, shiny gold pin.

A pin Brody recognized instantly.

"What's that?" Cade motioned to the object of Brody's focus.

Picking it up, he held it beneath the light to get a better view.

"Is that a Master Chief hat pin?" Jagger leaned over Brody's shoulder for a closer look.

He nodded, a nauseating acceptance running deep and fucking wide. "That's exactly what this is."

"Why the hell would someone leave that in your kitchen drawer?" Christian asked the obvious questions. "With a phone?"

Right on cue, the phone began to ring again.

Brody was no longer worried about prints or destroying evidence. He knew there would be none. Keeping the phone on the counter, he tapped the screen to answer the unknown number's call.

Putting it on speaker, he kept his voice low and steady. "What have you done with Ro?"

A deep chuckle from his past filled the speakers and beyond. "Damn, King. Is that any way to greet an old friend?"

Michael Ainsworth. Former Master Chief in the U.S. Navy, and Brody's former SEAL Team leader.

Despite already knowing he'd be the one on the other end of the line, the familiar voice sent a cascade of emotions racing through Brody's veins. Disbelief. Sadness. Anger. Betrayal. Guilt.

Every single negative feeling a person could have struck him all at once. *Hard.* With his fists curled painfully at his sides, he barely managed to control the murderous rage inside him.

"I'm going to ask you one more time, Michael. Where. Is. Aurora?"

"Relax, Your Highness. Your girlfriend's still alive. For now."

"You son of a bitch!" Brody leaned both palms on the counter. Never wanting to kill a man more, he warned his former leader, "Touch her again, and you're dead."

The bastard was a dead man either way. That wasn't even a question. He just didn't know it.

"You don't have to worry about that. Your *princess* is still fast asleep. Well she was as of thirty minutes ago, anyway. That was the last time I actually saw her."

"Where the fuck is she?" Brody's voice boomed inside his kitchen. Because yeah, he was starting to lose his shit.

"Three years, and that's all you have to say to me? No, 'Hey, Mike. How you been?' Or... 'What have you been up to since I got you kicked out of the Navy?'"

His entire team looked his way but remained quiet.

"You got *yourself* kicked out of the Navy, Michael. That shit wasn't on me, and you fucking know it."

"Still feeding yourself the same bullshit, I see. That what helps you sleep at night?" Another rage-inducing chuckle. "I bet that's the same story you told your girl, too, huh? Make yourself look like the big, bad Navy SEAL all-American hero?"

"I sleep just fine, asshole," Brody seethed. "As for my conversations with Ro, your name's never even come up."

A stretch of silence passed, and for a minute, he thought he'd fucked up and the asshole on the other end of the line had hung up. But then...

"Sorry to hear that." Another pause. "Guess there's still time, though."

"Time for what?"

"To share with your woman the *whole* truth about the man you really are. I would have told her myself, but sadly, she didn't wake up in time."

In time?

"The fuck you mean, 'in time'?"

"Oh, that's right!" Ainsworth's voice became animated. "We've been so busy catching up, I almost forgot to send the picture. I hope you don't mind. I only took a couple. To remember the occasion, of course."

More than done with the asshole's twisted game of cat and mouse, Brody got straight to the point. "You want me? You've got me. Tell me where you are right now, and I will come to you. Just...let Ro go. Please, Michael. She has nothing to do with this."

"She has *everything* to do with this!" The other man lost his cool composure. "I've been watching you for a while now, King. Not that you've noticed." A sarcastic huff. "Some security expert you are. Can't spot a tail if your life depended on it. Although in this case, your life isn't the one on the line."

"Goddamn it, Mike—"

"Tell you what." The deranged man interrupted. "I'll make you a deal. I'll send you a clue, and if you and your new team can find her...you can have her. Although if this really is going to be a fair game, you should probably know that your girl's only got about two and a half, *maybe* three hours of oxygen left. After that..."

Brody's stomach filled with a sense of dread like none he'd ever felt. "What are you talking about, Mike? What did…" His voice cracked, but he cleared it enough to go on. "What did you do to her?"

Seconds that felt like days passed before the other man spoke again. When he did, it was only to leave him with a taunting, "Clock's tickin' for your girl, King. Better hurry."

It was the last thing Ainsworth said before ending the call.

"Fuck!" Brody slammed his hands down onto the counter.

"Who the hell is Michael Ainsworth?" Cade asked. "And why does he think you got him kicked out of the Navy?"

"It's a long story." One he didn't really want to go into now.

"Well I hate to be the one to point this out"—Jagger spoke up again—"but until we have something more to go on than a phone call, there's not a whole lot we can do but wait."

"Maybe. Maybe not." Liam reached an arm between where Brody and Christian were standing. "Let me take a look. People buy these pay-as-you-go phones thinking they're impossible to trace, but that's not always the case."

"What good is a trace going to do?" Rocky joined in. "We already know the name of the person who took Ro."

"I may be able to use the phone's serial number to access its SIM card," Liam informed them all. "If I can, my system may allow for a trace of the incoming call's location."

"Okay, then." Jagger pulled out a chair and plopped down at Brody's kitchen table. "While we're waiting for Cutler to get his geek on, you can fill us in on exactly who it is we're dealing with."

Brody felt like he was going mad with the need to be out there looking for Ro. The fear he felt for her was so complete...so absolute...he felt as though his heart was physically being torn from his body.

Inch by agonizing inch.

But Jagger was right. Until Liam figured out a way to trace the call—if he could even do it in the first place—the only thing he could do was wait. And since knowing your enemy was the number one rule in warfare...

He walked over to the table and sat his ass down. Head pounding and body aching, he drew strength from the physical pain and emotional pain to do what was needed to help the woman he loved.

"Like I said, Ainsworth used to be SEAL Team 1's leader. About six months before he left the team, I noticed Mike acting...different."

"Different how?" Christian joined him and Jagger.

"He started getting these headaches. Then his personality began to change. He became more aggressive. Reckless." Brody ran a hand over his jaw. "I confronted him about it before one of our last missions together. Told him I was concerned, and I thought he should get checked for Breacher's Syndrome."

The unofficial term used for those suffering from repetitive TBIs—traumatic brain injuries. Pro football players, military...anyone at risk for experiencing multiple blows to the head was susceptible.

In Ainsworth's case—and countless others—years of being flash banged, coming close to a few RPGs, and constantly breaching doors with explosives had clearly damaged a once-sharp mind. Changing a once-great man into a deranged lunatic.

One who'd resulted in terrorizing and kidnapping an innocent woman simply as a pawn in his sick game of revenge.

"Let me guess." Jagger stared back at him from across the table. "Ainsworth screw something up on an op?"

Brody looked at his teammate and nodded. "He used to be the best, you know? From day one with the Teams, the guy took me under his wing." A humorless huff. "Asshole taught me everything I know about being a SEAL."

"So what happened?" Rocky asked quietly.

"He started taking risks. High risks, too. Gambling. Sleeping around on his wife. And then his shit spread over into the team. The guy started changing the game mid-op. Put himself at unnecessary risks."

"You talk to him?" Christian asked.

Brody forgot he'd never really gotten into any of this stuff with his best friend.

"I tried. Like I said, I went to him with my concerns. Mike blew them all off, of course." Guy always had an answer for everything. "He fucked up on that op, and I...I covered for him. Made excuses to the higher-ups. Blamed bad intel and poor communications. But it was all Ainsworth."

"That what ended his career?"

"No." Brody shook his head. "That was the last op he served as Team Lead. We were in Afghanistan, taking heavy fire. Orders were to hold in place until air support could arrive. Ainsworth goes off half-cocked...runs into a building we hadn't secured." His jaw clenched tight. "We were a team, so we went against orders and followed him inside. He'd gone up to the roof for a better vantage point, so that's where we went, too."

"You had his back," Christian rumbled.

A curt nod. "And it almost got me and another man on our team killed."

Sometimes in the dead of night, Brody could still hear

that bullet whizzing by his head. "On the chopper ride there, I'd already made the decision to tell Command what I'd witnessed. As soon as we got back, I was going to go in there and lay it all out."

"Weren't you worried about being labeled a rat?" Cade asked with genuine curiosity.

"Sure I was." Brody looked at the younger man. "But I was more worried about me and my teammates getting killed. Anyway..." A deep breath and harsh exhale. "I submitted my A.A.R. the same day we returned. So did the other guys."

"You let the report do the tattling for you." Jagger surmised. "And Ainsworth has been stewing about it ever since."

"That's what I don't get. This was what, three years ago?" Christian frowned. "Why now? Why, after all this time, has he decided to get his revenge on you now?"

"Who the hell knows what triggered the asshole?" Brody pushed himself to his feet and began to pace. "None of that shit even matters. We need to focus our attention on finding Ro. She's what's important here."

He'd barely finished his rant when a low dinging came from the other side of the room. Liam, who'd been using the laptop he'd brought with him to try to locate Ainsworth, stared at the phone before turning a paled gaze Brody's way.

"You just got sent two pictures."

Brody rushed to the other man's side. "Let me see."

"Okay, but first, I need you to promise not to lose your shit. We're going to find her. I just need a little more time to—"

He snatched the phone from the other man's hand and opened the new text feed...and the images he'd just received. A rush of bile hit the base of his throat, and it was all he could do not to puke all over his kitchen floor.

"Oh, my god."

"What is it?" Christian looked over his shoulder.

Surrounded by the entire team, Brody enlarged the image to see it more clearly. The first one showed an unconscious Ro. Her forehead was bloody and bruised and she appeared to be lying in some sort of metal storage trunk.

It reminded him of the one he had in the bed of his own pickup, only his wasn't metal. It was plastic.

"Ah, fuck." Brody opened the other image. Surely Ainsworth hadn't...

But he had.

The second image showed the metal trunk from a distance. It appeared to be in the middle of a large room in what he assumed was an abandoned building, and its lid had been shut and padlocked.

On both sides, set back several yards, were two tri-pod work lights. Same kind he had in his own garage. They were positioned in such a way, their glow illuminated the trunk as if it were on display.

That's because the bastard put it on display just for you.

"Jesus Christ." Christian spun away from the images. "So Ro's in there right now? Is that what he's saying?"

"Yeah." Brody's voice sounded wooden, even to him. "That's what he's fucking saying."

Your girl's only got about two and a half, maybe three hours of oxygen left. After that...

He looked at his watch, his pulse racing with terror. "He said she'd been in there thirty minutes. That was almost ten minutes ago, which means she's been locked in that fucking thing for forty." And that was assuming Ainsworth had been telling the truth. "That means Ro has, at most, an hour and a half of oxygen left."

"At most." Christian nodded.

Rocky's face fell with the gravity of the situation. "And we have no idea where to even start looking."

No, they sure as hell didn't.

"Fuck!" Brody slammed a palm against one of his cabinet doors. The damn thing cracked down the center from the blow.

"We're going to find her, Brody." Christian promised again. "We will. We just have to give Liam some more time to—"

"Ro doesn't have time," he cut his friend off short.

"Actually…" Liam inserted himself back into the conversation. "I think I might have a way to determine where she is."

All eyes went to Liam, who was staring back at Brody with an outstretched hand. "I have a program I can use to do a reverse image search."

"A what?" Brody handed his teammate the cell.

"Basically, I can use lighting, structure, and angles from the images he sent to triangulate possible locations here in the city. Assuming he's still here."

"He is." Brody felt confident in that. "One, it hasn't been that long since he took her, and two…he wants me to find her. Not in time to save her, I'm guessing. But Ainsworth wants me to get there. To see what my perceived betrayal to him cost. That's why he's doing this. He thinks I took everything from him, so he's going to try to take everything from me."

"Everything?" Rocky tilted his head with a searching gaze. "I thought you said you and Ro were just—"

"We were." Brody looked the man square in the eyes. "Now we're more."

"Hell yeah, you are." Christian actually grinned half-a-breath before taking on the role of Delta's leader. "All right, boys. It's game time, and Ro's life is the prize we *have* to win. Brody, why don't you and Cade grab some extra ammo. Just in case. In the meantime, we'll help Liam with whatever he needs to move the process along."

He wanted to argue but working on a task—even one as mindless as grabbing some boxes of bullets—may just be the thing he needed to wake his ass up and clear his mind.

Because right now, his one and only thought was Ro. Sweet, passionate, funny Ro who'd blown his mind in bed and taken over control of his heart. And if he lost her now...

I won't lose you, Princess. We're coming for you, so please. Just hold on a little bit longer.

He turned and marched his way out of the kitchen. Careful not to trip on the splintered wood and other pieces of his house still scattered across his living room floor, he maneuvered his way around the mess before taking the stairs two-at-a-time.

If Michael Ainsworth wanted a war, he'd damn well get one. Because Brody *would* find Ro, and he *would* take the bastard down.

Even if he had to burn the entire fucking world down in the process.

16

Two hours. It had been two full hours since Ainsworth's call. Since then...nothing.

And with each minute that passed, Ro was running out of time.

"Tell me you've got something." Brody looked up when Liam walked into the room.

"I've got something." The other man sat his laptop down onto the table. "I think. It's not one hundred percent, but it's the best shot we've got. I won't waste time going into detail, but basically, I was able to use the images Ainsworth sent to search potential locations in the city. Using the lighting, angles, and shadows, as well as estimated dimensions of the room, my program calculated all possible local structures."

"And?"

The man's almost golden gaze seemed hesitant, but then, "I think I know where she is." He spun the laptop around for Brody to see. "It's an old, abandoned building down by West Garfield Park. Stick-built, one-and-a-half stories. And it's sat boarded up and empty for the past two years."

"What the hell are we waiting for?" The first sliver of

hope he'd felt since regaining consciousness had Brody shooting to his feet.

"He's right." Christian set the cup of coffee he'd been sipping on down onto the table. "Let's load up. Liam can fill us in on the building's floor plan on the drive. We'll make a plan accordingly."

"Call Hansen," Brody told his friend. "Tell him to have his team and an ambulance meet us there. Ro's injured." Something he couldn't allow himself to think about. "She's gonna need medical."

"On it."

Armed to the teeth, the six-man team stormed out of Brody's house. He didn't think about the fact that his front door was non-existent, or that any idiot who drove past could see it and decide to traipse right in and help themselves.

Let them.

Brody didn't care about his things. Everything he owned could disappear tomorrow, and it would make no difference to him.

The only thing he wanted in this life...the only thing he really needed...was the woman he was hell-bent on saving. Things between them may have changed on a dime, but that didn't make the love he felt for Ro any less real.

And if he lost her...if they didn't make it in time to save her...Brody knew he would never be the same.

Breaking land-speed records to get there, Christian drove them into one of the more dangerous areas of Chicago. The location made sense for Ainsworth's plan.

Dark. Desolate. Everybody too busy worrying about themselves to care about an old building that's sat unoccupied for years.

"How sure are you that this is the right location?" Brody asked Liam, who was studying his tablet from the back seat.

"Sixty, maybe seventy percent."

He shot the man a set of arched brows from over his shoulder. "That's *it?*"

"I told you, it's not a hundred percent. But as far as statistical calculations and data-based theories, that's about the highest odds you're gonna get with something like this."

"Jesus." Brody spun back around and ran a weary hand over his face.

Ro's life was hanging in the balance, and they were banking on sixty percent?

"That's it right up there!" Liam pointed through the windshield at a shadowed building a block from where they were.

The entire area was building after building. Each structure more rundown than the last. Weeds had long-ago become overgrown, and the roads and sidewalks left much to be desired.

Brody didn't care about the neighborhood's aesthetics. He only cared about getting to Ro.

"Hansen just texted." Christian pointed to the wireless earpiece in his right ear that had presumably verbalized the message for him while he drove. "He and his team are headed this way, and he's put in a call for an ambulance."

"Lights and sirens?" Brody asked, praying the answer was no.

Christian shook his head with a confirmed, "They're coming in dark."

Dark was good, because it left them with the element of surprise.

"I'll pull in here in case he's watching." Christian turned

into an alley separating the two buildings just south of their target. "We'll walk the rest of the way."

Minutes later, the team was out of the vehicle and marching in a well-trained, hand-to-shoulder single file line. While they weren't wearing the usual combat gear they kept for situations such as this, the bullet resistant vests the team kept in the SUV would have to do.

Along with their pistols, and extra mags.

Keeping his left hand on Christian's shoulder, Brody held his Glock steady with his right as the team made their way along the buildings toward where he prayed Ro was waiting for him. He didn't let himself wonder how badly she was hurt, or whether she'd woken to find herself essentially buried alive.

His mind—his focus—was kept solely on getting into that building, getting her to safety, and taking down the threat. In that fucking order.

The team reached the side alleyway door they'd opted to use for entry. Looking back, Christian signaled Rocky to do his thing.

As the team's demolitions expert, the man had the tools and knowledge to check for possible triggers. Trip wires, stationary bombs...you name it. Right now he was checking the door to make sure Ainsworth hadn't set up a trap to take Brody and the others out in one fell swoop.

"All clear." Rocky stood from his crouched position.

"We can wait for Hansen if you want." Christian kept his voice low. "More back-up means more help for—"

"We've already taken too long." Brody moved around his friend and team leader and reached for the door. "Ro doesn't have time for us to wait."

He opened that door and stepped inside. It was dark and the place smelled like mold and mildew. Flipping on the light mounted to his weapon's barrel, Brody made his way through the small room where they'd entered and into a long, dark hallway.

The others followed, the team clearing every nook and cranny as they passed. With one door left to clear on the building's main floor, Brody ignored the terror sending his heart racing, and made his way across the open space toward it.

Emotions clogged his throat, but he swallowed them down. Terrified of what he'd find on the other side, Brody called upon every ounce of training he'd ever had to do what needed to be done.

The team waited with bated breath while Rocky checked for trip-wires or any signs of explosives present. When he gave the all-clear, Brody reached to open the door.

Sounds of his own frantic heartbeat rushing past his ears. With a final nod to the others—a signal to let them know he was ready—he turned the knob and went inside. There, in the middle of the room, was the locked and lidded trunk.

"Help me get her out!"

With no other hiding spaces in the large, open room, the team cleared it in seconds before racing to Brody's side. Using the bolt cutters he'd brought with him, he cut the padlock free and he and Christian shoved the trunk's hinged lid up.

"Aurora!"

Just like in Ainsworth's picture, she was lying on her back with her eyes closed. One side of her forehead was a myriad of purples and blues, dried blood smeared around a cut that was swollen up from the center of the bruise.

Her skin was paler than he'd ever seen it, and a bluish tint had begun to saturate her ruby lips.

"Get her out of there!"

Brody reached in to pull her from the makeshift coffin. With Christian's help, the two men carefully laid her on the tile floor.

She was so still. So quiet. And it wasn't until Brody looked at her chest that he realized—

"She's not breathing." He put an ear to her chest and listened. Seconds later, "She's not fucking *breathing!*"

His fingers flew to the side of her neck, a feeling of overwhelming loss consuming his very soul when he couldn't find one.

"No!"

Brody immediately called upon his training and began to administer CPR. Tilting her head back and her chin up, he ensured an open airway before sealing his lips to hers. He blew in two long, powerful breaths before lifting up and crossing his palms over each other in the correct area of her chest.

He began the compressions. Keeping the pace at one hundred beats per minute, he began counting in his head.

"Come on, Ro!" he shouted at her too-still form. "Don't do this to me. You have to make it. You *have* to!"

He couldn't imagine a world where she didn't exist.

Over and over, he pushed with bruising strength. Once he got to thirty, he stopped to give two additional breaths before returning to the steady, life-saving beats.

"You've got this, brother." Christian laid a hand on his shoulder. "It's Ro. If anyone can fight their way through this..."

"Come on!" Brody growled at her again.

His forearms and biceps burned from the strain, the pounding in his head growing exponentially with each and every compression. But he didn't stop. Stopping wasn't even a blip on his to-do radar.

This was Ro. His Ro. And he would never stop trying to save her.

Another thirty-count passed before he filled her lungs again. "Please, baby. Please stay with me." Tears fell from his eyes, but he ignored them and kept on.

"Why don't you let me take over?" Christian squeezed his shoulder.

But Brody jerked away and continued doing what he was doing. He'd put her in this position. His past had done this to her. So if anyone was going to save her...

"Goddamn it, Aurora! You have to breathe!" He shouted at his sleeping princess. "Fucking *breathe!*"

After yet another round of thirty compressions, he lifted a trembling hand to her neck. He held his breath and waited, silently pleading with God to save her.

And just when he thought all hope was lost...

There!

"She has a pulse!" he shouted to no one in particular. Tears of relief formed and he couldn't bring himself to care. "It's weak, but iI can feel it!"

I can feel her.

The entire team cheered, but Brody was too busy watching Ro's face to notice. Less than a handful of seconds later, her lips parted and her chest rose with a loud gasp.

The sound was rough. Desperate. Almost macabre in its delivery. It was also the most beautiful sound he'd ever heard.

"That's it!" Brody encouraged. "Just keep breathing, baby. That's it!"

Ro coughed and sputtered as her body regained its life. He was so overwhelmed by the relief he felt knowing they'd made it in time, he almost missed the slight squeaking noise coming from somewhere up above.

Tearing his eyes from Ro, he looked up just in time to see a shadow move past one of the opened room's second-story windows. What the...

Ainsworth.

"He's still here." Brody shot a look in Christian's direction. "I just saw someone right up there." He pointed. "I'd bet my ass it's Ainsworth."

"Guy like that...he'd want to stick close to enjoy the show." Jagger nodded.

He felt so torn. He wanted to stay with Ro...to make sure she kept on breathing. But he also knew this was his fight, and one only he could end.

"Go." Rocky knelt next to him. "I'll stay with her until the paramedics get here." When Brody didn't move, the other man shoved him to the side and said, "I've got her, now *go!*"

Taking precious seconds he may not have, he leaned down and pressed his lips to hers. "I'll be right back, Princess." Moving his mouth up to her ear, he whispered, "I love you."

It wasn't exactly how he'd planned to tell her the first time. Hell he didn't even have a plan for something like that. But Brody did know he wasn't going to let another second go by without her knowing.

Not after this. Not after being minutes—probably less—from losing her forever.

"You stick with her until I get back." An unwavering order meant for Rocky.

"You know I will."

With a nod in the other man's direction, Brody pushed himself to his feet and ran. Christian, Jagger, and Cade followed, leaving Liam and Rocky to keep Ro safe until their return.

"There!" Cade pointed to a set of stairs leading to the second floor. They were the kind that were exposed, running alongside the main area's interior wall and leading to a small platform at the top.

It had to be how Ainsworth got to the roof, which is where he'd been when Brody had seen him through the window.

The three men sprinted toward those stairs. Weapons in hand, their booted feet made a hell of a racket as they ran as fast as their legs would carry them up the metal steps.

Brody tried opening the door, but found it locked. One swift kick later, it was open and they were running inside.

As suspected, the area had once been an office. Probably the boss's, given the aerial view its small window gave of the main space below.

An old metal desk and worn and torn wheeled chair sat covered in dust, papers, and who knew what else. The floor was covered in litter from vagrants, and the walls had been stained from rain that had made its way in through the broken windows at the back and an unkept roof.

"He went out there." Cade motioned to a still-intact window that had been shoved open. "I'd bet money on it."

There was a lot more than money on the line with this one, but Brody had to agree. It was the only way Ainsworth could've gotten onto the roof from this part of the building.

He went to the window. Squeezing himself through, he immediately had his gun lifted and his head on a swivel. Brody waited until his teammates joined him before making his way along the roof's flat surface.

At first, he thought maybe the asshole had actually done

it. That maybe Ainsworth had managed to escape. But then, through the carrying of the evening wind, he heard it.

It was slight and he'd almost convinced himself he'd imagined it. But it was there.

Brody turned to his teammates and motioned to his right. Using only hand signals, they worked together to safely make their way around the opposite side of the elevated office's structure.

He cleared the corner, the breeze blowing harder with the wind block gone. And there, nearly reaching an exterior access ladder five yards away, was the man he was going to kill.

"Ainsworth!" Brody marched toward him with his weapon pointed straight at the man's head. "Don't fucking move."

Rather than appearing scared or panicked, Michael Ainsworth stared back at him and smiled. "Your Highness. I'm honored you could make an appearance."

"Shut the fuck up and drop the gun!"

Because Brody and the other men of Delta weren't the only ones armed. Ainsworth also had a Glock in his hand. A hand that, smartly, was still down at the other man's side.

"You know I can't do that."

"If you don't, you're dead."

"I'm as good as dead, anyway. At least that's what the cancer doc told me."

Cancer?

That might explain the man's sudden urge to act on his need for revenge. Not that Brody gave a damn either way. The only thing he cared about was downstairs right now, recovering from having literally *died* just minutes before.

"You killed her." He spoke through a set of clenched

teeth. "Ro was dead when we pulled her out of that fucking trunk."

"Was?" The other man tilted his head. "I'm assuming you and your merry group of heroes brought her back to life?"

"We did. So I guess this little plan of yours failed."

"Maybe. Or maybe it did exactly what I wanted it to do."

"Drop the gun." A muscle in Brody's jaw twitched. "I won't tell you again."

"See, that's always been your problem, King. You always thought you were the one in charge. But you're not. Not now. Not back then."

"Drop the fucking gun and get on your goddamn knees!"

But Ainsworth simply smiled. "You had promise, Brody. Real promise. I'm just sorry you never learned what being a true teammate really meant. Maybe someday."

He began moving backward. Not toward the ladder, but toward the roof's shallow ledge. Slow, purposeful steps that brought him closer and closer to escape. Only...

There's no way down from there. He'll have to jump.

Understanding struck in an instant. Ainsworth wasn't trying to escape. Not anymore. Men like him didn't want to be caught. Guys like that would rather die than go to prison.

Which meant...

"Don't do it, Michael! Don't you fucking do it!"

"Nice knowing you, Brody. While I have to admit, I hadn't planned on her surviving, I think you learned the lesson I was hoping for all the same. Keep watching out for that lady of yours. You never know what other enemies may come knocking."

Everything happened at once.

Ainsworth climbed up on the ledge. Brody and the others sprinted towards him, their shouted orders to get down filling the breezy night air. Ainsworth lifted a foot off the ledge.

He raised his gun. Started to point it in Brody's direction. Brody and the team opened fire, and the man who'd trained him to be the best damn SEAL he could be…fell.

Son of a…

Brody and the others closed the distance between them and the ledge. They all looked over and saw exactly what they expected.

Master Chief Michael Ainsworth. Former decorated Navy SEAL and leader of SEAL Team 1. Dead on a broken sidewalk in one of the worst neighborhoods in Chicago.

"Damn." Cade stared down at the dead man. "I really didn't think he'd do it."

"I knew he would." Brody turned away and headed back from where they came. "He wasn't going to prison. Not Ainsworth."

"Did you know he had cancer?" Christian asked as he stepped in line beside him.

"Not a clue. But I haven't talked to the guy in forever, so…"

Jagger snorted. "Yeah, doesn't sound like he was the type to have you over for Sunday tea."

"No, but the cancer makes sense." Brody approached the window. "I'm sure we'll find out once they do an autopsy, but if he was sick…if the guy *was* terminal…that may be what spurred him on in his plot for revenge."

"How so?" Cade followed him through the window.

"Probably wanted to get his payback before he died."

"I can buy that." Christian agreed. "Plus you saw the way he was at the end. One foot off the ledge. He was going off that roof whether we shot him off or he jumped."

"I think you're right." Brody hurried down the stairs to

get back to Ro. "But I think, there at the end, he didn't have the guts to jump."

"That's why he raised his gun," Cade agreed. "Suicide by cop. Well...not cops. But you know what I mean."

Yeah, Brody did know. He also knew Ro's nightmare was over. This part of it, anyway. The rest would depend on how well she recovered from the trauma of being kidnapped, beaten, and stuffed in a goddamn trunk and left to die.

She did die. For at least a few minutes, Ro was no longer with him. And that was a memory Brody knew he would never, ever forget.

He made his way into the room where she still lay. Only now, she was on a gurney, and about to be wheeled out into the ambulance.

"Wait!" He ran to her side.

Foggy blue eyes fluttered open and lifted to his. "B-Brody."

"I'm here." He took her hand and kissed her lips. "I'm right here."

The aching in his heart began to ease when he realized they were almost back to their original, kissable color. She was going to be okay. Physically, Ro was alive and was going to be okay.

As for the other, well. He would be just like he was now. Right by her side, every step of the way.

EPILOGUE

Three months later...

"Congratulations!"

Ro smiled wide hearing the joyful cheers and well-wishes. Today had been an absolutely perfect day.

Blue skies. Sunshine. White, puffy clouds filling the sky like the most perfect of paintings.

It reminded her of that day with her dad. By the pond when he'd asked her to take a selfie with him. That had been a perfect day, too. And now, thanks to the man dancing in her arms, Ro realized...

I have so many more perfect days ahead.

There'd been a time she hadn't been so sure. Right after Brody and the others had rescued her from that awful metal box.

She had no memory of her time inside there, thank God. Unlike being drugged at the bar, Ro was actually grateful the blows to her head had erased those terrifying moments in time.

But it still didn't diminish the residual terror the events

leading up to her kidnapping had left. Because those were memories Ro knew she'd never, ever forget.

The nightmares came less frequently now. During those first few weeks after Brody's former team leader broke into his home and took her against her will, they'd come for her every time she closed her eyes.

Megan had referred her to the therapist she'd turned to after her ordeal. Ro liked the other woman a lot, and felt their sessions had really started to help.

Brody had attended some with her. The man was a constant surprise of support and encouragement. He was also the sweetest, most amazing lover she could have ever asked for.

And he was all hers.

"Penny for your thoughts." His deep rumble brought her back to the present.

"Just thinking about how lucky I am." She smiled up at him. "After everything, we're both still here. Still together."

Minus the times when he had to go to work, they'd damn near been inseparable.

"You happy?" Those dark eyes searched hers for the truth.

Ro's lips curled into a wide, toothy smile. "Very."

And she was happy. A bit damaged, perhaps. But who wasn't?

Even Brody—a man she would have sworn could handle anything—had opened up to her about his own struggles with PTSD. Both during their shared sessions with her therapist and at home.

Home.

Almost immediately following her discharge from the hospital, they'd put her house up on the market and she'd moved into Brody's house with him. It had been Ro's decision. Brody had offered to move in with her.

But his house was bigger and needed less work, so it made sense that she be the one to move. Besides, something about living in a man's house surrounded by his things...

Or maybe it was just this man that did that *something* to her.

"I love you, you know?" She stared up at him and smiled.

Brody's bearded lips curled into a crooked grin that left her greedy sex craving what she'd already had just that morning. "I love you, too."

They said those precious words to each other every single day. Multiple times a day, most weeks. And every time she heard them falling off this man's lips, Ro felt as if it was the very first time all over again.

She'd heard him that day. She'd just come to, and he'd whispered them so softly. Ro was still struggling to comprehend what was going on around her, but she'd heard them.

I love you.

It was then she realized everything was truly going to be okay. Not just in that moment, but for the rest of her life.

"What do ya say? Want to scoot out of this shindig early?"

Ro took in the sight of the man holding her close. The man was mouthwateringly sexy in jeans and a t-shirt. But put the former SEAL in a tux, and he was like the absolute best version of suit porn she'd ever seen.

Let's see. Do I want to stay here and celebrate Megan and Christian's wedding, or do I want to take my man home and ravage that tuxedo right off him?

Decisions, decisions...

With a smile she hoped conveyed her answer, Ro pulled away, took his hand in hers, and led him off the dance floor.

After a few hugs and goodbyes to the happy couple and the rest of Delta, they took off for home.

Home.

With Megan and the men of Delta, Ro always knew she had her very own makeshift family. But with Brody, she'd discovered so much more.

Because as long as she had him, as long as this man was there, by her side…she knew there wasn't anything they couldn't conquer.

Even death.

READY FOR MORE DELTA TEAM?

Pre-order JOHN (R.I.S.C. Delta Team #3) for Rocky's story now!

https://amzn.to/3siAg9o

OTHER TITLES BY ANNA BLAKELY

<u>R.I.S.C. Delta Team Series</u>

Christian

Brody

John

R.I.S.C. Series (Alpha Team)

Taking a Risk, Part One

Taking a Risk, Part Two

Beautiful Risk

Intentional Risk

Unpredictable Risk

Ultimate Risk

Targeted Risk

Savage Risk

Undeniable Risk

His Greatest Risk

R.I.S.C. Bravo Team Series

Rescuing Gracelynn

Rescuing Katherine

Rescuing Gabriella

Rescuing Ellena

Rescuing Jenna

R.I.S.C. Charlie Team Series

Kellan

<u>Greyson</u>

Asher

Rhys

<u>Parker</u>

Marked Series

Marked For Death

Marked for Revenge

Marked for Deception

Marked for Obsession

Marked for Danger

Marked for Disaster

TAC-OPS Series

Garrett's Destiny

Ethan's Obsession

Eagle's Nest Securities Series

Keeping His Promise

Playing With Fire

WANT TO CONNECT WITH ANNA?

Newsletter signup (with FREE Bravo Team prequel novella!)
BookHip.com/ZLMKFT
Join Anna's Reader Group: www.facebook.com/groups/blakelysbunch/
BookBub: https://www.bookbub.com/authors/anna-blakely
Amazon: amazon.com/author/annablakely
Author Page: https://www.facebook.com/annablakelyromance
Instagram: https://instagram.com/annablakely
Twitter: @ablakelyauthor
Goodreads: https://www.goodreads.com/author/show/18650841.Anna_Blakely

Made in the USA
Middletown, DE
07 November 2023